Sherry Gottlieb

LOVE BITE

WARNER BOOKS

A Time Warner Company

Enjoy lively book discussions online with CompuServe. To become a member of CompuServe call 1-800-848-8199 and ask for the Time Warner Trade Publishing forum. (Current members GO:TWEP.)

WARNER BOOKS EDITION

Cover design by Diane Luger
Cover illustration by Mel Odum

Warner Books, Inc.
1271 Avenue of the Americas
New York, NY 10020

W A Time Warner Company

Printed in the United States of Amerca

First Printing: June, 1994

10 9 8 7 6 5 4 3 2 1

"*Your best defense is that people don't believe in vampires anymore . . .*"

"But if you let someone live after seeing your fangs, they'll start believing pretty damn quick. There's enough accuracy in the vampire literature available to the public to kill you, if you're not careful. So, even more important than learning how to keep them from doing it. You'll get the hang of it before long."

Two feedings later, Risha's fangs came out for the first time. Gregor said she could pass over any time now, but he wanted her to wait another week, just to make sure.

Finally the night came. "How will I go?" she wanted to know.

"My dear Risha, there's only one way to pass over: tonight, I drink all of you. And tomorrow night, when you awake, I'll take you someplace romantic for dinner. Afterwards, we can catch the Grateful Dead at the Avalon."

ʌʌʌʌʌ

"Los Angeles has a new Miss Lonelyhearts. . . one with fangs. Sherry Gottlieb has woven police procedural, love, lust, and lots of blood into a colorful, compelling tale."

—**Brent Monahan, author of**
The Book of Common Dread

Also by Sherry Gottlieb

HELL NO, WE WON'T GO!
RESISTING THE DRAFT DURING THE VIETNAM WAR

For the man I loved,
for inspiring me to murder

ACKNOWLEDGMENTS

My deepest gratitude to these who gave freely of their comments, experience, and love:

Frank M. Robinson, my beloved mentor;
Sandra Watt, my guardian agent;
Jeanne Tiedge, my editor at Warner Books;
Barry Fisher, Director, Los Angeles County Sheriff's Department Crime Lab, for anything I got right about police procedure;
Ellen Datlow, Wendy Fisher, Diane and Ron Schaffer, and Darryl Stanley, for early feedback and computer aid;
Pat Cadigan, Jordi Cosentino, Harry Gershon, Joyce Liddel, Jan and Howie Moss, J.J. Strano, Judith Waner, and Dennis Whitlow, for moral support.
The Grateful Dead, for the music.

CHAPTER
One

The night he died, Teece Cabot got the best ride of his life.

He didn't blame Charlie for stranding him at the Corral. He'd have done the same thing if he'd been the one the blonde had invited home. But now it was almost one in the morning, and Teece could either walk the five miles back through the dark canyon to the stable or he could try to hitch a ride. There wasn't much traffic on rural Topanga Canyon Boulevard late at night, but maybe someone leaving the bar between band sets would give him a lift.

At least the weather was pleasant, maybe sixty degrees. Somewhat shitfaced, Teece tried to look alert and harmless on the road across from the Corral, but only three cars had passed and no one had stopped. He'd been walking south for half an hour when he heard another car coming from behind him. He turned, stuck out his thumb, and smiled in what he hoped was disarming innocence. The Honda pulled over a hundred feet in front of him; as he trotted up to the open

1

passenger window of the car, he saw the only occupant was the young woman driver.

"Hi," she smiled, "where are you headed at this hour?"

"I'm just going up Old Topanga Canyon Road to the stable I work at. Can you give me a lift to the turnoff?"

"Sure, hop in." She picked up a camera case from the passenger seat and tossed it into the back as Teece got in. She was rolling before he got the door closed. He only got a glimpse of her before the car light went out, but she looked about thirty, slim, with dark hair in a single braid down her back. She was wearing a black denim jumpsuit unzipped far enough for him to see the tops of her white breasts, but it was the camera case that triggered his memory.

"Hey, wasn't you taking pictures in the Corral tonight?"

She took another look at him. "Yes, I was. I remember you: I took some photos of the group you were in at the bar. I'm not surprised you work at a stable—you look more like a real cowboy than most of the people there."

He got a kick out of that one—he'd always wanted to be a cowboy . . . and it sounded better than stablehand, which is as close as you could get in Los Angeles. "You like horses?"

"Sure—I love feeling all that power between my legs. A horse is warmer and safer than a motorcycle."

Teece wasn't too drunk to miss an opportunity like that. "A good man is friendlier than a horse, you want power between your legs."

She laughed in delight, "And I suppose you're a good man?"

They'd reached his turnoff.

"This here's Old Topanga Canyon Road. Whyn't you drive me back to the stable and decide for yourself?"

She made the turn without slowing. "Well, I suppose I could come in for a nightcap. What do I call you?"

"Teece, T.C., Top Cat—take your prick—I mean, pick." He grinned at her, sure that he was sweeping her off her feet. He'd heard of hitchhikers who'd gotten laid by cruising cunt; now it was going to be his turn. He hadn't had any pussy since before he got to L.A. two months ago; he figured she was going to feel power between her legs until she couldn't take any more.

"The stable's just past that rise—I got a bunk and a wood-burner behind the tack room. Got a bottle of tequila, you want a nightcap. Turn right here. You gonna tell me your name, honey?"

She parked the car where he indicated.

"Call me Rusty."

Teece laughed, "When I finish oiling you, you won't be rusty no more."

She smiled at that. He had it made. He led her through the stable to his room. She hesitated when she saw the bunk beds.

"Does someone else live here with you?"

"Just Charlie. He was at the Corral with me, but he won't come back tonight—that's why I was walking home, cuz Charlie got lucky, took a blonde lady home. You got me all to yourself, ma'am." He kicked the door shut behind him. "I'll build a fire in the woodburner. Won't take but a minute. The tequila's in the footlocker over there, glasses're on the sink."

Teece stacked wood and kindling in the stove and snapped a wooden match with his thumbnail. When he turned around, Rusty had completely unzipped her jumpsuit and the white V of her skin glowed through an opening unbroken by under-wear. Her ivory breasts were full and heavy, the nipples still hidden under the edges of the jumpsuit, the top of her dark bush just visible above the bottom of the zipper. His cock swelled and he felt it was all he could do not to throw her to the floor and nail her right there, but it had been a long drought and he wanted to take his time and turn this pussy inside out.

He rubbed his erection through his jeans with one hand as the flickering glow from the fire played on her skin. She smiled invitingly and that's when he noticed her eyes. They were so pale that they almost had no color, but they were hot, shimmering with anticipation.

She licked her lips.

Jace was lying on the floor of the living room of his mother's house. The furniture was covered with graying sheets, festooned with cobwebs and coated in dust. Spanish moss dripped from the ceiling. There were light rectangles on the rotting walls where pictures of the family used to hang. A miasma of decay lay over the whole room, and something else, something threatening, was just beyond his perception. He knew he had to leave immediately or whatever it was would get him. He told himself to GET UP NOW AND OPEN THE DOOR, but he couldn't remember how to stand up, couldn't get his body to respond. It was coming for him, he had to get away before it saw him. He could hear it coming, ringing loudly as it approached. He tried again to get up, but he couldn't move and it rang again, closer.

Ringing? It sounded like a phone. Suddenly, his hand was free and shot out from the sheets to stifle the phone and he woke, the receiver in his hand; the book he'd been reading when he had fallen asleep thumped as it slid to the floor.

He looked wildly about, then calmed as he realized he was

at home, in his own bed, covered with sweat, but safe. The same fucking nightmare he'd had regularly since his mother had died seven years earlier. He looked at the clock radio next to the bed: seven A.M. Why hadn't the alarm gone off? Sunday. It's Sunday—no work today. He took a deep breath, let it out slowly. What woke him? He remembered the phone, clutched in his right hand. He put it to his ear.

". . . Jace? Levy, you there?"

"Yeah," his voice creaked and he cleared his throat, "yeah, Liz, I'm here. What's up?"

"King just called. Malibu Sheriff Station's got a fresh stiff in Topanga, which sounds like it might tie in with the Cannon and Garcia murders. You want to see it *in situ*, I'll pick you up in fifteen minutes."

"Bring coffee." He hung up and got out of bed, his right foot turning as it hit the edge of the Stuart Woods novel on the floor. He tossed the book onto the bed and headed for the bathroom.

The Cannon murder was one of Santa Monica's cases last month. Gilvan "Boomer" Cannon had been a fifty-nine-year-old derelict who'd come to the bottom of his luck when he had been stabbed by person or persons unknown. He had bled to death through wounds to the neck and chest two days before he was found in a shallow grave under a lifeguard station. No witnesses, no leads. Jace and his partner, Liz Robinson, heard about the murder last week at the meeting of the Southbay Homicide Association.

Jesus Garcia was a nineteen-year-old crack addict who had been found at four A.M. three days ago, breathing his last on the lawn next to the east parking lot of the V.A. Hospital in Brentwood. He was smiling, but he didn't regain consciousness before he died. He'd been stabbed in the neck. Even though he'd been found within minutes of his murder, West L.A. Homicide didn't have any leads. Nobody had time to spare for the case. The only reason Jace and Liz noticed it was the neck-wound similarity to the Cannon murder.

Levy brushed his teeth in the shower, ran the electric razor over most of his lower face, and dragged his fingers through his silver-shot dark hair. He grabbed the gray cotton pants and wrinkled turquoise polo shirt from the chair where he'd dropped them the night before. He'd just finished tying his gray Nikes when Liz beeped the horn out front.

She was driving her red Miata with the top down. Tough life. Jace spent more time under his car than he did in it. When he got into his partner's car, she handed him a Winchell's Doughnut bag. The bag contained a large Styrofoam cup of coffee and an apple fritter.

"You don't look so hot. You feeling okay?" She pulled away from the curb and drove west while Jace drank coffee.

"Nothing to worry about. I had trouble sleeping—finally drifted off about four. Thanks for the caffeine and sugar."

Liz's short brown hair was freshly cut and shiny and she wore a light application of peach lipstick. Her beige wool slacks boasted a knife-edge crease and her tweed jacket picked up the pale yellow of her silk turtleneck. She was wearing small gold hoops in her ears, a delicate gold watch, and an abstract gold pin on her jacket. She was the best-looking detective at the station.

Jace gulped some coffee. "My, we're dressed well for corpse viewing, aren't we?"

She glanced in mock disdain at his wrinkled shirt and sneakers. "Well, I am, at least. Sandy's parents are in from Wichita, and we're taking them to the Westwood Marquis for brunch. I didn't know if I'd have time to change when we're through in Topanga, so I told them I'd meet them there after I drop you home.''

Liz had "married well," as Jace's mother used to say, two years earlier; Sandy was a successful civil litigation attorney who seemed to be able to handle having a homicide detective for a wife.

"Must be nice to be married to someone who can afford brunch for four at the Marquis. You could take me with you instead of leaving me home. You never take me anywhere," Jace whined.

"Actually, it's nice being married, period. You ought to give it a try. You're forty-two—it's time, Levy." She ignored his bid for brunch and turned the car down the California Incline to Pacific Coast Highway. "Anyway, I'm taking you to Topanga—what more could you want? You ready to hear about the stiff?"

"It's got to be better than a lecture on the virtues of matrimony." A lecture he'd seemed to be getting more and more the last few years. He tore off a chunk of the apple fritter and stuffed it in his mouth, spilling sugar flakes down the front of his shirt.

"Male Cauc, late twenties, stablehand at Whitfield Ranch. He was found in his room by his roommate, another stablehand, when he came home at dawn. Two obvious stab wounds—chest and neck.''

"Carotid again?" He ate another chunk of fritter, began to feel alert. He brushed the sugar off his shirt and onto his pants.

"Could be—he said right side of the neck. Maybe a bowie knife like the others. No sign of a struggle.''

"I suppose the other stablehand is alibied."

"We'll find out when we get there. That's all I know, Jace."

Even though it was still before eight A.M. and almost October, there was a fair amount of traffic on Pacific Coast Highway: families getting an early start on a day out of town, surfers with boards on top of their cars, tourists gawking at the Pacific Ocean. It had been in the mid-seventies the last few days, so the beaches would probably be crowded by noon.

They turned up Topanga Canyon Boulevard and left the noise and traffic behind. A rustic community in the Santa Monica Mountains, Topanga was home to artists, writers, horse ranchers, new age practitioners, nudists, ageing hippies, and their families. Few buildings were visible from the main boulevard, which ran from the coast to the San Fernando Valley. The mountains were covered with brown California chaparral. A creek bed—seldom carrying water during the five years of drought—meandered at the bottom of the incline next to the road. Jace smiled—to be riding through the sage-scented canyon in a red convertible sports car driven by a very attractive woman was a helluva way to do police work.

He spotted Whitfield Ranch as soon as they passed the rise; it would be hard to miss all the activity—sheriff's deputies and cars were all over the side of the road. A lanky, red-haired deputy guarded the driveway.

"Sorry, folks, the stable's closed today."

Jace showed his shield as Liz told the redhead, "Detectives Robinson and Levy, Robbery-Homicide, LAPD." They parked where the deputy indicated and walked toward the stable, Liz delicately sidestepping her low-heeled beige pumps past horse droppings.

"Levy and Robertson. To what do we owe this honor?" Liz bit her tongue at the mangling of Robinson while Jace shook the sergeant's hand.

Fred Waner was six-foot-five and weighed close to three hundred pounds. He sported a walrus moustache under an eagle nose and over thin lips. Jace had met him several times and liked him—he was a thorough cop and wasn't possessive about his cases—but Waner invariably irked Liz one way or another.

"There have been a couple of neck-stabbing deaths—Santa Monica and West L.A.—might be a pattern," Liz told him. "What have you got?"

"Come and see. The criminalist just finished and the coroner hasn't moved the body yet." Waner led the way past yellow crime-scene tape toward the tack room. "Victim is a twenty-six-year-old drifter from Florida; Thomas Cabot, known as Teece. He's been a stablehand here six weeks, lived in a room in back with the other hand, Charlie Haldeman." Waner tilted his head in the direction of a shaken pony-tailed young man outside the stable who was holding onto his coffee with both hands while he talked to a deputy writing on a clipboard.

"The Whitfields are due back from a week in Hawaii tonight. Haldeman found the body when he got home at six this morning. He and Cabot had been drinking at the Topanga Corral last night. Haldeman picked up a chick named Rachel and left about midnight with her to go to her condo in Canoga Park, leaving Cabot on foot at the bar. That was the last time he saw him. We'll check the broad, but my gut tells me he's straight."

They reached the bunkroom just as Josephann Tevis, the crime lab specialist, was coming out.

"Levy. Robinson." The criminalist was a chunky gray-haired black woman in her late fifties. "A little out of your jurisdiction, aren't you?"

"Just looking, J.T.," Jace said. "You going to be around for awhile?"

"Just until I finish talking to Waner. If you want to take a peek first, I'll wait."

Liz nodded and she and Jace entered the room. It was small and sparsely furnished. A wood-burning stove against the back wall had its door hanging open, a patina of fingerprint powder on the door and top. There was a doorless closet of a bathroom with a toilet, shower, and sink; a shelf between the sink and the shaving mirror held two glasses dusted with fingerprint powder, and various men's toilet items. A beat-up three-drawer dresser listed off the vertical against the wall to the left, and a closed footlocker was behind the open door to the right. A deputy stood away from the bunk beds; Jace noticed that both beds were made. A plaid Pendleton shirt had been dropped on one cowboy boot on the floor, the other was under the bunk.

The body was on the bottom bunk, his head on the blood-soaked pillow, his skin ashen, the dark-blond hair clotted with blood on the right side where a great bloody wound interrupted his neck. There was a knife hole on his bare chest about five inches down from his collarbone. The right hand hung over the side of the bed. A trail of blood zigzagged over his shoulder and ran down his arm to the wood floor, where it collected around a space between the planks. His jeans were unsnapped and unzipped; he wore no underwear. He was still wearing his white tube socks, both his feet on the bed. The blanket under him was only slightly rumpled.

"Looks like he never moved, like he just let it happen," Jace observed.

"Maybe he'd passed out before he was stabbed." Liz sketched the layout of the room and the body in her notebook, while Jace squatted down to peer under the bed and into corners. He saw nothing. Tevis was very thorough. "I've seen enough—let's see what J.T. has to say."

They found her and Waner talking next to the open driver's door of her county car.

"I can't tell you much until we get the work-ups," Tevis said. "We guess the time of death was maybe two-three A.M. King'll have a better idea after the post. The size of the punctures seems consistent with a bowie-knife-size blade. I'd say he had lost a lot of blood through the hole in his carotid artery before he was stabbed above the heart. The edges of the wound looked different. We got some trace fibers from the bed and some prints to check, but it'll be a while before we know if they're from the killer. Waner should have the photos by Tuesday."

After Tevis had left, Waner turned to them. "It seems he built a fire in the stove before he was killed; maybe he knew the knifer, someone who brought him home from the bar. No sign of forced entry, apparently no robbery. I'll send some men up to the Corral tonight to investigate, already got someone heading out to see the broad in Canoga Park. You want me to keep you informed?"

Jace nodded several times. "Yeah, we'd appreciate it, Fred." Waner walked them back to Liz's car.

"This what L.A. gives their dicks to drive? We get Mercedes, but mine's being hand-detailed today so I brought the Matador.''

"An active imagination must be a great comfort to you," Liz replied.

Jace threw off his clothes and jumped back into bed after Liz dropped him off, but he got up again ten minutes later when he realized he was no longer tired.

He picked up all the dirty clothes and stuffed them into the laundry bag. He had to admit the room looked better than it had in weeks, so on a roll, he confronted the rest of the small house, neatening stacks of reading matter, wiping off kitchen counters, taking out the trash and recyclables.

While he worked, the puzzle of Teece Cabot's murder kept his attention. Why would Cabot either let someone in in the middle of the night, or bring someone in with him? If it was a buddy to drink with, the killer had put the glasses away . . . or they had never gotten that far—have to wait for the prints to be checked.

A sexual partner might explain his semi-attire, but it was obvious they didn't get too far before the murder. Why would a woman go to a man's bedroom in the middle of the night and then stab him? Maybe an old girlfriend. Or attempted rape. (Then how'd she get to a knife?) Jace made a note to find out Cabot's sexual proclivities—maybe he was gay. And maybe Waner's men would find a witness at the Corral who knew who he left with.

Jace didn't vacuum or dust; he'd read somewhere that after four years, dust didn't get any worse, it just piled up in drifts. It occurred to him to call a maid service, a periodic idea that he usually failed to follow through on. This time, he wrote it in his notebook.

He opened the refrigerator, sighing at the selection. There were four bottles of Harp Lager, a jar of green salsa, and two cardboard containers of leftover take-out Szechwan food. He took out the *kung-po* chicken and a Harp and pulled up a stool to the kitchen counter.

As he picked out cold chicken with his fingers, he thought again about the crime scene. If Cabot brought someone home with him, he built a fire, took off his boots and shirt, unzipped his pants, and lay down on his bed and let the someone stab him without apparent protest. Didn't seem terribly likely.

On the other hand, maybe he came in alone, built the fire, and began to get undressed when the someone showed up . . . and then he lay down on his bed and let the someone stab him without apparent protest.

Why didn't the guy resist? Okay, there was Liz's theory, that Cabot was passed-out drunk and never knew what hit him: that would explain his being half-dressed and his not moving . . . if he were that drunk . . . or stoned; maybe he was a junkie. They'd have to wait for the autopsy. Jace had a strong hunch that Cabot's half-dressed state was a major clue.

He threw the empty food carton into the trash and took his notebook and pencil, along with another beer, into the living room. He had to move a stack of books and magazines off his recliner before he could sit in it. He decided that when he got to work tomorrow morning, he'd see what he could find out about other unsolved knifings in the county over the last year. If this was the same knifer as in the Cannon and Garcia murders, chances are there'll be others that match—and, un-doubtedly, more to come. Why did he stab Cabot in the chest after he'd already bled to death? Assuming it's the same guy, he might have done the same thing to Cannon. With Garcia, maybe he saw someone coming and didn't have time to deliver his *coup de grâce*, the chest blow. Jace made a note to find out if Cannon and Garcia were completely dressed, and to get all the police reports and autopsy results on the two cases from Santa Monica and West L.A. At this point, he just didn't have enough information to speculate further. It wasn't his case—and it was Sunday. Monday would be soon enough.

Deciding to save the crossword puzzle for later, Jace reclined the chair and picked up the new issue of *City of Angels* magazine from the stack next to him and began to leaf through it. It carried lots of glossy ads for rich, cool people who couldn't find enough to do with their money, but usually ran some first-rate fiction, articles, and art. There was an article bemoaning the demise of outdoor newsstands in L.A., followed by a short story by James Ellroy about the Hollywood blacklist during the McCarthy era. After a few more pages of ads that were so arty that the products were not immediately obvious, his attention was snagged.

On the next three pages were eye-catching black-and-white photographs under the heading "After Midnight in the City of Angels—One of a Series" by a photographer identified only as "Cadigan." There was no other text. The first photo had been taken at a meat-packing plant and showed beef carcasses being loaded into a refrigerated truck. The men loading the meat had a beefy look about them, their biceps bulging as they pushed the sides along. The next was of a hooker in front of the Wax Museum on Hollywood Boulevard, her underage appearance—short, low-cut white dress, black Mary Janes over white ankle socks, long bleached-blonde pigtails, and painted-on pout—belied by the old and wearied look of her eyes. She could have been as old as forty.

The last was at the counter of the Hollywood Ranch Market, an all-night attraction for the dregs of the area. A stooped elderly bag lady with a shopping cart piled high with her belongings had her hand out, palm up, to a black pimp with a shiny bald head who was festooned with gold and diamonds (or gold plate and cubic zirconia, Jace thought with a smile). The pimp was trying to look past her.

Jace thought the photos were outstanding and he flipped back to remember the photographer's name. Cadigan.

CHAPTER
Two

Rusty woke a little before seven P.M. Monday from a dreamless sleep. Instantly wide awake, she switched on the bedside light and got up. She didn't pull the blackout curtains, which were threaded on rods top and bottom so they didn't open. Elliott had anticipated her by running her a bath—his timing was impeccable: The Ombre Rose-scented water was exactly the right temperature and she settled in to read the mail and messages he invariably left for her at the side of the tub.

On top of the stack was a page from the *Los Angeles Times*. It was the last page of the Metro section; Elliott had circled a small news item with highlighter:

MAN FOUND MURDERED IN TOPANGA

The body of a stablehand who had been
stabbed to death was discovered Sunday morning

at a ranch on Old Topanga Canyon Road. The
twenty-six-year-old man had been attacked
sometime late Saturday night, and was found in
his bed by his roommate who returned home at
dawn yesterday.

Robbery was apparently not the motive for the
murder, said Sergeant Frederik Waner of the
County Sheriff's Station in Malibu. He declined
to identify the victim pending notification of
relatives. Waner said the man had been drinking
at the Topanga Corral, a club, Saturday night.
Sheriff's deputies are investigating the possibility
that the killer may have given the man a ride
home from the bar.

Rusty read the article, then balled it up and tossed it into
the wastebasket across the room; as usual, the cops had nothing. She smiled to herself. Even if they had everything, they'd
still have nothing because they wouldn't believe.

She had one telephone message—her agent had called to
say he liked the photos in the new issue of *City of Angels* and
that he thought there might be a book in it if the rest of the
series were as good. Rusty was way ahead of him—she'd
envisioned a book when she conceived the series—but she
was glad he was thinking in the same direction. Elliott had
noted on the phone slip that a return call wasn't expected.
There were a few bills for her to check and a couple of
mail order catalogs. There was a letter from the Erlich-Moss
Gallery in Pittsburgh thanking her profusely for the exhibit
and enclosing a check for $712 for the photos that had been
sold; they advised that the rest of the show was being returned

under separate cover and closed by asking for another show next year.

She finished bathing and washed her hair. Wrapping a towel around her head, she donned an antique Chinese silk robe embroidered with mythical creatures. She went downstairs to the living room and put *Workingman's Dead* into the CD player and upped the volume as "Uncle John's Band" began. The Grateful Dead was her favorite band—they reminded her of her Berkeley days . . . and Gregor. She still missed him terribly nearly two years after his death. It was ironic that she had only one photograph of him.

She found her assistant at his desk in the study. Short and stocky with glasses and a thin fringe of gray hair, he could have been anywhere from mid-forties to mid-sixties; he had looked middle-aged his entire life.

"Hi, Elliott. Have a good weekend?"

"Uneventful. I don't think I did anything."

"Sometimes, those are the best weekends." Rusty leaned past him to get a pen from the desk which she used to endorse the check. Elliott inhaled her perfume. "A check from the photo gallery in Pittsburgh—please deposit it to the local account tomorrow. And you can go ahead and pay these bills, too."

"I'll have the checks ready for your signature tomorrow. Is there anything you need me to do tonight?"

"No, thanks. I think I'll spend a few hours in the darkroom. I'm not planning to eat, but I might go out on a shoot. If you want to go out, you can take the Honda—I'll be using the BMW tonight."

"Thank you, but I'm going to stay in. There's a movie on TV I think I'll watch. Oh! I've developed the film you left this morning. The negatives and contact sheets are in the darkroom. Do you want me to bring them to you?''

Rusty shook her head no, and her turban loosened. "If you'll braid my hair before I go into the darkroom, I won't have to disturb you later.''

Elliott followed Rusty up to the dressing table in her bathroom. He no longer thought it odd that she had no mirror there—or indeed anywhere in the house outside of his quarters. When she sat on the upholstered stool, he stood behind her, comb in hand, and puzzled her wet dark hair into a perfect French braid. Her hair showed its red only when dry and under light. This was the only excuse he had to touch her and he looked forward to the ritual.

"Do you want make-up tonight?''

"Just a little shadow and eyeliner, I think.'' She pivoted to sit facing him, and he made up her face with the facile skill of long practice. Gregor had found a real prize in Elliott, who had been with him for years before Rusty came along. He'd be hard to replace. "Thank you. Have a good evening and I'll see you tomorrow night.''

When Elliott had left, Rusty traded her robe for jeans and a Dead T-shirt, and went to look at the contact sheets from the Corral shoot. She had a deadline coming up.

It was Thursday before Jace had a chance to return Fred Waner's call about the Cabot murder. He and Liz had been swamped with investigations into a new pair of drive-by shootings. Three people had been shot, one killed, in two separate incidents. The death was a seven-year-old girl who had the misfortune to be riding her bicycle Monday morning past a house frequented by Crips at the exact moment that a

passing car registered to a rival Blood opened fire on the
house with an Uzi. The Crip who had been standing guard
on the porch behind her was in critical condition at County
and wasn't expected to survive. The girl's aunt was less than
one hundred feet away when the child was killed, yet she had
had the presence of mind to note the license number of the
car. Tuesday night, they arrested two Bloods in connection
with the shootings.

They weren't as lucky with the other shooting: A pregnant
woman had been shot in the left shoulder with a small-caliber
bullet while driving north on the Harbor Freeway, but she
never saw the car that the shot was fired from. So far, no
witnesses had come forward, although the incident occurred
just before ten P.M. Tuesday and there were other cars near
hers on the freeway.

"Fred Waner, please. Detective Levy returning his call."
While he waited to be transferred to the sergeant, Jace pushed
papers aside and flipped his notebook to the questions he
wanted answered.

"There's not much, Levy. The broad in Canoga Park confirmed Haldeman's account, alibied him for the time of the
murder, which was about two A.M. A waitress at the Corral
saw Cabot leave the bar alone about twelve forty-five, but no
one saw him after he walked out the door. She said he'd been
drinking beer, but didn't seem particularly drunk. Coroner
didn't detect much alcohol in the autopsy; no plans to run
tox. Cause of death was exsanguination from the carotid
puncture. The only fingerprints in the bunkroom were Cabot's
and Haldeman's. No helpful trace on the body or the bed.
We do know that the assailant was one strong mutherfucker:
The hit to the chest was hard enough to crack the sternum."

"That lets out a woman, I guess." Jace rapidly made notes.

"Most men, too," Waner muttered.

"You think maybe Cabot was gay? Picked up some rough trade?"

"I thought of that. Haldeman said he 'didn't act like a fag.' We found some stroke mags in Cabot's footlocker—big tits stuff, all straight. We located a sister in Fort Lauderdale, said Cabot left Florida three years ago after knocking up a teenage girl. He's been bumming around since—New Orleans, Albuquerque, Flagstaff."

"Someone taking revenge for the girl?"

"Doubtful. The sister didn't even know he was in L.A. She said the girl had an abortion, went on with her life. We'll keep it open, but it looks like a dead end."

"Okay, Fred, thanks. Send me a copy of the report and autopsy, will you?"

"On the way. You think there's a connection with your other murders?"

Jace dug the Cannon and Garcia reports out from the mass of paper on the desk. "I haven't had a chance to look at the reports in-depth—I'll let you know if I find anything." He hung up.

Liz came back from a lunch with her husband, who was trying a case downtown, with a thick sheaf of computer print-out.

"I ran into Viramontes on my way up." She dropped the paper with a thud on the only bare spot on his side of the desk. "Knife assaults and homicides by knife, L.A. City, October 1990 to August 1991." Jace groaned at the size of the printout. Liz shrugged. "We're still waiting for the County readout—there'll be more." She went around to the neat side of the double desk—hers. "Did you talk to Waner about the Cabot murder?"

He filled her in, but before they could turn to the stabbing material, they got a call that a Korean grocer with a baseball bat had disarmed and severely beaten a black man with a gun who had attempted to force the grocer's daughter to turn over the till. There'd been a lot of racial tension in black areas with Korean business owners, particularly grocers, and Jace figured this one was going to find his store the focus of a neighborhood boycott by the end of the afternoon. As they left, he prayed for a black eyewitness to corroborate the grocer's account.

By the time they'd reached the Korean grocery, an angry crowd had collected and a brick had shattered the front window. It was nearly seven when Jace and Liz got back to the station. It would take an hour more to type up the report.

"If you want to go home, I'll finish the report," he told her in the station parking lot.

"I won't turn that down—you spell better than me, anyway. Thanks—I owe you one." Liz turned toward her car, then stopped. "You sure, Jace? I thought you had a date tonight."

He'd forgotten all about Ellen. Thank God Liz remembered. "Go ahead—I'll just be a little late."

After Liz left, Jace went to his desk and called Ellen to postpone their date to nine. A deputy district attorney, Ellen Fisher was Jace's "safe" relationship. For three years, they'd gotten together for dinner, conversation, and sex whenever Ellen's live-in boyfriend was out of town. Dennis was a musician. He and Ellen had an "understanding" about sex when they were separated: It was permissible as long as safe sex was practiced with others and outside love affairs did not interfere with their primary relationship. Jace always thought it a strange arrangement, but it seemed to work for Ellen and Dennis—they'd been together eight years. And it worked fine for Jace, too; he was able to have a safe sex life that didn't carry the risk of romantic involvement. He and Ellen were friendly lovers, but emotionality was never part of the package. He didn't know if she had other lovers or not, and he didn't care. She never asked if he was seeing anyone else, although he usually wasn't. He never initiated contact, leaving it to Ellen to call when Dennis was gone and she wanted to see Jace. The sex was great—maybe the best he'd ever had, the conversation comfortable. He was looking forward to the evening; when Ellen called that morning, she'd promised to model "a hot new teddy" she'd just bought.

When Rusty woke Thursday night, she was ravenous. Tonight, she thought, she'd really pig-out. What would it be? Soul food? Mexican? She was awfully tired of eating alone—it wasn't any fun, it was just "feeding." She and Gregor had usually gone out to eat together, often splitting meals. She remembered how they took joy in the sharing of the experience—talking over where they would go and what they would choose, even if it was just grabbing a bite after a movie. They used to attend things all the time—plays, concerts, gallery openings, the ballet. When they lived in Berkeley, sometimes they'd go to Marin County just for dinner and the drive.

On the nights they stayed in, they would play Scrabble, or Gregor would read while Rusty worked in the darkroom. He had always been interested in seeing her latest work, in hearing how she found her subjects. He had a good eye, and she valued his opinions. She'd had no one to share with since he died. It was time to meet a new man, someone who enjoyed the same pleasures she did, someone who would never leave her.

She opened the bedside table and reread the personals ad that would run in *What's Up/LA* this weekend:

> WHAT WOULD YOU DO TO LIVE
> HAPPILY EVER AFTER? MYTHICAL
> CREATURE SEEKS MATE WHO CAN
> BELIEVE. I AM PRETTY SWF,
> INTELLIGENT AND SUCCESSFUL. YOU
> ARE SWM, BRIGHT, ARTICULATE, FUN,
> AND CAPABLE OF SERIOUS LONG-TERM
> COMMITMENT. I CAN OFFER THE RIGHT
> MAN SOMETHING NO OTHER WOMAN
> CAN—WOULDN'T YOU LIKE TO KNOW
> MORE? LETTER WITH P.M. PHONE TO
> BOX #.

She smiled to herself. The ad would probably bring letters from nuts of every description, but it could also attract a real mate. She hoped to have her first responses sometime next week.

After her bath, she put on a black velour running suit with red trim and the $200 French sneakers she'd ordered from a catalog. Elliott was in the study unpacking the photos from the Pittsburgh show. He practically snapped to attention when she entered.

"Did you find the prints I left on the table?" Rusty asked.

"Oh, yes! I thought they were excellent. Are they for the next spread in *City of Angels*?" Elliott thought all of her photos were "excellent." She'd take more pleasure in the compliment if he had only once admitted to not liking one.

"Deadline's tomorrow—please wrap them and take them over in the morning. They'll choose three out of the five— I've numbered them on the back in my order of preference."

"Yes'm. Anything else?"

"I don't think so. I'm going out to eat—I'll take the Honda." She got the car keys off the hook in the kitchen. "Oh, Elliott?" she called as she passed the study, "would you also get a copy of *What's Up* tomorrow?"

Tony Flores and Spiker Jackson didn't have enough cash between them to buy a spoon, so they had to settle for glue. They were in their usual spot among the debris on the west side of the Venice Pavilion, with their backs to the wall. They'd found nearly a half a fifth of vodka in the litter of bottles, cans, cigarette butts, and used condoms, but it was hardly enough for a buzz for one, let alone two. The moon had already gone down, the beach was mostly deserted, although here and there they could see mounds marking the presence of the homeless who slept on Venice Beach.

Spiker had pushed the opening of the bag around his mouth and nose and was sucking noisily at the glue fumes when Tony spotted the lone jogger pacing down the path. He elbowed Spiker and jerked his head towards the runner.

"Kind of stupid, running alone here this late." The figure passed under a light and Tony saw it was a woman. Even better. "Mebbe we oughta teach her a lesson, huh?"

Spiker pulled his face out of the bag and looked vaguely in the direction Tony had indicated. "D'ya say sumpin', man?"

Tony looked around: no one else in sight. He untied the sock full of sand from his belt, and made sure the knots were secure. "C'mon. Mebbe she's got some bread, man; we could get some spoons from Chico, don't have to sniff this shit."

She was still a block away. Tony got up and went around to the water fountain, where he soaked the sock in the trickle of water. When he got back to the wall, Spiker was blearily watching the woman jog, but he hadn't moved. Tony kicked Spiker's foot and said, "Axe her a question, man; I'll sap 'er." When Spiker nodded, Tony ducked behind the trash bin next to the path.

The jogger passed Tony's hiding place and came even with Spiker, who was still sitting. "Uh, 'scuse me, ma'am . . ." he began, having no idea what he was going to say next. Rusty stopped and looked at Spiker, who stood up unsteadily, still grasping his glue bag. "Uh, you got any spare change?"

Before she had a chance to respond, Tony brought the beachjack down hard across the back of her head, and she crumpled to the ground, motionless.

"Drag her over there to the light, man; let's see what she's got."

Spiker put down his sack, and picked up the chick's hand to drag her. She was wearing a watch and he pulled it off and stuffed it in his pocket as he dragged her. What Tony didn't know wouldn't hurt him. Before he dropped her arm, he realized there was no pulse in the wrist and her pale eyes were staring blankly. "Jesusfuck, Tony, you kilt her!"

"Don't be stupid—I dint hit her that hard. See if she got a wallet." He tied the sock onto his belt, the wet sand soaking through his pants.

"I ain't touchin' no dead chick, man. This Bud's for you." Spiker snatched up the glue bag. "You get some spoon, I be at the garage.'' He took off, heading around the building in an arrhythmic lope, his hand clutching the pocket with the watch in it.

When he had gone, Tony squatted down to search the woman for money. Before he knew what had happened, he was on his back and the chick had him pinned to the ground. Fuck, she was strong! She had both his arms immobilized as she sat on his chest, and he couldn't buck her off. And the weird part was, she was smiling! Just before she lowered her head to his neck, Tony thought he saw two of her teeth lengthen, extending just like a cat's claws. He felt a sharp pain in the side of his neck, but it stopped almost instantly. He could smell the musky rose scent of her perfume and his vision began to swim. He stopped struggling as impossible colors danced in his eyes, mandalas of rotating intricate patterns that spiraled in and out to the beat of his blood. He could hear his pulse sounding like a tom-tom in his ears. As she sucked on his neck, he felt a surge in his throat that was almost orgasmic. He tasted a cloying sweetness in his saliva that hadn't been there a moment before, and then he gave himself up to the best high he'd ever had.

When she'd drunk enough blood to sate her, Rusty lifted her head and licked the blood off her lips. Her fangs had retracted. The punk was smiling but unconscious, still alive, the hole in his carotid already closed. Still straddling his limp body, she pulled up the right leg of her sweat pants and took the bowie knife from its holster. She placed the point precisely between the fang marks, and pushed the knife into his throat until both holes were swallowed by the sides of the blade, a trick she'd learned from Gregor. When she pulled it out, the rest of his blood spurted out rapidly and puddled on the sandy pavement; his smile faded. Grasping the knife handle firmly in her right hand, she raised her arm and stabbed him hard, once, in the chest. By the time she'd retrieved the knife, he was dead. She lifted his body and dumped him in the trash bin. "You picked the wrong woman to fuck with, asshole."

She walked the few feet to the sand. While shoving the knife in and out of the sand to clean it, she could see from the grit clinging to her shin that her left pant leg was wet. She brushed off the sand and smelled the moisture on her hand. Not blood. She must have been kneeling on his wet beachjack. Well, blood didn't show on black, anyway. She reholstered the blade and headed back the way she'd come, to the Honda and a stop home. She was high from the kill and it wasn't too late to go on a shoot.

She never saw Spiker's stunned face at the far corner of the Pavilion.

As soon as Jace got to work Friday morning, he began studying the Cannon and Garcia files. The blood on the necks of both men's shirts, along with no notations to the contrary, seemed to indicate that they were not undressed to any extent like Teece Cabot. However, the neck wounds were identical in all three cases. Apparently, "Boomer" Cannon had not been buried under the lifeguard station as Levy had originally believed—he had merely been covered with his urine-stained sleeping bag. Enough sand had been thrown on the bag to make it look like it had been there a long time. No one had bothered to look under the lump until the lifeguard had noticed the growing smell of "something rotting" and had gone to investigate the source of the odor.

The phone rang. "Robbery-Homicide. Levy."

"Levy, this is King. We just got in another stabbing victim; this time from Pacific Division. Knife to the carotid and left lung. The neck wound is only an inch and a half deep; the chest wound seven inches, buried to the hilt, judging by the bruising. Male Hispanic, no I.D., looks to be early twenties, six-one, two hundred and ten pounds. I've got him on the table now.'' Jace took notes rapidly.

''Is he completely dressed?''

The medical examiner laughed, ''No, Levy—it's kind of hard to do a post on a dressed stiff. But he was wearing a dark blue T-shirt, dirty jeans with a braided leather belt, white socks and gray sneakers, no underwear. He's got a few tracks, none fresher than three days.''

''Who's assigned to the case?''

''Ghiz and Sale at Pacific. I told them you had a pattern and would probably be in contact. I'll be done with this by lunchtime, then I'm gone for the weekend; McIntyre will have the file if you've got any questions.''

Jace thanked the M.E. for calling and looked up the number for Pacific Division—it was still listed as Venice Station. He found that Detectives Ghiz and Sale were on their way back from the crime scene, so he left word that he would meet them at their station in half an hour.

''Hey, Liz—that one you owe me for doing the report last night?'' His partner looked up with a crooked expectant smile. ''Pacific has another neck-knifing. I'm going to see what they know. We really should start going through this''—he hefted the computer printout—''and see what connects. How about getting started on it while I'm gone?''

Liz sighed and took the stack from Jace. ''What do you want flagged?''

''Neck wounds consistent with a bowie knife, particularly in connection with a chest wound. Pay close attention to male victims, indigents, Westside divisions, night assaults—not

just homicides—maybe one of his victims lived, and you'd
better check the clearances, too, in case he got bagged for an
attack.''

"That's a lot of work, Levy. There must be eight thousand
knife assaults here. Don't expect me to be finished by the
time you get back. Hey! How about bringing some Killer
Shrimp from Venice for lunch?'' She handed him a twenty.

"You're on.'' He put on his Bogart voice, "Thanksh,
Liz—you're just about aces with me.''

She smiled. "I should have known it would cost too much
to leave you with that report last night.''

Even though her back was to the door, Liz knew when Jace
had returned by the smell of Killer Shrimp, from the restaurant
of the same name. The only thing on the menu, the shrimp
swam in a hot, spicy garlicky sauce she'd have to be dead to
miss. By the time he got to the desk, she had cleared the open
printout and her notes to the side.

"God, that smells great!''

"It was hell in the car—my mouth watered so much, my
shirt is wet.'' Jace gave Liz a ten, poured the shrimp into the
disposable plastic bowls, and handed her a spoon and a bag
of French bread. He took his to his side of the desk. Liz got
two soft drinks from the vending machine in the hall.

When she sat down, Jace told her about the body from the
Venice Pavilion. "They got an I.D. from a uniform who
recognized the stiff. His name's Antonio Vincente Flores,
and he's a piece of garbage, in more ways than one. He's
been popped for mugging joggers on the beach, possession
of speedballs and dust, B and E, vagrancy, and indecent
exposure for pissing in public. Sometime after midnight at
the Venice Pavilion, the assailant punctured his carotid—on

the left side of the neck this time, another puncture to the left lung. Flores bled to death on the ground. Then, our strongman picked up two hundred and ten pounds of dead druggie and deposited him where he belonged, in the nearest trash receptacle—ten feet away.''

Jace soaked a piece of bread in the shrimp sauce and shoved it in his mouth, spilling sauce down his chin. Liz passed him a stack of napkins.

"How big do you have to be to carry two hundred pounds of dead weight ten feet? Any witnesses? Suspects?"

"*Nada, muchacha*. Flores had a damp beachjack tied to his belt. Victor Ghiz said there was hair on it. The lab's got it. Might be Flores was stoned enough to try to mug one of the Gold's Gym bodybuilders. Ghiz and Sale are on top of it; they're also checking out who he hangs with. I'll check with them Monday. You find anything?" He indicated the printout.

"Yeah—our guy has been busy. I started with the uncleared homicides—over three hundred of them." She pulled over her notes so she could refer to them while she ate. "Out of a hundred and twenty-three knife homicides, twelve had carotid punctures, eight with chest wounds; three had carotid slashes, none with chest wounds. Of those fifteen, one was killed by an awl—neck, shoulder, and eyes; two were women—both hookers; nine were homeless, and ten were on the Westside. I haven't started a chart yet, but I will. I called Viramontes, and we'll have the printouts for the rest of the county by the middle of next week if he can get the computer time. I think we're onto a serial killer, Jace. You want to talk to Cosentino, get us assigned to this?"

"Let's see what we can distill from this stuff first. Can you work with me this weekend?"

"Sandy will be thrilled. He was complaining about my overtime before this happened." She frowned. "I can come over to your place in the morning and we can work on this part of the day tomorrow and Sunday—but I have to go to Sandy's partners' dinner tomorrow night or I won't have a husband to go home to."

"If this is a serial, he better get used to it. We can see Cosentino Monday and show him what we have." Liz dumped the empty lunch containers in the trash and gave part of the printout to Jace.

Al Watt entered the room and sniffed loudly. "Hey! Who's got Killer Shrimp?"

"You're too late, Watt—the killer's already been executed."

CHAPTER
Three

At fifty, Rusty was a very young vampire, but she was the oldest one left . . . at least for the last two years. Gregor had passed the three-hundred-year mark before he died, and he had been certain that, before Rusty, he was the last of his kind; he'd said that it had been over a century since he'd known of another. Never a widespread phenomenon, vampirism was an anomaly of "unenlightened" past centuries. It all came down to lack of belief, he'd explained: both his personal longevity and the general demise of the species.

Contrary to popular fiction, there are only three ways to "kill" a vampire, one of which works only with very old vampires. Since none of them are modern methods of either murder or execution, a vampire is unlikely to be killed by anyone who does not believe in the ancient race and act accordingly. No civilized judicial system executes by decapitation anymore (although Gregor said that several vampires had been lost to the French guillotine two hundred years ago).

No lynch mob would still think to kill with a wooden stake through the heart.

Gregor told her that once in the thirties, he had been caught by a contingent of the Ku Klux Klan which accurately suspected the foreigner of foul play in connection with the death of a Klan member's daughter. It was midnight when they took him out into the woods and beat him to (what they thought was) death. Then they tied a noose around his neck and hung him from a tree and left him there. As soon as they were gone, he tore the rope apart and was safely out of the area long before dawn. Exposure to sunlight doesn't directly kill vampires, but the ultraviolet will age them very rapidly to their actual age—a method not yet fatal to Rusty, but Gregor could have been turned to dust in minutes.

Belief was also the necessary element that made vampires so scarce. If every feeder automatically became vampiric, the planet would have run out of humans long ago, belief or not. But becoming a vampire is a deliberate act, taking a fair amount of time and care—time for the venom to cause its changes, care that the thrice-weekly feedings be limited in amount so that the novice vampire doesn't die prematurely of blood loss before his own venom sacs have developed. Once the sacs are functional for feeding, it takes another ten years before the venom is sufficiently potent to cause sac development in another. Enlistees were never rarer than in the enlightened twentieth century. Gregor had been searching since the mid-nineteenth century for a companionable mate eager to persevere through the process when he met Rusty in a cloud of tear gas.

*   *   *

She was twenty-eight in 1969, taking photography courses at an art college in Oakland and working nights at Moe's Books in Berkeley.

Although no longer a virgin, Rusty could still count the number of men she'd dated on one hand and her lovers on two fingers. Forty pounds overweight for most of her life (that had changed when she switched to a diet of blood), she'd felt unattractive to men and kept to herself, preferring the safety of observing people to the risk of disappointment inherent in contact. Men had always abandoned her if she trusted them. Her beloved father left her and her mother when Rusty was ten, never to be heard from again.

Her high school sweetheart, to whom she'd given herself in the back seat of a Rambler in the belief that they would marry upon graduation, stood her up on her eighteenth birthday. She'd bought a new dress and had her hair permed in anticipation of the romantic dinner out that he'd promised. She waited four hours for him before going to bed in tears. The next day, she'd heard that he'd gone back to an old girlfriend; their engagement was the talk of the school.

She'd had a few more dates over the next ten years, but most of them appeared to be interested only in sex, and didn't call again if she wouldn't sleep with them; the one she did sleep with never called again, either.

It was late spring when the People's Park demonstrations got out of hand. Telegraph Avenue ("Telly") was frequently a morass of protesting students, "outside agitators," and observers facing off against Berkeley Police, the Oakland Police's brutal Tac Squad, and, eventually, the National Guard. The demonstrators chanted, carried signs, and used their sheer numbers; the police used batons and tear gas. Telly had been filled with the noxious gas so often that year that the fumes seeped into the bricks of the buildings lining the street and lingered on the trees for days after a confrontation.

Rusty was about to close up Moe's for the night when several people burst through the front door, yelling "Tear gas!" They were fleeing from the gas-clouded street and the pursuing masked police.

While one of her co-workers got a bucket of water and paper towels for the blinded protesters, Rusty locked the door and stuffed wet towels into the cracks. She tried to get plastic dropcloths over all the books closest to the door to help prevent the fumes from getting into the paper. A man was helping her, but it wasn't until she'd run out of sheets that she took a look at him.

He was older—maybe mid-forties—and quite distinguished-looking with dark, piercing eyes and shoulder-length silver hair that contrasted with the relative youth of his lean, pale face. He was wearing a Grateful Dead lightning-skull T-shirt and jeans under a tweed jacket. He smiled at her.

"It would be a catastrophe for that terrible odor to get into these lovely books. I expect that should do it as long as no one opens the door until the gas dissipates." He had an unusual accent which she couldn't identify.

"I don't think anyone's in a hurry to go out there." She realized that she wouldn't be able to go home for at least an hour. "Thanks for helping me. Would you like a Coke? We've got a few in the office fridge."

"No, thank you—I'm fine. My name's Gregor Bathory. May I know yours?" She was entranced by his manner, so unlike that of other men she'd met.

"Rusty. Risha Cadigan." Belatedly, she put out her hand to shake.

He took her hand, and raised it to his lips, lightly kissing the back of her hand; before he straightened up, he turned her palm up and pressed his lips briefly to the inside of her wrist. A quick thrill coursed through her body, and she blushed in confusion when he released her hand. She tried to cover herself and abruptly asked the first thing that came to mind.

"Where are you from? I can't place your accent."

He laughed. "Originally, I come from a part of Eastern Europe that is sometimes Rumania, sometimes Hungary. But I've spent many years in both America and England, which has diluted my accent, I believe. I'm here for a year from Cambridge as a visiting lecturer on film from literature—I was walking home from my evening class when I got caught in all that." He gestured to the street outside. "Are you a student?"

"No. I mean, not at Cal. I take some classes at the art college. I do photography"—she dipped her head in self-deprecation—"or at least I try to."

"I'm sure you're quite adept. Perhaps you might show me some of your work—I enjoy photography as an art. I have a small collection of photographs, some quite valuable, including some by Stieglitz and Cartier-Bresson. Unfortunately, I can't offer to show them to you just now as they are in my residence in London, but I've recently acquired a delightful Brassaï which I have here. I would be honored to have your opinion sometime."

Within the hour, Telly had emptied of both people and gas fumes, and those who had ducked into nearby buildings came out to go home. Rusty unlocked the doors of Moe's and let everyone out. Everyone except the charming Gregor, who had asked to be permitted to see her "safely home."

Rusty thought that the eight-block walk to her apartment

went altogether too fast. Gregor was a skilled conversationalist and he quickly put her at ease. He seemed truly interested in her and listened intently whenever she spoke. She couldn't remember anyone ever paying so much attention to her before. It was hours later that she realized how little he had talked about himself.

By the time they reached her building, Rusty was nervous about what she should do and say at the door. Although she wanted to talk more to him, she was afraid of intimacy should she invite him up to her room. She needn't have worried. When they got to her door, Gregor took her hand.

"It's been a long time since I've met such an intelligent and vital woman that I'm actually quite grateful for the tear gas that brought us together. Please—may I see you again?" Rusty didn't trust herself to answer him with the same grace he exhibited, so she nodded. A beat later, she remembered to add a smile.

He looked quite pleased. "Do you work the same hours at the bookstore tomorrow night?"

"No, I only work until six on Saturdays."

"Excellent! If you're free tomorrow evening, perhaps you'd care to accompany me into the City. Do you like music? The Grateful Dead are playing at the Fillmore. Or we could find some jazz in North Beach if you prefer?"

"Could we really go to the Fillmore? I've never been to a rock concert before."

He arranged to pick her up at eight the next evening. Then he kissed her hand once again, and was gone.

Jace and Liz were well-suited as partners and had developed a division of labor that played to their strengths. Liz was logical and her skill in organizing the chaotic mass of information produced in a homicide investigation verged on the miraculous. Several times, Jace had overlooked a key clue in the evidence until he'd seen it in the context of one of Liz's lists or charts. Jace's aptitude was his synthesis of crime-scene observation with an almost instinctual recognition of patterns of human behavior. He relied on her thoroughness, and she honored his "hunches"; Frank Cosentino once described Liz as the objective side of a case, while Jace was the subjective. When they'd first teamed up five years ago, others referred to them as The Odd Squad—and as Princess Yuppie and The Jew—and subjected them to a fair amount of derision. As their clearance record surpassed that of the other homicide detectives, the nicknames were dropped and the derision turned to grudging respect.

Frank Cosentino was the homicide coordinator and their immediate boss. Son and grandson to New York cops, he was raised in New York's Little Italy; in spite of nearly thirty years on the LAPD, he still sounded like a New Yorker. He'd been a three-pack-a-day smoker until the police doctor told him seven years ago that he could either give up cigarettes or his job. Cosentino quit smoking cold and hadn't had a cigarette since, but when Liz and Jace told him they thought there was a serial killer working the Westside, he began to absently pat his pockets in search of a smoke.

"What do the victims have in common so far?" He stopped patting his pockets and got a piece of sugarless gum out of his drawer.

"Aside from the neck wounds? For one thing, none of the fourteen probables had any defense wounds," Liz ticked off points on her manicured nails as she spoke, "in spite of often being stabbed repeatedly. Secondly, all were apparently killed after midnight. Next, most of them were on the Westside:

Santa Monica, Redondo Beach, Topanga, Brentwood, West
L.A., Palms . . .''

''. . . and Venice,'' Jace added. ''Flores of the trash bin
is the most recent one we know of.''

''Right.'' Liz continued ticking off points. ''Most of them
were homeless or drifters. I think that's about it so far.''

Cosentino popped his gum thoughtfully. ''No leads on any
of them?'' Liz shook her head. ''Okay, look. We'll put it out
on the Teletype, let the other stations know what you're
looking for. But I can't spare you full-time on derelict murders, not with the load we've got right now. Do what you can,
when you can. In the meantime, I've got another homicide for
you—it was called in just before you came in. A twelve-year-
old boy just shot his ten-year-old brother with their father's
gun. It's probably accidental, but check it out. Here's the
address.''

Jace took the note, and he and Liz turned to go.

Cosentino added, ''Keep an eye on the knifings. If he starts
getting citizens, it'll be your game.''

The Teletype about the neck knifings brought reports of
other probable victims from recent months.

An investigator in Long Beach called about two victims
they'd found separately in August who'd died of blood loss
due to bowie-knife-size neck wounds. One had also been
stabbed in the chest, apparently as an afterthought. Both in
the middle of the night. Both were men. One was a black
sixty-two-year-old night watchman at a construction site
whose body was found in his shed the next morning. There
was no evidence of a struggle. The other was a thirty-four-
year-old white schizophrenic who had been picked up several
times for bear-hugging any woman within his reach, some-

thing that apparently occurred whenever he stopped taking his medication. The investigator said the man was known to be nonviolent in spite of his propensity and he'd always obeyed promptly if the woman told him to let go of her. He'd been found in a dumpster, stabbed twice. He also showed no defense wounds.

Inglewood had a case from April where the victim was a seventeen-year-old car thief who was found dead in the back seat of a Volvo he'd stolen the day before.

Police at Los Angeles International Airport reported an uncleared case from January when a routine morning patrol discovered the body of a forty-six-year-old welder shoved under his car in LAX's employee parking lot. The pattern of wounds was the same as in the other cases.

The lab report came in on the beachjack found on Tony Flores's body. The two hairs found on one side of the sock were dark auburn and one was just over ten inches long. A few fibers were found on an adjacent side of the sock, and so weren't necessarily from the same auburn-haired person who'd been hit with the beachjack; two matching fibers were found on Flores's T-shirt. The fibers were short black velour. Neither hair nor fiber had been Flores's.

As the crime scene and forensic reports began to pile up, Liz managed to requisition a computer terminal to organize all the information. Terry Viramontes, the station's computer expert, set up a database for her to cross-reference the evidence, but the work was going slowly and Liz was frustrated.

"We've got nineteen probables at this point and more printouts due from County any day now," she told Jace. "And that's just the homicides. God knows what's in the assaults lists. There might be a lot more homicides if I had the time to go back even farther than fall 1990, but I can't even get what we have entered in the database. It seems that every time I think I'm on a roll, we get sent out on another case. I need more time on this.''

Jace snapped, ''What the fuck do you want from me? I've been working overtime to field the incoming calls and handle all the other reports and I spent nearly an hour trying to get Cosentino to assign us to this full-time. I just get the same broken record: not a priority. You think I've been sitting here with my thumb up my ass?''

Liz stared open-mouthed at Jace's uncharacteristic outburst. ''Chill out, Levy. I wasn't blaming you. What's with you today?''

He looked at Liz, shoved his chair back, and got up. Without answering her, he went to the men's room and locked himself in a stall.

What *was* with him today? He was overworked and tired, but he'd been that way many times before without jumping on Liz. He hoped it was just fatigue, but he knew there was always the possibility that it was what he feared most, something even scarier than his nightmares. Several times in the last year or two, he'd thought of confiding in Liz; he knew he could trust her not to tell anyone his secret—after all, he trusted her with his life—but he didn't know if he could say it out loud. He never had before.

It was becoming too much of a burden to carry alone. Maybe it was time.

''Dear Mythical Creature,'' the letter read, ''I enjoyed your ad in the current issue of *What's Up/LA*, and I am eager to find out what you can offer me that ''no other woman can'' (I sure hope it isn't a penis!). My name is Les Kaufman, and I'm an attorney, but don't hold that against me. I'm thirty-seven, semi-handsome, 5′11″, with curly dark brown hair (what's left of it) and green eyes, and I live in Marina del Rey. I've never been married, but am willing to make a commitment with the right woman. My interests are my work, golf, movies, and moonlit walks on the beach with a lovely lady. (You don't say what kind of mythical creature you are, but I hope it isn't a cyclops!) I can be reached evenings at the number above. I look forward to meeting you.''

Rusty had a date to meet Les for drinks at Babar's, a restaurant in the Marina, at 8:30. She hadn't been on a date in years, and she changed her outfit three times before finally settling on a black silk jumpsuit accented with a long yellow-and-black silk scarf. By the time Elliott had finished doing her hair and make-up, she'd developed a fair case of nerves. During the twenty-minute drive to the Marina, she kept readjusting her zipper between too little and too much cleavage; the last half-inch adjustment in favor of modesty occurred as she locked the BMW.

Les recognized her from her description as soon as she entered the restaurant, and steered her to a table in the bar. By his third double Glenfiddich, he had propositioned her four times ("Why don't we just go back to my place and get it on?") and had talked incessantly about himself and his possessions. Rusty resented the time and emotional energy that she'd spent preparing for the date, and hoped that the other responses to her ad wouldn't turn out so disappointingly.

As she followed his Mercedes back to his condominium, she thought that the evening wouldn't be a total waste—at least she would get a dinner out of it.

Rusty had been out with Gregor eight times in a three-week period and he had been A Perfect Gentleman. He always offered her a choice of activities for the evening; they'd been to the Fillmore and a play at The American Conservatory Theater in San Francisco, as well as a play and two movies in Berkeley. He brought her flowers and invariably kissed her hand when they met. He made it quite clear that he was taken with her and looked forward to their time together. Rusty was happier than she'd ever been and thought she might be falling in love. However, his goodnight kiss lasted only a moment longer than a peck; he'd never made a pass. She began to fear he might be gay. She knew she ought to take the initiative or at least bring up the subject of sex before she fell much farther, but she was afraid of the answer. If there was something Seriously Wrong, all the fun she'd been having with him would have to end . . . and she wanted it to go on forever.

They were at Gregor's rented Victorian playing Scrabble and smoking pot in front of the fireplace the night she broached the subject.

"I've been having the best time with you, Gregor." She twisted her shirt hem while she tried to figure how to phrase what she wanted to say. He took her active hand and held it between both of his.

"I'm very glad to hear you say that. I'm quite enchanted with you, Risha." No one had called her Risha since her father had left. She was pleased that Gregor used it. "You've been on my mind at the most inappropriate moments, like during a lecture I was delivering on Brecht," he laughed. "I'd been looking for you for many years, and now that I've met you, I can't stop thinking about you. Do you mind that I said that?"

Rusty beamed. She couldn't help it. "I was afraid you weren't . . . attracted to me. I mean, I knew you were having a good time, but you've never . . ." she trailed off, hoping he'd catch the gist.

Gregor looked down for a moment, silent, and then apparently made a decision. Standing up, he gently pulled Rusty to her feet, and led her into the bedroom. He put his arms around her and kissed her full on the mouth, his cool lips sending a hot rush through her body. But when they stopped, he took her hand again and led her into the bathroom. He flipped on the light, backed her up to the sink, and kissed her again. She began to feel confused. Why were they in here?

"In some ways, I am unlike anyone you've ever met before, Risha, and perhaps it's time you find out why." Putting both hands on her shoulders, he turned her around to face the large mirror.

For a minute, she didn't know what she was supposed to see. Surely, he couldn't be showing her how fat she was. Then she realized what she was seeing and she turned back to him, then back to the mirror.

"I . . . I don't understand. Is it a trick mirror?" Standing behind her, he encircled her with his bare arms. The image didn't change: she alone was reflected.

He took her hand again. "Let's go sit down. This will take a while."

CHAPTER
Four

Jace stared at the page without comprehension. He made it a matter of habit to scan each notebook before he began a new one. He couldn't believe the note to himself to call a cleaning service out to the house, but not just because he hadn't done it yet. What bothered him was that he had no memory of writing the note. It was definitely his writing and he could tell from the pad's chronology that the reminder was written immediately after Teece Cabot had been found in Topanga—but it wasn't reminding, he could swear he never wrote it.

The memory lapse, not his first, in addition to his outburst at Liz two days before, scared the hell out of him. Nothing had frightened him like this since he was six and thought a monster hid under his bed at night. Even though there was nothing she could do about it, he resolved to talk to Liz by the end of the day. If nothing else, he thought it would make him feel better to be able to tell someone.

When he returned to his desk, Liz was concluding a phone call, writing rapidly as she spoke. When she hung up, she said to Jace, ''Don't sit down—we've got a call.'' He stuck a fresh notebook in his pocket and got his gun out of the desk drawer while she got her purse. ''Detective Ghiz from Pacific. They've got another one.''

Liz drove, as she usually did. On the way across town, she told Jace, ''He was calling from the Marina; he and his partner just got there, but he knew it was our guy as soon as he saw the neck puncture. It's a citizen this time, Levy. Ghiz said the housekeeper found him in the bedroom of his condo and called 911.''

Like several other large condominium developments on the Westside, Admiral's Rest in Marina del Rey was a warren of identical ''unique'' three-story buildings separated by extensive faux rain-forest landscaping, with picturesque footpaths and bridges over burbling *koi*-filled streams. It took Jace and Liz nearly fifteen minutes after they'd parked to locate the crime scene.

''For what they pay, they ought to get some of those 'you are here' maps around this place,'' he complained.

''It's probably part of their security system. A burglar would get caught before he found his way out of the complex. Here we are: building H. Ghiz said number 17 on the second floor.''

The patrolman at the door had been told to expect them. He directed them to Ghiz and Sale in the master bedroom, warning them that they'd just started dusting for prints. An Hispanic woman was lying on the living room couch with a wet facecloth over her eyes. ''The housekeeper,'' the patrolman explained. ''She's been fainting.''

They found the two Pacific Division homicide detectives

talking in the hallway outside the bedroom. Victor Ghiz was in his early thirties, short and slight of build, with dark good looks and a small moustache; his partner, Patrick Sale, tall, blond, and tanned, looked like an overage surfer. Jace introduced them to Liz. After a round of handshaking, Sale went to talk to the housekeeper and to ask the criminalist to check the vacuum cleaner bag. Ghiz filled them in.

"Lester Kaufman, attorney at law. Thirty-nine years old, single, lives alone. The maid found him when she arrived at nine-fifteen this morning." Ghiz checked his notebook. "Her name's Merla Ramirez." He smiled. "The first thing she did when the officer came was show her green card. She comes in for half a day each Monday and Friday while Kaufman's at work. She's got her own key, has been working for him three years. Unfortunately for forensics, she'd already cleaned the living room before she entered the bedroom. She washed and dried two glasses, vacuumed and wiped all the surfaces in the room. Apparently did an excellent job," he added ruefully.

"I ought to get her number," Jace muttered.

"The coroner is on the way, so 'you can look, but you'd better not touch.' "

Ghiz led them into the bedroom. Curly haired and mustachioed, Les Kaufman was lying on his back on the blood-soaked king-size waterbed. He was completely nude, his hands tied together with a black-and-yellow silk scarf. The knot had been slipped over a large open hook set into the headboard. He had a stab wound on the right side of his neck. His penis was missing.

"Jesus! What happened to his cock?" Jace winced involuntarily.

"Makes you shrivel right up, doesn't it?" Ghiz sympathized. "It's on the floor on the other side of the bed. Looks like the killer just cut it off and threw it away. He was probably unconscious or dead by then, or he would've unhooked his hands."

"The housekeeper say whether the hook was there before?" Liz asked.

"It's been there as long as she's been working for him. We also found this." Ghiz pulled open the bedside drawers with the end of his pen, so Jace and Liz could see inside. The top drawer contained condoms, a couple of vibrators, a black sleep mask, some wooden clothespins, a tube of KY Jelly, some hospital-style leather restraints, and a rolled-up suede belt with no buckle. The bottom drawer held a copy of *The Story of O*, a book called *Pecker's Bad Boy*, an issue of *What's Up/LA*, and a box of Kleenex. "She doesn't recognize the scarf. He must've got kinky with someone who wasn't just playing."

When the coroner's investigator arrived to examine and bag the body, she told the detectives that the type of bruise and small amount of blood at the stub indicated that Kaufman was already dead when his penis was amputated. "The waterbed isn't leaking. You can see that it was done with an upward-cutting motion, probably while holding the head of the penis with the other hand." She estimated the time of death at between eleven P.M. and midnight the night before.

Eventually, Kaufman was untied. Jace caught a faint whiff of rose. No one noticed the single auburn hair that slid from a fold in the scarf before the scarf could be placed in an evidence bag. It joined the lint and other hairs collecting between the waterbed mattress and the frame.

By the time Jace and Liz had left, they'd found Kaufman's

calendar with a notation for the day before that said simply, "Rusty—8:30." Not even an indication of A.M. or P.M. The name appeared nowhere else on the calendar. His personal telephone directory yielded no Rusty, but Sale planned to contact everyone in the book anyway. Officers had already started canvassing neighbors. Ghiz and Sale were going to Kaufman's office to talk to his co-workers and promised to call Jace and Liz late that afternoon.

"Cosentino has to give us this full-time now," Liz insisted as they got into the car. "He's finally killed an upstanding citizen."

" 'Upstanding' is a poor choice of adjective, given the circumstances, Liz," Jace said wryly. "But I'm beginning to be not-so-sure about the killer being a 'he.' 'Rusty' could be either a male or female name . . . if it's even the killer. Both Cabot and Kaufman were straight, judging from the porn they kept around. Cabot was partially undressed and Kaufman was nude—and they were killed on their own beds. At least Kaufman had probably been planning to have sex with his killer. And there's the scarf. That's definitely a woman's scarf."

"But what about the cracked sternum on Cabot? And Flores's body being thrown into the trash bin? A woman just wouldn't be strong enough."

"Shit, Liz, maybe she had help. A male accomplice who hides until the victim is unconscious? And that hair on Flores's beachjack was long for a man."

"We don't even know if the hair belonged to the killer. And there are a lot of long-haired men on the Westside," Liz observed. "Isn't a collaboration rare for a serial killer?"

"Almost as rare as a female serial killer, but not unheard-of. Don't forget Bianchi and Buono.'' Kenneth Bianchi and Angelo Buono were the cousins known as The Hillside Strangler; they'd killed ten women in the Los Angeles area in the late seventies.

Liz nodded thoughtfully as they stopped at a light. "Hey, you want to pick up some Killer Shrimp to take back?''

"Let's eat there instead. I want to talk to you about something . . . personal.'' She turned west toward the restaurant.

Although Liz thought of her partner as a good friend, she realized he seldom talked to her about his personal life. She knew he'd been sleeping with Ellen Fisher, who apparently lived with another man, and thought that might be what he wanted to discuss. He was obviously having a hard time getting started, and ate most of his lunch in silence.

"So, what's on your mind?'' Liz dipped the tip of a piece of bread in shrimp sauce and nibbled it, looking at Jace expectantly from under her brushed eyebrows.

Jace sighed, and put down his spoon. "It's hard for me to talk about this—can you promise that what I say will stay between us?''

She put down her bread and crossed her heart, her expression serious. "Hope to die, Jace, you know that. Are you in some kind of trouble? If it's money . . .''

Jace waved off the offer. "I wish it were that easily fixed. Actually, it can't be fixed at all.'' He looked at his bowl, drank some water, glanced at the other patrons—anything but meet Liz's eyes.

She took a deep breath. "You want another partner.'' A statement in monotone.

He looked at her then. "God, no, Liz—you're the best partner I've ever had, and damned near my only friend. It doesn't have anything to do with you.'' He took a deep breath.

"Have you ever heard of Huntington's chorea? Huntington's disease?"

Liz shook her head.

"It's a rare genetic disorder, not contagious. It's a horrible, insidious disease that attacks the nervous system—it usually begins with mental disturbances—memory lapses, irritability, inability to concentrate, stuff like that." Jace spoke evenly, almost a cold recitation. "Movement disorders develop over the next several years with muscle weakness, spasms and jerky movements, slurring speech. Dementia and paralysis eventually set in. Between five and thirty years after onset, it's fatal. It's always fatal." He paused. "It usually starts at around forty years of age." He stared, unseeing, into his bowl of shrimp. "My mother died from it seven years ago."

Liz was stunned. "Do you think you've caught—inherited it? Have you seen a doctor?"

"I have a fifty-fifty chance of inheriting it, and there's no way to tell in advance if I'm going to get it. There are no effective treatments."

Liz reached across the table for Jace's hand. "God, Jace, I'm so sorry. How are you dealing with it?"

"Not very well, I'm afraid. I've been having a lot of nightmares—monsters trying to kill me and shit like that," he laughed mirthlessly. "To tell you the truth, I'm scared shitless, Liz. My mother's death was almost a blessing after the deterioration that preceded it."

Liz squeezed Jace's hand tightly. "Are you afraid that no one will be there to take care of you?"

Jace had never articulated that particular fear, but now that it had been voiced, it washed over him like a tidal wave. He fought to hold back tears; unable to speak, he nodded.

"You're not alone, Jace—you have to know that. I'll always do what I can, and so would a lot of other people."

Jace was deeply touched by Liz's words, but again he could only nod.

"Look, Jace, whether you inherit it or not, you've got to get some outlet for the stress, some way to blow off the panic. Have you talked to the department shrink?"

He found his voice. "You're the only person I've ever told . . . and you promised this would stay between us. If the department finds out, I'll be forced into retirement. I don't even know if I have it yet, Liz. I just needed to tell someone I could trust. You'll tell me if it starts to affect my work, won't you?"

"Of course." She smiled reassuringly. "And you talk freely about it to me whenever you want; don't worry that you're dumping on me . . ."

"That's what friends are for, right?"

Rusty would have been sure that Gregor was either joking or crazy, except for that weird trick with the mirror.

"A vampire? You mean like Dracula? A guy with a cape and fangs who sucks blood and turns into a bat?"

Gregor smiled. "I can't turn into a bat, and it's been many years since capes were in fashion for men, but yes, Risha: like Dracula. The historical model for Stoker's book was Vlad IV, a fifteenth-century ruler from a region not far from where I was born two hundred years later. My grandfather's second cousin, Elizabeth Bathory, was walled up in 1610 by the king of Hungary when one of her feeders escaped. I crossed over in 1729, when I was forty-seven years old."

"You're telling me that you're—" Rusty did some fast calculations "—almost three hundred years old? C'mon, Gregor, nobody can live that long!"

" 'Live' is a relative term, my dear. In the most common sense of the word, I am not alive. My heart beats twice an hour, I breathe once in that time, my blood is different from yours. I'm not subject to disease or age and I heal almost instantly from injury. I have the strength of three men and could conceivably outlast every human on earth, but not for long," he laughed, "as I need humanity to survive. Do you remember last week when we went for a hamburger after the movie and I didn't eat? I told you I was on a special diet. The diet consists of fresh human blood, Risha. It's all I eat. I had to sacrifice a varied menu for immortality."

Rusty could tell Gregor believed what he was saying, but she wasn't so sure she could. "You kill people for food? Is that what you're telling me?"

"Is that so very different from killing cows and chickens for food? Nearly every animal on the planet is food for another one. My feeders happen to be human."

"Yeah, well, if you're a vampire, where are your fangs?" Rusty laughed, peering at Gregor's mouth. She thought this joke of his must have a helluva punch line. He didn't disappoint her. He opened his mouth and sneered back his upper lip. While she watched, his canine teeth lengthened from his colorless gums until they were nearly an inch long. A drop of clear fluid appeared at the tip of each fang. Gregor wet his forefinger with the venom. His fangs retracted. He closed his mouth and looked at Rusty. Her mouth was open in astonishment. He gently traced the drop of venom along her lower lip. She licked it. It was sweet. Very sweet.

"I want you to join me, Risha. I'm the only vampire left. I've seen everyone I've known grow old and die for nearly ten generations. You can't realize how incredibly lonely I am. I have wealth—you'd never want for anything. I could show you the world by night, more fascinating than you'd ever imagine. We'd be together forever, watching the world age while we stay eternally young. Trust me, Risha. I love you.''

Two years later, in Amsterdam, Rusty asked him, "After telling me your secret, what would you have done if I hadn't accepted?''

"Regretfully, I would have had you for dinner, my dear.''

Cosentino muttered, "Shit," and crumpled the empty gum package. "You got any gum?" Jace shook his head while Liz rummaged in her purse, eventually surfacing with the last third of a roll of wintergreen Certs.

"Close as I come." She passed the roll to Cosentino, who put two in his mouth. "You said on Monday that if he kills a citizen, it would be our case. Lester Kaufman wasn't homeless, a drifter, or a bottle baby. He was a tax-paying home owner. And he wasn't just stabbed—he was mutilated. It's going to be about twenty minutes before the press finds out about his murder, even if they don't know about the others."

"That makes it less than thirty minutes before Bradley calls Gates and the chief calls me. Who's handling the case at Pacific?"

"Victor Ghiz and Patrick Sale," Jace answered. "They're thorough, but in over their heads with this one. They also got the call on Flores in Venice last week."

"I'll call the captain over there and see what we can work out."

"Sergeant Frederik Waner at the Sheriff's Station in Malibu has the Topanga case," Liz added. Cosentino nodded and made a note.

"As of now, you two are the task force on this killer. Try

not to step on anyone's toes at the other precincts; you're going to have to depend on them a lot for footwork. I want frequent verbal reports on your progress—the capos are going to be breathing down my neck and I want to be able to let them know we're on top of this.

"Keep the . . . mutilation . . . out of circulation, *capisce*? And the longer the press takes to find out we have a serial killer loose, the better. We don't need the kind of panic we saw with the Night Stalker. Who's been handling this at the crime lab?" Cosentino patted his pockets absently, then ate two more mints.

"Josephann Tevis from County was on the Cabot case; Ronnie Schaffer had the Venice and Marina cases; King did all the posts," said Liz.

"Sharp people. Josephann," Cosentino mused, "they sure come up with some strange names. Okay, I'll see what I can do about drafting them for calls that fit the pattern. For now, maybe you should treat the—Kaufman?" Jace nodded. "—the Kaufman case as a single. There's always the possibility that the killer offed the others to make this look like one in a motive-less string, while Kaufman was the target all along.

"Meanwhile, it wouldn't hurt to query a profile from the ViCAP unit at the FBI. It didn't work out with the Night Stalker case, but you never know. Have you ever seen the form?"

"I've read it. It's a muther," Jace said. "Must be at least two hours' work. Twenty-five-page booklet. For each case."

"I'll handle that," Liz volunteered. "I'll start with Kaufman, then do Cabot and Flores."

"Okay, boys and girls. You need anything, let me know—and I'll let you know why you can't have it. Go catch this bastard."

* * *

It was just before four when Victor Ghiz phoned from Pacific.

"Captain said to report to you on everything concerning the Kaufman case, but to continue our investigation. What we got so far is a load of nothing. It's a small office, two attorneys and a paralegal who share a receptionist and a secretary in Culver City. It's all civil stuff, lawsuits and divorces. His partner says Kaufman's current case load was pretty light—the biggest case he had was a dispute over a severance package with a former VP of a client's resort and condo company and they were close to settling for something in the vicinity of $20K. The partner wants a court order before he turns over any more info about Kaufman's cases, but he made it pretty clear that it wasn't going to be worth the hassle. Kaufman just didn't get involved in the kind of cases someone would waste him over. Do you want the court order?"

"Hold off on that for now. But, you'd better check into Kaufman's finances, see if he was into anything hinky. Did you find financial records?" Jace asked.

"Yeah, a couple of boxes in a storage closet. Sale'll call his accountant." Ghiz was silent for a moment as he made a note. "Kaufman came into work yesterday about ten A.M., which doesn't preclude an 8:30 A.M. appointment, but he had nothing scheduled for before or after work on his office calendar. He left around six, without mentioning evening plans to anyone. There was nothing unusual about his mood at the office. No one there recognizes the name Rusty, and it wasn't one of the names in his Rolodex. Sale's going through that and his home phone book anyway, but it's going to take most of the weekend."

"So you have no clues to his activities before ten or after six?"

"Nil. I've got calls in to his credit card companies to see if there were any charges yesterday," Ghiz added.

"Good. It'd be a good idea to get his phone records for the last week or so, too," Jace suggested.

"Right. As far as personal motives go: Both the partner and the secretary said Kaufman didn't have an ex-wife or a steady girlfriend; in fact, he avoided commitment like the plague, and the secretary got the impression he never went out with the same woman more than a couple of times."

"I know that syndrome," Jace observed.

"You're not the only one," Ghiz laughed, "I still haven't figured out how my wife, Deborah, caught me."

"Ask Sale to flag any interview reports with former lovers, male or female. I may want to follow up on those in person. Also, keep an eye open for these names: Antonio Flores; Thomas Cabot, also known as Teece; Gilvan "Boomer" Cannon; and Jesus Garcia. They could be in either set of contacts. See if the partner will tell you if any of them were clients." Jace paused to interpret a signal from Liz, ". . . and Robinson will need a complete list of both his home directory and his office Rolodex for the computer." Liz nodded.

Jace jotted a quick note to call Fred Waner to see if Cabot had a phone book to compare with Kaufman's.

"It'll take a while—we both type slower'n snails. Anyway," Ghiz continued, "the neighbors saw and heard nothing Thursday night, although the old lady whose bedroom shares a common wall with Kaufman's says things got noisy over there several times a month."

"What did she mean by 'noisy'?"

"Near as I can figure, it was just lovemaking noise. Oohs

and ahs and oh Gods, thumping, that kind of stuff. Apparently, Kaufman bellowed when he came and that often woke the old lady up. Occasionally, she'd go over to complain that his stereo was too loud, but he'd always apologize nicely and turn it down. She's seen him entering or leaving with different women, but never saw the same one twice, and she couldn't describe any of them.''

"Did he bellow Thursday night?''

"If he did, it didn't wake her up. She said she was asleep by nine-thirty. That's it, Levy. So far: no witnesses, no leads, no motive. Oh shit, I forgot! We found two grams of coke and a half-ounce of weed at Kaufman's,'' Ghiz said.

"You think there's a possibility he deals or got it from Flores?''

"Not much. Flores couldn't afford a hit of this stuff, but I'll check with the narcs. It was a small stash, and the only cash in the condo was the $125 in Kaufman's wallet, so Kaufman probably wasn't dealing.

"As far as the Flores hit goes, there were no mugging reports from Venice that night, so whoever he hit with the beachjack didn't report it. He had less than seven dollars on his body when he was found, so it doesn't look like he scored. The uniform who recognized him said he's seen Flores hanging with a two-bit Mex dealer named Chico and black kid named Spiker, but we haven't found either of them this week. No one's picked up any street talk about Flores, either. He was small potatoes, Levy; no one cares.''

"Okay, thanks, Victor—good work. Liz and I are talking about calling a Homicide Association meeting soon to pool what we have. We'll let you know. In the meantime, keep a lid on this for me, will you?''

"You got it. Captain already got a visit from the *Times* on

Kaufman, but he didn't tell them about the bondage or his cock. As far as we know, the press hasn't linked Kaufman and Flores—in fact, they may not even know about Flores.''

"Keep it that way. Until you hear otherwise, the Kaufman case stands alone. You have my home number if something breaks when I'm off.''

Jace called King to find out what he had on Kaufman, but the M.E. had already left for the day; Jace left a message for him to call Monday. He knew it was too soon to expect anything from the lab. He made a note to find out if the combings of Kaufman's body had yielded any evidence.

"Looks like that's it for now, Liz. It's been a long week. What do you say we get out of here, maybe go get a beer?''

"You go ahead," she said as she continued to enter data in the computer, "I'm going to spend another hour or two on this. I told Sandy I wasn't cooking tonight, so he said he'd take me to Rockenwagner. Our reservations aren't until nine. I can get a lot done by then.'' She never looked up from the computer. He was almost at the door when she called to him. "Hey, Jace—try not to worry too much about that other thing, huh? Call me if you need to talk. Any time.'' Jace waved an acknowledgment as he left.

On the way home, he picked up a TV dinner and a couple of six-packs of Harp. When he got in, there was a message on his machine. "Jace, it's Ellen. I just missed you at the station. I realize this is short notice, but if you're free this evening, please give me a call.''

It was a tough choice: a TV dinner and recaps of the Thomas-Hill hearings—or a restaurant dinner followed by sex with Ellen. He could catch up with the hearings tomorrow. He picked up the phone.

* * *

"Where's your ashtray?" Ellen fished the cigarettes out of her purse on the floor next to the bed.

"Wherever you left it last weekend." Jace wiped the sweat off his chest with the end of the sheet. Ellen found the ashtray under the bed, still containing the butts of the cigarettes she'd smoked the week before. While she was hanging over the edge to retrieve it, he kissed her bare ass. She wiggled appreciatively, and straightened up. She lit a cigarette.

"You ever think of cleaning this place up?" She brushed his hair out of his eyes affectionately.

"And destroy all its charm? You've got to be kidding."

"I can't spend the night, Jace."

"Just because I haven't cleaned? Shit, Ellen, *Chez Miserables* has never been clean when you've been here. I changed the sheets," he pointed out.

Ellen laughed, "No, it's not that. Dennis's gig was local. He'll be home by three, and I should be there."

"I thought you didn't go out when he was in town."

"I don't usually. I thought we . . . you and I . . . should talk." She pushed the old butts aside with a fingernail and knocked the ash off the cigarette absently.

"Something up, Ellen?"

"I want to have a baby."

Jace was stunned. He'd never thought he was anything more than a casual lover to her; this came out of left field.

"I don't know what to say. Didn't you know that I had a vasectomy?"

"Not with you, Jace—with Dennis. I'm almost thirty-four years old. I can't wait any longer. It could be too late already." She took another drag on her cigarette. "Dennis has been talking about getting married. We're finally making enough money to be able to afford a baby, and we both want to have kids. It's time for me to get on with the rest of my life. I've gotten the career, now I want the family. I'm going to accept, Jace. I didn't want to tell you over the phone, but this was our last time. I won't be seeing you again." She didn't look at him. "I'm sorry." She stubbed out the butt.

"Hey, at least you fucked me first, right? The modern version of a kiss-off." All of a sudden, Jace felt very much alone in the world. Ellen hadn't been that important to him, yet he felt rejected and abandoned.

"That's not fair, Jace. You always knew about Dennis. I never misled you." She got up and headed for the bathroom. "You ought to have a woman of your own, not just one you borrow periodically." She closed the door behind her. He could hear the shower running.

Jace got up, dug his bathrobe out from the tangle of bedding at the foot of the bed, and put it on without tying it closed. He took the ashtray into the kitchen and emptied it into the wastebasket, then thought better of it and tossed in the ashtray. He got a Harp out of the fridge and downed it like medicine, without tasting it.

He was slumped on the couch finishing his second bottle when Ellen came out of the bedroom, fully dressed, purse in hand. He plucked out a gray pubic hair. It hurt. She came over and sat next to him.

"Look, Jace, we had a lot of good times together and I don't regret it for a minute. I hope you don't, either. We both got what we wanted out of this. Please try not to take it personally. I certainly had no intention of hurting you."

He knew he should say something, make it easier for her, but not knowing what he was feeling and why, he couldn't talk. He searched for more gray hairs. The silence screamed. Finally, Ellen leaned over and kissed him on the cheek. He pulled away. She got up and walked to the door.

"Goodbye, Jace." She opened the door and was gone.

CHAPTER
Five

Elliott was permitted to use the Honda during the day and whenever Rusty didn't want it for the evening. Most nights, he preferred to stay close to the house in Beverlywood, just in case she wanted him. But he often spent his mornings seeing movies around town. He had a love-hate relationship with the romantic films he often chose to see: Although they promoted a fairy-tale view of love that he found appealing, they made him yearn for a relationship he believed he would never have.

Elliott had never actually had sex with a woman, but as Woody Allen had said, he practiced a lot when he was alone. The image he always practiced with was Risha. He had loved her ever since Mr. Bathory had brought her into his home, and he knew how lonely she'd been since the loss of the old vampire. For the last two years, Elliott had waited patiently for Risha to get over her grief and to notice him. He would never press suit, but he thought that she would eventually realize that he was the only person who knew what she was and that he didn't judge her for it. He didn't want to become a vampire because then he wouldn't be able to take care of her; it took a very special person to handle his responsibilities, and he was proud of what he did. It was not worth immortality to leave her without a daylight guardian.

But now she was obviously looking for a mate. He'd gone through the singles ads in the issue of *What's Up* until he located the one he thought she'd placed. The packet of letters from the magazine that arrived at the mail drop that week confirmed it. He had thought about sending a response himself, but he couldn't figure out how he would handle it if she chose to answer.

It concerned him that she would be meeting strangers who answered an ad. It wasn't that he feared for her safety, because he knew she was more than capable of defending herself. He was afraid that she would tell the wrong man her secret and jeopardize her existence . . . and the reason for his. He couldn't let her be involved with anyone who didn't have her best interests at heart. He would never let anyone hurt her like Gregor Bathory had.

He'd been in the Honda when he followed Rusty the night she'd gone to Babar's in the Marina, and then tailed her BMW following the man's Mercedes. Elliott missed the light and lost them near Admiral's Rest in the Marina around eleven P.M. He'd gone home, waiting up until one, when he heard Risha close the car door and enter the house. She went to work in the darkroom, which was unusual because Thursday would have been a feeding night. She fed every two or three nights, and he was sure the last time had been Monday. She must have had the man from the Mercedes. Elliott would remember to check the papers for knife deaths in the Marina area.

While she slept during the day on Friday, Elliott read the letters from the first batch of responses to her ad. They were in her bedside drawer, the first place he looked. He needed to turn on the lights in the adjoining bathroom and leave the door ajar to have enough light to find them. She didn't stir. She never did. Sometimes, Elliott would watch her for hours by the light from the door.

He took the letters to the study. There were seven of them, and two envelopes bore the squiggle Elliott recognized as Risha's "OK." The first of them was the letter from Les Kaufman, whom Elliott surmised was the date from last night. The other OK was on the letter from a Marshall Wilkins, who said he worked the P.M. shift in the lab at a Veterans Administration Hospital. He listed international politics and science fiction as hobbies. Elliott could tell why she passed on the other candidates: two were crassly sexual, one was from a semi-illiterate cabbie from Orange County, another was "interested in finding a woman to have my children," while the last already had a child for whom he was looking for a mother. He copied down Wilkins's phone number and address and put the letters back the way he'd found them.

On Friday evening, Rusty put on jeans with a green sweater and told Elliott not to bother with the make-up, so he knew she didn't have another date that night.

He turned on his TV, but watching the Hill-Thomas hearings upset him; he didn't like the way the senators treated Anita Hill. He decided to watch his video of *Ghost* again.

It was close to three A.M. Sunday when Marshall Wilkins walked Rusty back to her car from his Fairfax District apartment. It had been a delightful evening, and Rusty was looking forward to seeing him again. They'd spent the first hour discussing the hearings, agreeing that they believed Hill and didn't think that Thomas belonged on the Supreme Court.

Marsh was a fascinating conversationalist. He'd spent quite a lot of time studying the Asian steppes, and was simultaneously entertaining and instructive about the different subcultures involved in the Soviet dis-Union. Although he tended to be a motor-mouth, Rusty quickly discovered he didn't mind if she interrupted when she had something to say . . . and he was almost as good a listener as he was a talker.

He was attractive, too, with long, strawberry-blond hair and a trimmed red beard and moustache. In spite of his intellectual bent, he had an aura of physical power that Rusty found comforting for some inexplicable reason. They'd met at Canter's, the all-night delicatessen on Fairfax, at ten; by midnight, they were at Marsh's, continuing the conversation over coffee and a joint.

The only reason Rusty didn't stay longer was hunger. Pot always gave her the munchies, and it had been two nights since she'd fed on that creep in the Marina. She had only a few hours left before dawn to eat, or she'd have to wait for Sunday night.

"So, you want to do this again?" he was asking.

"Sure. When is good for you?"

"The only nights I'm off are Friday and Saturday, but maybe we could meet for lunch one day next week," Marsh suggested.

"Uh . . . lunches aren't really good for me. I generally work all night and sleep in the daytime," she explained. "How about after you get off work one night?"

"I don't get off until eleven-thirty. Do you really want to get together at midnight?"

"My favorite time of day."

They made a date for Wednesday night, and Rusty left, driving north in the BMW. She was oblivious to her own Honda, following a block behind. She turned east on Fountain, trolling for dinner along dark Hollywood streets sprinkled with drug dealers and prostitutes of both sexes; the Honda turned west, back toward Beverlywood.

Steve Avallone was a little surprised when the trick in the BMW turned out to be a woman, but she didn't flinch when he said the price was fifty bucks, so what-the-hell. He didn't tell her he was HIV-positive, but, then again, she didn't ask. She turned north on Vermont and headed into Griffith Park, mountainous and secluded, except for the hustlers turning tricks. Steve knew all the back roads through the park, and directed her to a favorite spot. There were no other cars around.

Rusty popped the trunk release and turned off the ignition. "I've got a plastic dropcloth in the back."

Steve carried the ground cover, leading Rusty through the scrub and trees to a small clearing invisible from the road. The clearing was littered with bottles and used condoms. Steve kicked a bottle out of the way and spread the plastic out over the smaller debris. He unbuckled his belt.

"What's your pleasure?" he asked.

"Take off your shirt, and lie down."

He did as she requested, and lay belly-down, spread-eagled on the dropcloth. Rusty laughed.

"Honey, your ass doesn't do a woman any good. Turn over." She dropped down beside him as he flipped, a sheepish grin on his face. He reached for her.

When she had finished feeding, Rusty had to go back to the car to get the bowie knife and a penlight from under the driver's seat. She returned to the clearing. Steve was unconscious, breathing shallowly, his pulse slow. The punctures in his neck had closed, but she knew they were still visible. He was smiling.

"Glad you enjoyed the meal as much as I did," Rusty said as she knelt next to his head, on the side away from the punctures. Although her night vision was much better than it had been when she was alive, it was not good enough to find the punctures in the unlit and moonless grove. She held the penlight between her teeth as she placed the knife point in the proper position to obscure the fang marks.

When she pulled out the blade, Steve's remaining three quarts of blood spurted out onto the tarp, pooling in the folds. His smile faded rapidly, and he was gone. Rusty got up, avoiding getting any of the spilled blood on her clothes. She wasn't wearing black tonight. She tucked fifty dollars into his pocket.

"Thanks. You were very good."

She cleaned off the knife in the dirt, turned off the penlight, and returned to the car. It was time to head home.

When Jace awoke, his heart was pounding and he was wet with sweat. He'd had the same nightmare—helpless in the decaying ruins of his mother's house with Something Awful out to get him. Jace didn't need a shrink to tell him the dream was about his fear of inheriting his mother's deadly disease, but understanding the dream had no effect on it. It still terrified him, every time—and he was having the dream more often. It wasn't death itself that frightened him—it was that kind of death. And there was nothing anyone could do to help him.

Unbidden, the image of his mother's last days burst into

his mind with the brightness of a flare: He saw her lying in her bed, nearly paralyzed except for the jerking head covered in thin gray hair, the hair that had once been a rich brown, perfectly coifed each week. She'd had to wear diapers by then, because she'd lost control over all her body functions. She could no longer talk, but Jace didn't doubt that she was delusional. She didn't seem to recognize anyone, but her eyes would often widen in fear for no external reason; sometimes she smiled to herself, the scary smile of a bully planning an ambush. Now Jace knew the ambush was Huntington's, and it was set for him.

He opened his eyes to banish the image and looked at the bedside clock: seven-thirty. Sunday. He couldn't go back to sleep—what if he had the dream again?

When he got up, his legs cramped, and his arms felt like they'd been coated with lead. He thought he might have overdone it yesterday. He'd spent most of Saturday working out at the police gym, trying to sweat out the time bomb implanted in his genes; he should have gone more slowly, he thought ruefully—it had been six months since he'd gotten any real exercise.

He ran a hot bath while the coffee was brewing, then soaked until his mug was empty. By the time he got out, his muscles had loosened a little. He threw on a pair of jeans and an Amnesty International T-shirt; the organization had been in L.A. recently investigating police brutality, so Jace kept his membership a secret at work.

He turned on the hearings, got the Sunday *Times* from the front step, poured some more coffee, and began the crossword puzzle, one of his most treasured rituals. He even had a special red pen he used; the challenge was to complete the puzzle flawlessly, no corrections. He aced it about a third of the time, but not this time; he erred halfway through.

The hearings kept his interest for a few hours, but once he'd concluded that he didn't believe Clarence Thomas, he found the senators' behaviors annoying, and turned off the TV. He picked up the new Andrew Vachss novel, but discovered he wasn't in the mood to read. He was wondering how Ghiz and Sale were doing with the Kaufman investigation when the phone rang.

"Levy? Pat Sale from Pacific."

"Shit—you clairvoyant? I was just thinking about checking in with you guys. You got something?"

"Maybe. One of the names in Kaufman's home phone book is an ex-girlfriend named Joyce Stein. Victor is going to talk to her at noon. I've got to stay on the phone here; he thought you might want to go along."

"Damned straight I do. Where does she live?"

"In Mar Vista. Do you know the area?"

"I live in Mar Vista, a few blocks southeast of the Santa Monica Airport. Just give me the address."

When Jace parked in front of Joyce Stein's apartment building, Victor Ghiz was waiting for him.

"Fuck. You've got balls, Levy." Jace was confused until Ghiz indicated the T-shirt under Jace's jacket with a grin.

"Oh, shit. I forgot what I put on this morning. Don't tell anyone, man."

Ghiz laughed, "You owe me."

As they entered the building, Jace asked, "Does she know Kaufman's dead?"

"Yeah. She said she saw it in the *Times* yesterday. She's not upset by it, said she'd be happy to talk."

Joyce Stein was a tanned, shapely woman in her early thirties, not more than 5′2″ tall, with permed red hair. She was wearing a sea-green running suit and apologized for her appearance by explaining that she was going to Holiday Spa after the interview. She showed the detectives to seats in the living room, where the TV was on the hearings, and offered coffee and soft drinks, which they declined. She turned off the TV; once they were settled, Ghiz began.

"Miss Stein . . ."

"Oh, call me Joyce."

"Okay, Joyce. What can you tell us about Lester Kaufman?"

"What do you want to know? I dated that scum for eight months; I know a lot about him."

Jace said, "I take it you didn't have an amicable parting?"

"Amicable—that's a laugh. Eight months, he doesn't introduce me to any of his friends or family, but he tells me his 'intentions are honorable.' What does that mean to you?" Before anyone could answer, she continued. "Well, it meant to me that he was serious about our relationship, that he was considering marriage. I trusted him! I introduced him to my friends, to my family! That shit. Excuse my language."

"What happened?"

"I'll tell you what happened! I spent all day baking him an apple pie from scratch—from scratch! Rolling out pie crust, peeling and coring apples, all that stuff. Because it's his favorite, right? And I finished at, like, four in the afternoon, so I took it over to his condo to surprise him. I had a key—he gave it to me."

"When was this, Miss . . . Joyce?" Ghiz asked.

"Last April. The twenty-fifth. Anyway, I'm standing there balancing the pie on my arm and trying to open the door with the key, and the chain lock is on. So I know he's home, right? So I call through the crack. It takes about a minute, and then this . . . this woman," she made the word sound like an epithet, "peers out at me, then slams the door."

"What did she look like?"

"Like a cheap slut—that's what she looked like! I pounded on the door, and yelled for Les, but no one came back to the door. Finally, I was so mad, I dumped the entire pie on his doorstep and left. As soon as I got home, I called him, but he wouldn't talk to me. He said he'd call me later. He never did."

"Did you call him again? See him?" Ghiz asked.

"I tried! His secretary wouldn't put me through, he never answered the phone at home, he wouldn't return my calls. That sonofabitch cost me a fortune in therapy bills! Not to mention the fact that I haven't been able to even think about trusting a man again!"

"Just how angry were you? Did you . . ."

". . . kill him? No. I could never do that. I'm a pacifist. I don't even eat meat. But I sure could have yelled him to death if I ever got a chance to. Tie him to the bed with his damned handcuffs and tell him what a shit he is." She shook her head. "Now he's dead and I'll never get 'closure.' "

At the reference to bondage, Jace and Ghiz looked at each other. The *Times* report had said nothing about the circumstances of Kaufman's death.

"Handcuffs?"

Joyce looked down at the rug. "Handcuffs, blindfolds, spanking—he liked to play games in bed. He even had a hook in his headboard. He liked to be tied up. Hell, half the time, he couldn't get it up without that stuff. It's not my thing, but I didn't mind doing it for him, because he really liked it."

"Joyce, do you have any idea who the woman was in his condo that afternoon?"

"No, but she was wearing his robe, so I'm sure they were playing games in the bedroom. I guess he couldn't come to the door himself because he was tied up," she smirked.

"Do you know of anyone who might have wanted to kill Kaufman?"

"Any woman who's had the bad luck to fall in love with him. Otherwise, I don't know of any enemies." She looked at her watch. "Look, I've got to go soon. Is there anything else?"

"Just one thing. Where were you last Thursday night?"

"I was in New York, visiting my parents. You can call them if you want. I got back yesterday."

They took her parents' number and flight information, and stood to leave.

"May I use your bathroom?" Jace asked.

"It's at the end of the hall."

Jace passed Joyce's bedroom door on the way—there was an open suitcase on the floor containing a pair of sneakers and a paperback romance novel. The bathroom counter held her open, but still unpacked, cosmetic case. Her hairbrush was on top. Jace pulled out several of her red hairs from the brush, wrapped them in a tissue, and put it in his pocket. He flushed the toilet, ran the water in the sink, then returned to the living room, where the TV was on again, Joyce engrossed in the testimony.

"Thank you for your cooperation, Joyce. We may call you again, if we have any more questions."

She waved a hand, "Yeah, whatever." She opened the door for them. "I really believed him when he said he loved me."

Ghiz walked with Jace back to his car. "I don't think she's involved with this, Levy, but I'll check out her alibi when I get back to the station."

"That's my take, too. Did you find anything that indicates where Kaufman got his sex partners? Phone records of calls to House of Domination or call girls? Bar matches? Box rental receipts from sex papers?"

"Sale's still matching up all the numbers on his phone bill with his directory and Rolodex. We haven't even gotten to his receipts file yet. I don't know about the matches—you want to go over and take another look around?"

"You got the key with you?"

"No, but if you want to follow me back, I'll give it to you. If you don't need me, though, I've got a lot to handle at the station," Ghiz added.

"No problem. See you there." Jace turned to his car, then stopped. "Uh, Victor . . . Would you mind bringing the key out to the car? Otherwise, I'll have to go home and change first."

Jace spent two hours searching Les Kaufman's condo for clues to where the lawyer found his playmates while he listened to the hearings on the radio.

The copy of *What's Up/LA* in the bedside drawer was a possibility, but the biweekly free newspaper was used as often for movie and concert listings as it was for singles ads; none of the ads in Kaufman's copy had been marked, and Jace considered it a source only because of where it was kept.

In a closet, he found a package of letters, some with photos, addressed to Box #3948 and forwarded from a now-defunct Orange County sex publication called *Matches*. They were dated two years before, and apparently were in response to an ad placed by Kaufman for "a strong, sexy woman." Jace doubted that any of the four women (and two men!) who wrote would be eager to discuss the matter with the police, but he took the letters for follow-up.

A kitchen drawer produced six matchbooks, one with a "Draw This Girl" cover, and the rest from local restaurants; two were from Babar's, half a mile from the condo. Jace made a note to see if Kaufman was enough of a regular at any of them to be recognized by the staff, then dialed Pacific Division from the kitchen phone.

"Have you gotten the credit card records yet?" he asked when Ghiz came to the phone.

"Some of them. We've got his AmEx, Visa, and Mastercard—no charges last Thursday at all. But it's hell trying to get readouts on the weekend from Diner's Club, Carte Blanche, and the gas and store cards. He had so many cards, he kept them in a separate wallet. We should get something tomorrow morning on the rest of them. Did you find anything?"

"Some sex letters from two years ago. How long are you going to be there? I'll drop them off with the key."

"Pat left an hour ago, and I was just about to leave. Deborah hasn't seen me all week, I've missed the hearings, and I'm getting punchy here. I need sleep. If you want to come by now, I'll meet you out front."

"Be there in ten minutes. And Victor? Bring me a photo of Kaufman. I want to show it around some local restaurants."

Late Sunday afternoon was a busy time at Babar's. Weekend sailors with salt-spray-tousled hair and expensive casual clothes mixed with upscale families having an early dinner with the kids and couples having drinks. Although Jace had never eaten there, he had the impression that the restaurant's popularity had more to do with its Marina-view atmosphere than its surf-and-turf cuisine. The bar TV played PBS's coverage of the Hill-Thomas hearings.

He took an empty stool at the end of the bar and ordered a Harp Lager. The bartender, a tall man with a *café-au-lait* complexion and green eyes, put the change from Jace's ten on the bar.

Discreetly, Jace showed the bartender his badge, then the photo of Kaufman. The man nodded.

"Double Glenfiddich, straight up."

"He come in often?" Jace took a sip of his beer.

"I only work Fridays, Saturdays, and Sundays, but I see him about three times a month."

"You notice who he's with?"

"He only sits at the bar when he's alone, Officer. He's got someone with him, he takes a booth over there." The bartender indicated the area ajacent to the bar.

"Who's the waitress for that station?"

"It varies, depending on shift. Tonight it's Elaine, the tall girl with the big earrings."

"Do you know who worked last Thursday night?"

"Not offhand, but I can check the schedule. Can I make these drinks first?"

Jace nodded and watched the hearings while the bartender poured wine coolers and buzzed piña coladas in the blender. When he returned to Jace, he had the schedule in his hand.

"What shift Thursday are you asking about?"

"What hours are you open during the week?"

"Eleven 'til midnight. Two overlapping shifts: ten to seven and four 'til one."

"Who worked the late shift Thursday?"

"Howie Erlich tended bar. He's off tonight—he'll be back tomorrow at four, if he makes it—"

"Is that in doubt?"

"Janyce, the early shift Monday-through-Friday, was complaining that he doesn't even call if he's going to be late. I get the impression she's had to cover for him a lot. Listen, Officer, I don't want to get him in trouble. Maybe you ought to ask the manager about Howie."

"Who was the waitress for the bar tables Thursday night?"

"Wendy Nee was on 'til seven, Elaine Notkin worked the evening shift."

"Did I hear my name?" Jace swiveled on his stool. A black waitress with big silver earrings was towering behind him. "Tanqueray-rocks, and a Diet Coke," she told the bartender.

Jace showed his badge to the waitress. "Could you spare a moment, Ms. . . . Notkin?" She half-nodded, but looked wary. The bartender poured the drinks.

"What's this about?" she said, putting the drinks on a tray. She garnished the gin with a twist, and the Coke with a wedge of lime. "Can I serve these first?"

"Go ahead. I just want to ask you about a customer." Jace signaled the bartender for another Harp and turned back to the TV.

When the waitress returned, Jace showed her the photo of Lester Kaufman.

"Les? Has he done something?"

"You know him?"

"Well, not . . . socially, you know. He comes in once or twice a week. Double Glenfiddich, straight up." She looked reluctant to talk.

"Do you remember if he was here last Thursday night?"

"Thursday? Let me think. Yes! He was here about nine, I guess." Jace could tell she was curious why he was asking, but he didn't volunteer any information.

"Was he alone?"

"No, he was with a woman. I don't think I ever saw her before, but that isn't strange. Les always met different women here."

"He picked her up here that night?"

"No. He probably had a date to meet her here—they walked from the front door together. They didn't seem to know each other very well."

"Can you describe her?"

She looked up at the ceiling while she thought. "White, dark hair, about thirty." She shrugged, and her eyes returned to Jace. "It's dark in here after sunset. You can't see much."

"What was she wearing?"

"Jeez, I don't remember. Wait! She was wearing this neat silk scarf—yellow and black. I remember because I was thinking it would look good with this yellow dress I just got." Jace stopped writing.

"You're sure of that?"

"The scarf? Yeah. They were here a couple of hours."

"Would you recognize her if you saw her again?" The waitress shook her head. "Did they leave together?"

"Yeah. Les left me an extra five bucks on the tip. He only does that when he's got a hot one. When he strikes out, I get fifteen percent—to the penny. You gonna tell me what this is about, or do I have to ask Les?"

He stood and added a dollar to the change on the bar. "Les won't be in again, Ms. Notkin. He died Thursday night." He handed her his card. "If you remember anything else, please call me. Thank you for your cooperation."

Jace nodded to the bartender as he left, but the gesture went unseen. Everybody was watching TV.

When the hearings concluded for the night, Jace became engrossed in the Vachss novel for a few hours, then went to bed. He was too jacked up to sleep. Convinced that Kaufman's killer was the woman Elaine Notkin had seen with him at Babar's Thursday night, he was equally sure that a woman hadn't killed Cabot and Flores . . . at least, not without help. Was it possible the deaths were unrelated? His instincts said they were all the work of the same killer, but how could a woman have the strength exhibited in the other murders? Could a woman have overpowered the others so effectively that they couldn't defend themselves—or even move!—when she stabbed them?

He was still running in mental circles at two A.M. when Pacific called. They had someone who claimed to have witnessed Flores's murder.

CHAPTER
Six

When Rusty woke up Sunday night, her stomach was upset. It was unusual for her to feel ill, but it happened sometimes if she fed on someone who was sick. Maybe the hustler last night had the flu—or AIDS. It didn't matter, because viruses couldn't live long in her body, but it was an annoyance. She soaked in her bubble bath while she did the Sunday *Times* crossword puzzle, but didn't feel any better when she got out. Usually, illnesses in her feeders didn't affect her for more than a few hours—that guy must have been seriously diseased. Gregor had once been so sick from a feeder with tuberculosis that he'd regurgitated the meal and then was too weak to feed again, and she'd had to bring him a Jehovah's Witness who was working their neighborhood. It was the major drawback to feeding on the street.

She decided to stay in. Elliott was watching *Body Heat*, and she joined him in the living room. By midnight, she was feeling nearly normal, so she spent the rest of the night work-

ing in the darkroom, thinking about Marshall Wilkins. She
was looking forward to seeing him again on Wednesday. It
had occurred to her that, working in the V.A. lab, he must
have access to human blood, but Gregor had warned her
that the anticoagulants used in blood banks interfered with
digestion. Maybe she could get him to bring her some to
taste, if their relationship continued. At least, they screened
the blood for disease there—on the streets, it was potluck.

It had taken Rusty nearly six weeks to become vampiric.
Gregor fed on her every other night during that time, taking
only about a pint at a time. He said that the transformation
could theoretically be done in half the time, with longer
feedings, but there was a danger of dying from blood loss
before the protective venom sacs developed. Rusty didn't
mind the wait at all, so pleasurable was the process.

The night he "proposed" was the first—and most intense—feeding, an experience Rusty was sure she'd remember until the end of time.

They'd kissed, passionately, on the bed, his cool lips
against her hot ones; her heartbeat racing, his still. She
started, afraid, when his lips touched the hollow at the base
of her neck, but he continued the trail of cool kisses along her
collarbone without stopping. He gently removed her clothing,
licking her lightly as he bared her; she fumbled eagerly at his
buttons until he stood to remove his own clothes.

He stood before her, his slim white body golden in the candle-
light, his long thin cock at rest against his thigh. She was suddenly
conscious of her own plumpness, afraid that her rounded stomach
and ample hips were a turnoff to him. She smiled nervously at
him, wanting him, wanting him to want her.

"Risha, you're so beautiful. You're warm, and round, and

full of life. It's selfish for me to take that away from you. You deserve a lover with hot blood stiffening his cock, not a man who hasn't had an erection in two hundred and fifty years,'' Gregor said wistfully. ''I don't think I've ever wanted to make love to a woman as much as I want you now.''

At that moment, Rusty knew she loved Gregor, would always love him. She opened her arms to him, and he came to her. He was slow and tender, kissing and licking and nibbling her, until she was nearly panicked in frenzied anticipation. His cool tongue played on her clitoris, his fingers darting in and out, and she experienced the first (but not the last!) orgasm of her life, the explosive spasms radiating over her as he held her buttocks cupped in his hands. When she'd stopped shaking, he'd begun again, sucking on her hypersensitive nipples, bringing her swiftly to another peak. He moved his mouth to her neck, pressing his body along the length of hers, his limp cock pinned by her legs against her pulsing vulva.

She felt his lips cool against her hot neck, and—just for a second—a sharp pinch; but somehow, even that pain was pleasure, and she came again, the multicolored hallucinations exploding under her closed eyelids echoing the exquisite explosions in her groin.

When she was once again aware of her surroundings, she was lying with her head on Gregor's chest, his arm close around her shoulders, their legs entwined. She turned to look at him. He was smiling at her.

''Still lightheaded?'' he guessed.

She grinned, ''Maybe a little. I see two of you.'' She'd never felt this content and safe in her whole life; the feeling was so good, it brought tears to her eyes. Gregor wiped one errant tear from her cheek and tasted it.

"Maybe we should go look in the mirror and see if only one of me disappears. The high from the venom should wear off in about an hour. I didn't hurt you?" he asked in concern. She shook her head, vehemently.

"Can we do it again?" she wanted to know.

Gregor laughed, a rich, deep sound. "Some of it, yes. But no more blood-venom exchanges for forty-eight hours. I don't want to lose you now."

By the end of a month, Rusty had been able to taste venom in her own mouth, the sweetness like an intangible candy in her saliva. She began to become sensitive to bright light, wearing dark sunglasses from dawn to dusk, unless she was in the school's darkroom. The semester was nearly over, and she wanted to finish her classes before she died. She'd already quit her job at Moe's and moved in with Gregor.

"It's happening, Gregor!" she had announced excitedly one night. "My teeth are tingling, and the sweetness is really strong! How come it doesn't zone me out, having all that venom in my system? Am I ready now?"

He was delighted with her enthusiasm. "Slow down, Risha—one question at a time. The venom doesn't knock you out because you manufacture it; after you cross over, you won't taste the sweetness anymore, but you'll feel a rush when you feed that you'll come to love. Show me your fangs," he suggested.

She pulled back her lip, then closed her mouth again, and looked at Gregor. "How do you make 'em come out like that?"

"It's kind of hard to explain—you sort of . . . stretch with your gums, and they just kind of come out." He grinned as she tried to force her fangs out, without success.

"You're just not ready yet. After you cross over, and until you get the hang of controlling them, they'll come out whenever you're hungry and near a human—like, within two feet. It can be a little embarrassing—and dangerous, if you can't feed then and don't remember to keep your mouth closed. Your best defense is that people don't believe in vampires anymore, but you let someone live after seeing your fangs, they'll start believing pretty damned quick. There's enough accuracy in the vampire literature available to the public to kill you, if you're not careful. So, even more important than learning how to make your fangs lengthen, is learning how to keep them from doing it. You'll get the hang of it before long."

Two feedings later, Rusty's fangs came out for the first time. Gregor said she could cross over any time, now, but he wanted her to wait another week, just to make sure.

Finally, the night came. "How will I go?" Rusty wanted to know. "Shall I jump off the Golden Gate Bridge?"

"What? And end up in a morgue? Or worse, at sea? No, my dear Risha, there's only one way to cross over: tonight, I drink all of you. And tomorrow night, when you awake, I'll take you someplace romantic for dinner. Afterwards, we can catch the Dead at the Avalon."

Hollow-eyed from too little sleep, Victor Ghiz filled Jace and Liz in while they headed for the interrogation room where Spiker waited, chain-smoking.

"His name's John Kennedy Jackson, but he only answers to Spiker. Black, twenty-two years old; rap sheet's got two possession charges—smack and ice—and one count of furnishing liquor to minors. He was picked up with Tony Flores on one of the dope busts. Uniforms popped him about an hour

and a half ago and found crack and glue in his pocket—
apparently, he's an equal-opportunity druggie. He was spac-
ing-out when they brought him in, but he got lucid in a hurry
when he was charged. He said he saw Flores murdered on
the beach ten days ago. He wanted to make a deal to have
the drug possession charges dropped completely, but settled
for having the charges reduced to public intoxication.''

"Anybody questioned him yet about the murder?" Liz
asked.

"No. Datlow made the deal, then left him to sweat in
Interrogation while they called us." Ghiz led them into the
adjoining room to check out Spiker through the one-way
glass. "He's been Miranda-ed, hasn't asked for a lawyer
yet."

Spiker was seated alone at the table, next to an overflowing
ashtray. He crumpled an empty cigarette package nervously.
His hair was styled in a buzz-cut a week old, the outline of
a hypodermic syringe above his left ear and "Spiker" shaved
across the back. "Man obviously believes in advertising,"
Jace observed.

Spiker wore a small iron loop in his ear, a faded and torn
red T-shirt, and dirty jeans. His face was acne-scarred, and
the left side of his mouth drooped like a stroke victim's.

"Looks more like a public service message to me," Ghiz
said. "You want the white hat or the black one?"

"Your territory, your choice."

Ghiz opted to be the "bad cop" if Jackson proved difficult,
and handed Jace a pack of Marlboros and a lighter. They
entered the interrogation room, while Liz stayed behind to
watch.

Jace identified himself to Jackson. Victor leaned against

the door, arms crossed over his chest while Jace pulled up a chair opposite the punk.

"Cigarette, Mr. Jackson?" Jace offered the pack.

"Spiker." He took a cigarette and Jace lit it for him.

"Okay, Spiker. I understand you have some information on a murder for us." Spiker's hands were shaking.

"He tole you about my deal, righ'?" When Jace nodded, he continued, "I seen who killed Tony Flores at da Pavil'on."

"You witnessed the murder?" Jace asked. Spiker nodded several times. "When?"

"T'ursday night—not last T'ursday, da one afore. Mebbe 'round midnight . . . I dunno da time for sure, man. I on'y 'member what day 'cause my momma's county check come next day, an' it allus come on Friday." He dragged hungrily on the cigarette.

"Okay, that would have been October third. Start at the beginning and tell me everything you remember. Were you alone?"

Spiker thought about that one for a second too long before replying. "Yeah, man, but I know Tony a long time; we kinda hang, y'know? In fac'," he suddenly improvised, "I was gonna meet him dere, so thass how come I seen him offed."

"What did you see?" Jace prodded.

Spiker took a deep breath, followed by another drag on his cigarette. "A' firs', I t'ought she was fuckin' him—y'know, he was onna groun' an' she was ridin' him an' kissin' his neck an' stuff, y'know?" He took another drag, even though the cigarette was down to the filter.

"She? You saying it was a woman?" Jace traded a brief glance with Ghiz.

"What you t'ink? M' man don't be no fairy-boy. But she wasn' fuckin' him, 'cause she was wearin' dis, like, runnin' suit, but she was sure kissin' his neck an' he look like he gettin'-off, y'know? wit' her sittin' on him, an' all, doin' all da work." He dropped the smoldering filter into the ashtray.

"What happened then?"

"Dat when it get real weird, man, but, I swear it be da trufe. Den she take out dis blade an' she push it inna m' man's neck, y'know, where she was jus' kissin' him afore— an' den she stab him again here!" Spiker pointed to his own chest. "You got anot'er smoke, man?" Jace passed him another cigarette and lit it for him.

"What was Flores doing when she stabbed him?"

"He wasn' doin' nothin', man! He was jus' layin' dere, smilin' at her like she was some queen pussy an' he jus' got 'lected tomcat. Den—oh, man, you ain't never gonna believe me, but I swear it be trufe!—she pick him up like he be some bedroll or sumpin' an' t'row him over her back an' she t'row him inna trash bin! I ain't never seen no pussy dat strong in my life, man, and dat be trufe!"

Ghiz spoke for the first time since they had entered the room. "Levy, this guy's handing us a load of shit to get a deal. I think he killed Flores, not some chick. Your deal doesn't include immunity on murder, Jackson."

"Hey, man, chill! You t'ink I gonna make up a dumb story 'bout some pussy kilt my man, it ain't true?" Spiker's defiance was genuine. Jace put up a hand to stay Ghiz's questioning.

"I know you didn't kill Tony, Spiker. But we need some more information. What did she look like? She must have been big to be able to pick Flores up."

"No, man! I tellin' you, I dunno how she pick him up.

She be normal chick-size, mebbe come up to here.'' Spiker stood up and held his hand a little over five feet off the ground. He dropped into his chair again. "She be white pussy, too, in her 'spensive runnin' suit.''

"What color suit? What color hair?"

"Shit, man, I dunno. I don't see no colors, much.''

"You're colorblind?" Ghiz looked unhappy.

"Yeah, man, dat's da word. I t'ink her car be red, t'ough, on accounta dey on'y comes in red an' gray, I t'ink. I us'ly see red—oh! I 'member!—she have some red on her suit, 'round her neck an' . . .'' he indicated his wrists. "She got dark hair—it be long, but she have it braided inna back, y'know?''

"How did you see her car?" Ghiz asked.

"Af'er she dump Tony, I follow her. She parked down da block, an' I see her get her car, den she drive away, an' dat's all.''

"What kind of car was it? Did you get the license plate?" Jace asked hopefully.

"Y'know, man, I 'membered to look at da plate, but I forget what it say. It be from here, t'ough, not one o'dem outer-state jobbies. An'way, de car be one o'dem Honda Accords—thass why I t'ink it be red, on accounta dey on'y comes in red an' gray, righ'? I mean, you ever seen one of dem wasn'?''

"Do you remember anything else about her or the car? Did the car have any bumper stickers, something in the back window?''

"I dunno, man. I tole you all I know. You got a smoke?''

It was nearly dawn when Jace got home. Further interrogation of Spiker Jackson had been fruitless, except for identifying the Honda as "old," and the killer as "mebbe twenny-fi'." Neither Jace nor Victor Ghiz believed that Spiker just happened on the scene at the time of the murder, but he was sticking to his story. Jace peeled off his clothes on the way into the bedroom, and dropped onto the unmade bed.

He'd slept for almost three hours before the phone rang.

"Were you still asleep?" Liz sounded surprised.

"I'm not as young as you—I need at least a couple of hours a night. What's up?"

"We've got another victim. Griffith Park." She gave him directions. "Get a move on, Jace."

They were waiting to bag the body of Steve Avallone until Jace showed up. Liz was talking to Ronnie Schaffer, the lab criminalist, an attractive middle-aged woman with graying light-brown hair and glasses. They stopped to accompany Jace into the clearing to the body.

"He's been dead at least twenty-four hours," Liz said. "A park maintenance man found him. No I.D. Fifty-dollar bill in his pocket. It looks like the neck wound is the only one this time."

After Jace had a look around, he signaled the coroner's assistant to move the body. Jace made sure he'd be called to see the autopsy.

When the body had been removed, he joined Liz and Ronnie near the bloody tarp. Liz told Jace that there were no distinguishable fresh car tracks nearby, and only one clear footprint, belonging to the victim's right shoe. Ronnie kept looking at the yellow tarp, a puzzled look on her face.

"You see something?" Jace asked her.

"No animal tracks."

"So?" Liz asked.

"This site hasn't been disturbed since the murder. Look at the blood on the tarp." Jace and Liz looked. The blood formed a zigzag pattern, characteristic of arterial spurts. It had all collected on the tarp next to where the body had lain.

"You mean the zigzag?"

Ronnie shook her head. "No, that's consistent with the wound. You see that all the blood is on the plastic? None on the ground?"

"Yeah. So?"

"That look like six quarts' worth to you?" Jace and Liz stared at the blood, then at the serologist. "It doesn't, to me—nothing like that much. I'll have a better idea once I get the tarp into the lab, but this is really weird."

Jace called the photographer over to get shots of the tarp without the body. "It looks like only half that much. What happened to the rest of his blood?"

CHAPTER
Seven

By three-thirty Monday afternoon, Jace had a raging headache that analgesics couldn't touch. Liz was busy entering data in the computer when the fingerprint I.D. on the Griffith Park stiff came in: Stephen Michael Avallone, twenty-four, address in Glendale, five arrests for prostitution, one for public indecency. A homosexual now? Instead of getting clearer with each victim, things were getting more confusing—and trying to find the pattern was making Jace's head hurt even more. He rubbed his eyes and sighed.

"Do you want me to go to Glendale with you?" Liz asked Jace.

"No—you can keep on with that stuff. I'll go after I check with King." He picked up the phone and called the deputy medical examiner who would be doing Avallone's autopsy.

"I was just about to call, Levy," King said. "I got the I.D. from the lab."

"I just heard. You scheduled the post yet?"

"I'm clear to handle it now if you want to come down."

"Wouldn't miss it, Doc." Jace hung up and turned to Liz. "King's ready to go. I'll check back with you before I head out to Glendale. Jeez, I love attending posts with a headache," he muttered as he left.

Darrell Stanley King had become a county forensic pathologist after returning from a stint as a medic in Vietnam. A wartime explosion had left the forty-five-year-old doctor completely deaf in his left ear with the hearing in his right ear dependent on the hearing aid he wore clipped to his belt. The lanky black man had Avallone on the table by the time Jace arrived.

"Dress-out completely, Levy. The stiff's a known hooker with an anus as wide as the Ventura Freeway—and probably as heavily traveled. If you're a 'toucher,' you ought to forgo it this time."

"I'm a 'looker,' but thanks for the warning." Jace put on a surgical gown, booties, mask, and gloves.

King began the examination, narrating into a mike as he went. He began with the wound. "Incision in neck three-point-five centimeters in width; depth: four-point-seven centimeters; angle of entry—hmmm. That's interesting. Levy, look here. See the top edge of the wound?" Jace looked where King pointed. He didn't see whatever the M.E. was indicating, and shrugged. "Here, let me re-aim the light. See that shiny orange smear?"

Jace saw the tiny smear King had noticed. "What is it, Doc?"

The pathologist took another photo of the wound, then scraped the skin to collect a sample. "Won't know for sure until the lab has a chance to look at it."

"How about an educated guess?" Jace prompted.

"Educated guess?" King adjusted the volume on his hearing aid. "I think it's lipstick."

"The lab won't have the results on the smear for a few days," Jace told Liz two hours later, "but King thinks it might be lipstick."

"What's a male hooker doing with lipstick on his neck?"

"Damned if I know." Jace took three more aspirin. His hand was shaking. "Avallone was high-risk for AIDS. There wasn't enough blood left in the body for type-and-tox, but King said they can use the spleen. Complete tox will take at least a month, but he'll try to get HIV results for us this week."

"What else?" Liz asked.

"The entry angle of the wound confirms he was already lying on his back when the knife went in, and the size of the wound was consistent with the other murders. King said the trauma indicates the knife was pushed rather slowly into his neck; he wasn't stabbed with force. No defense wounds at all. He had a two-day-old hickey on his ass. Right cheek. We'll have to wait for the protocol for the rest." Jace stood. "I guess I'll get into rush-hour traffic out to Glendale." He rubbed his face wearily.

"Headache still bothering you?"

Jace nodded.

Liz hit a few keys on her computer and turned it off. "I'll drive. I've had enough screen-staring for now."

Jace kept his eyes closed on the ride, and by the time they got to the address they had for Steve Avallone, his headache had mostly subsided. He was grateful that Liz had driven.

The building was a forty-year-old tract home in need of paint, the brown remains of a lawn leading up to the three rickety steps. An old beige Volkswagen bug was parked in the driveway, and a little white-haired woman in a housedress was taking a bag of groceries out of the passenger seat when Jace and Liz arrived.

Liz showed the woman her badge while Jace relieved her of the groceries. "Thank you, dear," the woman told him gratefully. "The kitchen's through here."

She led the way into the house, which smelled faintly of mothballs and cabbage. There were lace doilies on the arms and backs of the old furniture.

The woman didn't seem to care why the police had come to see her. She put the food in the refrigerator, and said to Liz, "A policewoman? How exciting! Just like Angie Dickinson!" Liz smiled. "Now, can I offer you two a nice cup of tea? Or a glass of milk? I have some Oreos here somewhere . . ." She rooted through the cabinet.

"No, thank you, ma'am. We'd just like to talk with you, if you don't mind," Jace said.

"Mind? Of course I don't mind! We can sit right here. It's nice and homey to visit in the kitchen, don't you think? I love to have company, but Stevie's the only one who ever visits me, and he didn't come yesterday." They sat on wooden chairs that had lost their edges to multiple repaintings.

"Is that Stephen Avallone?" Jace asked.

"You know Stevie? He's my grandson. I'm Bitty Avallone. What are your names, dears?" Liz told her again. "Oh, this isn't your husband?" Liz shook her head. "Does this have something to do with Stevie?"

"Mrs. Avallone, I'm afraid we have some bad news for you."

"Don't tell me Stevie's in trouble. I just can't afford to bail that boy out of jail again. Was it jaywalking? I keep telling him to wait for the light, I don't know why he doesn't remember—"

"No, ma'am," Jace interrupted. "It's not jaywalking. He's been murdered."

The announcement of her grandson's death hit the old woman hard; while Liz comforted her, Jace called her nephew in San Francisco. By the time he'd found a neighbor to stay with her until the nephew could arrive, Mrs. Avallone had regained her composure and had talked to Liz.

Liz filled Jace in during the drive back to town.

"He hasn't lived there since he was sixteen, but he visits her two or three times a month, usually on Sundays. She said he lives in Hollywood with a 'nice roommate,' a girl named Erica who she never met—she talked to her on the phone once last year, when she called Stevie. She doesn't know the address or her last name, but she gave me their phone number. She has no idea of what kind of life he led, Jace. Aside from the phone number, she's a dead end."

It was nearly nine P.M. when they returned to the station, and Jace's headache was back.

"That's it. If I don't get some sleep, my head is going to explode."

"Leave your car here. I'll take you home and pick you up in the morning." Jace was too wiped to argue.

The pile of mail next to the bathtub included a thick envelope from *What's Up/LA* with twenty-two more letters responding to Rusty's ad. Elliott had slit open all the other mail as usual, but had left the letter package unopened; Gregor's silver letter opener sat atop the bundle, its Bathory family crest freshly polished. Elliott excelled at discretion, and Rusty saw it must have won an internal battle with his penchant for organization; otherwise, the letters would have been sorted like the rest of her mail. Rubber-banded stacks labeled in his tiny print—"bills," "catalogs," "photo-related"—might have included stacks of personals responses sorted into "definites," "promising," "maybes," and "feeders." Rusty smiled at the thought of having her assistant screen her dates for her. She began to read.

By ten P.M., Rusty had set up dates to meet seven men: two were "definites," three were "promising," two were "feeders" scheduled three days apart. The other letters could wait. With luck, she'd be spending more time with Marshall Wilkins after their date Wednesday.

She realized that it wasn't a bad idea to get her feeders from the ad responses which she had decided were "no's"— there might be less chance of tainted blood than in accessible street people. While she was dressing, Rusty mentally composed an ad for her other need: BLOOD DONORS WANTED BY LAST "LIVING" VAMPIRE—NO EXPERIENCE REQUIRED. IMMORTALITY AVAILABLE TO RIGHT PERSON. Gregor would have gotten a kick out of it. If it didn't jeopardize her existence, she would have been tempted to run it just to see what kind of response it got.

Tonight, however, she wasn't going to eat. For some time, Rusty had been curious about Chippendales, the club on Overland which specialized in male strippers for female audiences. She hoped they allowed cameras. It was time to do some new photos.

* * *

The dream had changed. Jace was still trapped, paralyzed in the surrealistic ruins of his mother's living room, with its dripping ceiling and moss-hung walls. But this time, he was tied up, naked, his wrists and ankles anchored by black-and-yellow silk scarves to iron rings in the floor. He could smell the faint odor of dusty roses. He realized he wasn't alone. Ellen knelt nude next to him, rubbing her nipples across his bare chest, stroking his penis until it was rock-hard erect. She smiled, a knife in her hand. He didn't know what he wanted from her first—to lower herself onto his rigid cock, or to cut the binding scarves to free him—but when she took the head of his cock in her other hand, he was suddenly afraid of her. She put the edge of the blade against his cock, and he screamed wordlessly until the sound woke him.

It was four-fifteen. Liz wouldn't be by to pick him up until eight, and he desperately needed more sleep, but the nightmare shook him. He needed something to help him sleep for a few hours. He thought of taking a Valium, but knew it wouldn't wear off soon enough to ensure lucidity in the morning.

He remembered confiscating a joint from the ten-year-old boy down the block a couple of months ago. A few tokes of grass might be just the ticket. Had he thrown it out or kept it? Ten minutes later, he found it; twenty minutes later, he was dreamlessly asleep.

"You look a lot better this morning," Liz observed when Jace got into the car. "Get enough sleep?"

"I haven't gotten enough sleep since I joined Homicide, but yeah, I feel better."

"Good enough to talk to Avallone's roommate? I got an

address to go with the phone number; I thought we might stop and see her before going into the station.''

"Drive on, MacDuff."

The building was an old duplex on Wilcox in Hollywood, the address belonging to the upper unit. Jace knocked on the door, but it was solid wood, and the sound was muffled. There was no bell. Jace pounded again, this time with closed fist. After a third knock, they heard a woman's voice say, "I'm coming!"

The door was opened by a tall, square figure in an open, pink chenille bathrobe, platinum hair in curlers, traces of old eye make-up smeared under puffy eyes. Small breasts and rounded jawline were belied by the obvious male bulge in the black cotton bikini underwear and the stubble of chest hairs.

"Who are you?" s/he asked, pulling the robe shut.

"Police." Jace flipped open his badge. "We need to ask you about Stephen Avallone."

"He's not here. I haven't seen him since Saturday." S/he began to close the door. Jace put out a hand to stop the door's movement.

"This won't take long, Miss. We'd appreciate your cooperation." Hostility somewhat diffused by Jace's acknowledgement of her chosen gender, the transsexual shrugged, opened the door, and gestured them in with a graceful wave.

"I'm not saying anything about Steve until you tell me what this is about." She crossed her arms theatrically over her chest.

"We're investigating Stephen Avallone's death this weekend."

"Steve's dead?" She dropped onto the couch, stunned, her hands forgotten in her lap. "Migod, what happened?"

"Are you Erica?" Liz asked.

"Erica Michelle. It's my legal name," she added defensively. "Was it a car accident?"

"Someone murdered him, Miss Michelle," Jace said softly. "He was stabbed in Griffith Park. Do you know anyone who might have wanted to kill him?"

Tears formed in Erica's eyes, and she wiped them on the sleeve of her robe. "I told him to be careful, but he was sure he could take care of himself. He must have picked up a rough trick. Or some fag-basher got him. Poor Steve. Migod—dead!" She began to sob.

"What can you tell us about his tricks, Miss Michelle?" Liz said, handing Erica a tissue. Erica blew her nose loudly, and collected herself. She sighed.

"He doesn't—didn't—have any regulars. He just trolls— he'll blow any man with a twenty. I told him it was dangerous . . ."

"Does he have a phone book?" Liz asked. Erica nodded and got it for her.

"Did he ever trick with women?" Jace said.

"Steve? He wouldn't know what to do with a vagina. As far as I know, he's never even seen one. His gran'ma and me are the only women he knows." She barked a short laugh. "We're not exactly representative, huh?"

On the way to the station, Jace was quiet. Liz suddenly said, "I just thought of something."

Jace nodded. "That's what I was thinking." Liz looked at him to find he wasn't kidding. He explained, "You figured out that a transvestite would have the upper-body strength of our killer and still might be mistaken for a woman, right?"

"No shit, Sherlock. No wonder they made you a detective."

Jace mused, "That theory could account for Elaine Notkin

thinking Kaufman was at Babar's with a woman—it's dark in that bar, and she maybe wouldn't be able to see well enough to tell it was a man in drag. The lighting where Spiker saw Flores killed wasn't much better."

"Chopping off Kaufman's dick was symbolic of something for the killer—maybe it was male-to-female surgery." Liz was getting excited that they might be onto something. "The chest wound could stand for a broken heart."

"You're forgetting that all the victims before Avallone were straight. The only way a straight guy is going to pick up a drag queen—"

"—is if he thinks it's a woman," Liz finished for him. "It wouldn't be the first time a man put his hand in his date's panties and found a cock. We might be dealing with someone who passes really well for female, not like Erica. The killer might have stabbed them because they knew."

"This sounds like *Dressed To Kill* or something. Life imitates art? You know how many drag queens there must be in this city? Not to mention West Hollywood?" Jace thought for awhile. "That still doesn't explain the lack of defense wounds. That one's really bothering me, Liz. Why didn't any of these guys fight back?"

"I think we ought to get toxes on all the victims. We have no way of knowing if they were drugged when they were killed."

When they got to their desks, Liz found a message to call the psycho squad of the FBI in Quantico.

"Kevin Brenner," the well-modulated voice answered.

"Agent Brenner, this is Detective Robinson at the LAPD returning your call. My partner, Jacob Levy, is also on the line. Are you calling about the reports I sent in?"

"Yes, Detective. I'm afraid I haven't got a profile for you

yet, but we're working on it. Have there been any more killings since?''

"We had another this weekend. I'll try to have the report to you by the end of the week," Liz said.

"Good. Everything you send us can help us develop a more accurate profile. The reason I called . . . This is probably just a strange coincidence to this case, but we've got a similar M.O. in the archives. Seven bodies in Binghamton, New York; all derelicts—decimated the homeless population there at the time—drained of blood, stabbed in the carotid. It wasn't publicized, but one of our agents' fathers worked the case.''

"That sounds like our killer. Why do you think it's a coincidence?" Jace asked.

"Because it was thirty years ago, and the one eyewitness described the perpetrator as a man close to fifty. If it isn't a coincidence, there's an eighty-year-old serial killer loose in L.A. who's been working undetected for thirty years.''

"I see what you mean. Is there a file you could send us on it anyway?''

"There's not much. The police file is lost, and the investigating officer dead. But our agent found some notes in his father's files and a sketch of the suspect. I'll fax them to you.''

Three pages arrived from Brenner shortly after they hung up. The first had locations and dates for the murders (spanning from late November 1960 through early January 1961), the names of the victims, and the location of the wounds (all but the first on the right-side carotid). The second page was an artist's composite sketch of a lean-faced Caucasian male with gray hair and a trimmed moustache. The eyes were dark and somehow intense. The third page was a handwritten summary of an interview with the eyewitness to the third murder, a habitual drunk named Sassy Dann, who was himself the sixth victim. According to the policeman's notes, the eyewitness was totally unreliable, babbling incoherently about were- wolves and vampires while in the throes of DT's. God knows how they got a description out of him.

"Brenner was right. There's nothing here," Liz sighed. "It's just as well. Couldn't you just see Cosentino after we tell him we're looking for an eighty-year-old transvestite vam- pire?"

"Let's go see him anyway," Jace said. "It's time we called a meeting on this; get everyone involved: Ghiz and Sale, Fred Waner, someone from each homicide department; maybe see if we can get Tevis, Schaffer, and King to come in, too. We're going to need help on this."

Gregor told Rusty that there was an advantage to wintering in the north: the long nights, the sunless days—for a vampire, it meant being able to enjoy a day 20 percent longer than the usual ten to twelve hours, hours that could be spent perusing art and literature and theater.

"Unfortunately, these places are seldom cultural centers— at least in America," he had laughed. "I spent a turgid six weeks in upstate New York once, where the big cultural events of the holidays were the bowling championships. The snow was hip-deep and it was hell trying to find feeders. I ate about once a week, but even at that, I couldn't drain them—I had to leave some blood on the snow so the cop wouldn't figure out it was being drunk. I think they had only one cop—the only advantage to small towns. Usually, strangers stand out too much, but this was almost a small city. That's when I started using a bowie knife to cover the fang punctures. You wouldn't believe the selection of knives you can get in hunting areas. I finally got back to civilization and the next time I wanted a long night, I went to Stockholm.''

"Was that better than New York?'' Rusty asked.

"Stockholm's a wonderful place in the winter. There're only about three hours of daylight in a city filled with museums, galleries, theaters, and concerts. Most Swedes know how to keep busy in the winter—those who can't, get drunk and suicidal: easy meals. Shall I take you to Stockholm this winter, my dear?''

CHAPTER
Eight

As soon as Liz came in Wednesday morning, Jace knew something was wrong. His partner's usual careful application of makeup was missing entirely, her eyes were puffy, and her hair finger-furrowed. She dropped—rather than placed—her purse in the bottom drawer of her desk and then kicked the drawer shut with a semi-vicious push of her Reeboks. Athletic shoes? Jace had never seen Liz in anything but leather pumps before. She wore heels to stakeouts, ferchrissakes.

"Mornin', Liz," he ventured.

"Die, male scum," she hissed. She dropped into her chair and banged her keyboard until the computer gave in and hummed to life. "Fucker," she muttered under her breath, angrily tapping keys.

"Me?"

"Sandy." She didn't look up from the computer. "I figured out why men are such asses."

Inwardly, Jace groaned. Why was it that women always seemed to blame the entire male sex when one man pissed them off?

"Testosterone poisoning," she announced, "the male equivalent of PMS. You go a few days without sex and it backs up in your system and turns you into gorillas, pounding your chests and marking your territory. Like it matters."

"Hey, I've gone without sex for—" Jace calculated, "—five days now . . . and I haven't beat my chest once; my meat, maybe, but not my chest," he finished weakly. "I gather you and the counselor have had a spat."

Liz took her hands off the keyboard and sighed deeply. She finally looked at Jace. "Sorry. I didn't mean to take it out on you. Yeah, we had a humdinger this morning, before he left for San Francisco on a case. He started out complaining about the hours I've been working—"

"Every detective has had that one with a Significant Other, Liz, you know that. It comes with the territory."

"Yeah, yeah, I know," she waved off his comment. "It's not like it's never come up before, but this time, he was really crazy. I don't know what's gotten into him." She paused as if unsure she should continue. "I've been pretty wiped out by the time I get home lately, and I just . . . haven't felt like . . . making love maybe quite as often as he wants. You know how it is."

"Naw. I always feel like it." Liz scowled at him. "Joke, Liz. So that's what it was all about—insufficient sex?" Jace was a bit uncomfortable with the topic, but she'd listened to his problem, so he owed her.

"Not quite. Seems my beloved husband isn't so much pissed that he's not getting it, but that someone else is."

Jace was stunned. Liz Robinson was the last person he'd guess was having an extramarital affair. He wondered who the guy was, if he knew him.

"You're having an affair?" he asked, trying to appear disinterested.

"Sandy thinks I am."

"Are you?" He wasn't sure he really wanted to know.

"I'm considering it." She paused. "Well, not really; but it'd serve him right for not trusting me. Jesus, when does he think I have time for an affair? I work twelve-hour days—more, since this serial started—and I'm with him all night when we're not on a case."

"You pointed that out?" Jace asked, fascinated in spite of his reluctance to become involved. Relationships were always interesting from a distance.

Liz grinned ruefully. "At the top of my lungs. I guess he figures I have a lot of nooners." She suddenly looked even more distressed. "You don't think he's projecting his own guilt, do you? It never occurred to me that he might be . . ."

"Whoa, Liz, hold down the paranoia. He probably just misses you—don't make a federal case out of it. Sandy loves you, and he's a good man, you know that."

"You wouldn't say that if you heard what he said about you."

"Me? What have I got to do with anything?"

Jace had a sinking feeling that he knew what was coming next. He was right.

"You're the one he thinks I'm screwing," Liz said. She turned back to the computer. "He thinks you'll be spending the night while he's in San Francisco," she told the keyboard.

* * *

Jace found Ronnie Schaffer at her bench in the lab, eyeing a test-tube containing an inch of blue liquid. The serologist looked surprised to see him.

"You didn't have to come here—I could have told you over the phone," she said. She put the test tube in a rack and made a note on her work sheet.

"I needed some air. Life was getting a little confusing at the station. What did you find?"

Ronnie rotated on her stool. "You're going to love this one, Detective. Your killer apparently stole about three quarts of blood from Avallone, Stephen Michael; and I can't figure out how he did it."

"He did have a gaping wound in his neck," Jace pointed out.

"The pattern on the tarp had no interruptions in the spatters—the flow was unimpeded from the moment he began to spurt until his heart stopped. There were no smudges in the pooled blood. For all the evidence shows, no one was there when he bled to death. He sure as hell didn't normally have half as much blood as everyone else, but there's no way anyone could have collected some of his blood. He couldn't just put a container under the fountain without leaving some track on the tarp. You're the detective; you tell me," she shrugged.

"Lemme use your phone." Jace dialed the number for the coroner. "Darrell King," he told the person who answered. It was several minutes before the doctor picked up the line.

"Were there any other punctures on Avallone besides the neck wound?"

"You were at the post, man. That was it."

"I know that was the only knife wound, King. I'm talking about needles."

"Jeez, Levy, I didn't see any. I would have noticed any near the wound or on the insides of his arms; he didn't have any tracks, arms or legs, if that's what you mean." Jace told him what Schaffer had found on the tarp. "You wanna know did someone tap a vein before they stabbed him? Shit, it's possible, Levy, but if so, we've got a major problem."

"What do you mean?" Jace asked.

"I got the HIV results on him. His blood is lethal."

The briefing room was filled with handshaking homicide detectives, primarily from various LAPD precincts (mostly the Central and West Bureaus), but Fred Waner and another homicide sergeant represented the Sheriff's Department, and there were detectives from the Santa Monica and Long Beach Police Departments. Ronnie Schaffer, the criminalist, had arrived with Darrell King. Jace and Liz had expected ten to fifteen to attend; they had close to thirty. Folding chairs were brought in.

Liz passed out collated sets of maps and data summaries while Jace finished tacking photos of the victims and crime scenes on a large bulletin board. Liz got a clerk to run off a dozen more sets.

Frank Cosentino tapped a pencil against his water glass. "Let's get started." The hubbub stopped as the detectives turned to the front. "Before we get to specifics, I want to make one thing clear. There are to be *no* leaks to the press, *capisce*? What you hear today has not been made public—and we want it kept that way, at least for now." He scanned the room, looking for a weak link, then nodded. "Okay.

Jacob Levy and Elizabeth Robinson are running this case—''
Cosentino gestured and sat down. He took a pack of gum out
of his pocket and unwrapped two sticks.

Jace took over. ''We've got at least six—and possibly as
many as twenty-two—murders with the same pattern in less
than a year's time. All the victims are male, killed at night.
All were stabbed by a bowie-sized knife in the carotid. Some
have one additional wound—usually in the chest, but in one
case, there was a . . . penis amputation.'' A few men
groaned. ''None of the victims bore any defense wounds.''
He paused to let that sink in.

''Kaufman, the vic who was . . . mutilated,'' Jace continued, ''was seen three hours before he died in the company of
a woman wearing a scarf later found at the scene of the crime.
The particulars are in your packets. A less-than-reliable witness to the Flores murder swears a woman did that one, too.
The only description is white, dark hair, twenty-five to thirty
years old.''

''Ah, a *femme fatale*,'' a cop named Liddel wisecracked.

''There's no such thing as a female serial murderer,''
Waner said, ''is there?''

''What about that woman they just picked up in Florida?
Waronos or whatever her name is? She offed something like
seven or eight men,'' Cosentino said.

''We're not sure ours was really a woman,'' Liz offered.
''Flores weighed two hundred and ten pounds and his killer
picked up his corpse and tossed it into a trash bin.''

''The druggie who saw the murder said the woman hoisted
him like he weighed nothing,'' Jace added. ''We suspect we
may be dealing with a transsexual, or a man in drag. Another
victim, Cabot, had been stabbed in the chest so hard, it

cracked his sternum, right, Doc?'' Jace looked to King for confirmation.

The doctor shrugged. ''It was a pretty hard blow even for a man.''

Victor Ghiz spoke up. ''At least the two vics we had were straight, Levy.''

''Yeah, I know, but even straight men have been known to pick up drag queens—either they don't know . . . or they don't care. We had another vic this last weekend in Griffith Park—a gay hustler named Avallone. His roommate is a queen, a pre-surgery hormone junkie.''

''Suspect?''

''No, we don't make him for it. Besides, nobody'd take him for a woman. He said Avallone didn't swing both ways; he'd never gone with women.'' Jace scratched his cheek reflectively. ''Avallone had AIDS. Which brings us to another problem. Somehow, the killer took about half his blood from the crime scene.''

Everyone began talking at once. Cosentino rapped on his glass until the room quieted.

''It's possible we might have some kind of weird gay terrorist running around—maybe taking revenge for being infected or something. In any event, someone out there has''— Jace sought visual confirmation from Ronnie Schaffer as he spoke—''three quarts of AIDS-infected blood, and we don't know what they plan to do with it.''

''What about the other vics? Did they have AIDS too?'' a cop Jace recognized from Hollenbeck asked.

King said, ''I'm running tests on them now. I have to use the spleen because none of the bodies had enough blood left to collect.''

"Was blood taken from the other bodies?" Fred Waner demanded. "I don't remember J.T. saying anything about that on the body we had in Topanga."

"We can't tell on the others. All the victims bled to death, but some were on sand—Cabot bled through a wood-slat floor into dirt," Jace reminded Waner. "We just lucked out with A'vallone because he was on a plastic dropcloth which caught the blood that was left."

For the next hour, the detectives discussed the evidence, and theories ranging from the outré to the absurd; this was like no case they'd ever heard of. No one was looking forward to finding out what the killer wanted with AIDS-infected blood.

Rusty dried her hair, singing "Good Lovin' " with enthusiasm, if not on key. Tonight she'd see Marshall again; they were meeting at midnight, and this time she wouldn't have to leave early to eat.

Last night's "date" had been one of the responses to her ad who had been immediately classified a feeder. Kelly Lamont was an unemployed printer who apparently "partied down" as a way of life. He asked Rusty to pick him up because he'd stopped making payments on his car after his license was suspended for DUI and the vehicle had been repo'd that week. Although the bulbous-nosed, greasy-haired man had not bothered to shave within three days of their date, he did have a clean (although wrinkled) T-shirt smoothed over his ample gut and tucked into the stained jeans he wore under his belly. The T-shirt read "Moustache Rides 5 Cents." Although he had claimed to be "good-looking" and twenty-eight in his letter, he was neither.

He didn't invite her in, muttering vaguely about trouble

with "the dude what lives here"; he suggested they drive out to a biker's bar he knew out at the far end of Mulholland Drive, where there was always a party. The drive involved a one-way trip of nearly twenty-five miles; although Rusty consented, she had no intention of driving that far in the company of a meal with the intellectual development of a chicken.

As soon as she'd driven into the hills, she pulled off onto a dirt lane.

"Somethin' wrong wit' your car?"

Rusty smiled with what appeared to be lust, but which she knew to be hunger about to be appeased, and opened her arms to him. Kelly looked like he'd just found El Dorado and lunged for her. The gearshift in her ribs reminded Rusty that it would be easier to get him out of the Honda on his own steam, and she breathlessly urged him outside where there was room to maneuver. She didn't have to ask twice.

When he grabbed her, she dropped to the ground, bringing him with her. Reluctant to be kissed on the mouth by him again, she turned her head to the side and, without preamble, planted her fangs in his neck. He moaned with pleasure as soon as the venom injected. Rusty could tell from the wet spot on his jeans that he'd ejaculated. His hot blood spurted, filling her mouth with its lovely copper taste as she gulped it down.

"Take it all, baby!" he yelled, just before he lost consciousness.

Rusty was hungrier than usual, and when she stopped feeding, only a few pints of blood followed the knife puncture. She hoisted up Kelly's drained corpse and tossed it down a gully, where it came to rest at the bottom, invisible in the tangle of deadwood and leaves. On the way back to the car, she scuffed the ground where his body had been, dispersing the blood through the dirt.

It was only ten P.M., so Rusty had decided to continue on to the biker's bar anyway—and was glad she had. She got some great photos.

Tonight would be different.

As Elliott applied blusher to Risha's cheekbones, he thought again how lovely she was. He was particularly enamored of her eyes, somehow simultaneously pale and deep, like non-reflecting mirrors. He remembered falling into them the first time he ever saw her, and he didn't think he'd ever climbed out.

She'd looked different twenty years ago—not younger, just different. She'd been heavier by some forty pounds, but even then she wasn't chunky; she was round in a comforting sort of feather-pillow way. The dark-auburn hair he delighted in braiding had been worn in a short, shapeless cap then— she began letting it grow after she had crossed over.

Her personality had changed, too. The woman Gregor Bathory had brought home was shy, quiet, and lacking in confidence. But under their care and tutelage, she had come into her own. The old vampire had encouraged Risha to express herself, both verbally and photographically. As her work began to sell to publications and through galleries, she gained self-respect. She began to ask Gregor to travel to specific places she wanted to see, rather than merely following his lead. The year they'd spent on various Caribbean islands had been her idea. Although Gregor had been bored with only reggae and calypso clubs for entertainment, he'd had to admit that some of her best photographs had been taken there.

When Elliott started to braid her hair, she stopped him.

"I'm going to wear it down tonight; maybe just put a comb in it?"

He opened the dressing table drawer where she kept her hair accessories. He took out the comb that had belonged to Gregor's mother—a carved ivory piece with a silver Bathory crest on the crossbar, but she shook her head.

"Not ivory—it's politically incorrect."

"I take it you're not planning to wear your sable tonight, either?" Elliott asked with a smile. "Afraid he'll throw animal blood on you?"

"It's a shame I can't drink it—I could feed by wearing my fur to animal rights meetings," she laughed. "Use the jade comb, Elliott. I don't think anyone's down on jade."

Rusty was so eager to see Marsh that she was fifteen minutes early. She rang the bell at his apartment, then knocked, but there was no response; he must not be home from the hospital yet. He said he didn't get off until 11:30; it took at least twenty minutes to get to the Fairfax District from Brentwood. Rusty went back to the BMW to get the book she was reading—a new anthology of vampire stories called *A Whisper Of Blood*—and took it back to read in the light over Marshall's door.

It was 12:20 when she finished the first story and Marsh still hadn't appeared. She began to be concerned. She hadn't given him her phone number, which was unlisted; he would have had no way to contact her if he'd had to cancel. On the other hand, if he'd known in advance that he couldn't make it, wouldn't he have left a note? Maybe he just got tied up at work. She started the next story, sure he'd arrive before she finished it.

Fifteen minutes later, she decided to find a phone. Maybe

he had left a message for her on his machine. She walked over to Fairfax Boulevard and found a pay phone at a gas station and dialed his number. It rang eight times before she hung up. Was she dating the only person in L.A. without a phone machine?

She returned to his apartment and started to write a note on a scrap of paper, but then it occurred to her that he might have returned while she was gone, and she rang the bell again. This time, he opened the door.

"God, I'm sorry," he blurted. "I figured you got pissed off and left. Please come in. You wouldn't believe the night I've had. Do you want a drink?"

Rusty was relieved that he hadn't stood her up. She sat on his couch, a homemade wooden platform with a six-inch foam pad covered by a faded pink sheet, while he poured her a scotch and topped off his own.

"This is the day we do dialysis, and the lab was swamped all day. Then the computer went down, and I spent three hours accumulating data that I had less than an hour to enter once the system got back up. The guy who takes over from me at shift-end called and said his car broke down and he was coming by bus; he didn't get there until after midnight. By then, I knew you'd be here, and I had no way to reach you. So I make the fifty-yard dash to the car, and while I'm putting the key in the lock, some wino tried to grab my backpack and I had to deck him. I think I broke his nose, but I wasn't going to spend time taking him into the hospital and making reports and all that, so I just left him there. I would have done seventy on the way home, but the way my day was going, I would've gotten pulled over, so I behaved myself . . . sort of." Marsh shrugged. "When I got here, you were gone, so I figured I fucked up royally.'' He took a gulp from his drink.

"Luckily, I had a book with me,'' Rusty said.

"What are you reading?'' Marsh took the book. "*Eighteen Stories of Vampirism*,'' he read. "You into this stuff?''

"It's sort of a hobby of mine. Wouldn't you like to be immortal?'' Although her questioning appeared to be casual, Rusty was eager to hear his answer.

"Great topic for the middle of the night,'' he laughed. "I imagine living forever could have its advantages, but I'm not so sure the world is turning into something I'd want to see a few hundred years from now.'' Marshall put his arm around her. "Besides, blood is high in cholesterol; what's the good of being a vampire if you've got blocked arteries?''

"I don't think vampires have to worry about disease,'' Rusty said, snuggling into him. "Would you be able to kill people if it meant you could live as long as you wanted?''

"If I could choose the people, you bet! I'd start with Jesse Helms, I think . . . oh, shit! That wouldn't work, either, because then he'd turn into a vampire; the only thing worse than Jesse Helms is an immortal Jesse Helms.'' He laughed again. "Well, we don't have to worry about it—it's all make-believe anyway, right?'' He lifted her chin with his finger and kissed her.

Rusty turned to look at the bedside clock: 4:20. She knew she should leave. Marshall was sleeping, his silky strawberry-blond hair strewn across the pillow. It had been over two decades since she'd actually been fucked and this had been a glorious return to a pleasure she'd experienced too seldom before it was gone.

She had delighted in his firm cock, hot and pulsing with blood. It had been exquisite torture for her to keep her fangs retracted while she was fellating him; she thought it must be somewhat the same thrill some people got from bondage. Although he was a skilled lover, in the end, she was unsatisfied because she couldn't bite—it was like sex without orgasm: pleasurable, but not complete.

She got out of bed carefully, so not to wake him, and got dressed in the dark. She found a pad of paper in the kitchen and wrote a note: "Vampires must be home by dawn. This weekend? I'll call you." She left it propped against the bedside clock, and tiptoed out.

CHAPTER
Nine

Rusty's first feedings were not what she'd expected, nor what they would eventually become for her. In later years, she and Gregor had had several heated discussions about his decision to not allow her to watch him feed until after she herself had crossed over; she finally conceded to his contention that she would have changed her mind about vampirism when confronted with the reality of the hunt.

Gregor had chosen a prostitute that first time in San Francisco, a pretty Chinese woman named Lauren who thought she was being hired for a *menage-à-trois* with the lanky gray-haired gentleman and his plump lady.

In the small room near the Wharf, Gregor had paid the hooker a hundred dollars. He sat on the bed, his back against the wall, with Rusty between his outstretched legs, her back against his chest. He told Lauren to undress—slowly—and as she unzipped and bared herself, Gregor opened Rusty's shirt to pinch and tease her nipples with his cool fingers. By the time the Chinese girl was down to only a black lace thong, Gregor had hiked up Rusty's skirt, and was fingering her moist opening, their eyes glued to the sensuous striptease Lauren was performing.

Rusty was becoming overwhelmed by excitement, unable to differentiate between lust and hunger, but knowing that she wanted Lauren *now*.

"Play first," Gregor whispered, "make her blood rush." He got up, and pulled off Rusty's clothes, directing her to take his place sitting back to the wall. Gregor put Lauren in the position Rusty had been in before, her back against Rusty's breasts, her legs open between Rusty's. Gregor knelt and began to lick the hooker's clitoris. Rusty put her hands on Lauren's breasts, caressing the nipples with increasing pressure, and Lauren leaned her head back against Rusty's shoulder, her neck scant inches from Rusty's lips.

Rusty felt her fangs extend, the venom dripping into her own mouth; she closed her lips before she realized Lauren couldn't see her fangs from her position. She caught Gregor's eye, and opened her mouth again to reveal her fangs. He nodded imperceptibly.

Rusty bent her head to Lauren's neck and sunk her teeth in the spot where the blood smell was strongest. The hooker shrieked and pulled away.

"That hurt, you bitch! I don't do that shit—this is gonna cost you plenty!" She put her hand to the spurt of blood that had escaped before the punctures sealed. "Fuck, I'm bleeding!" Lauren tried to get off the bed, but Gregor had her pinned, and before she could shift, he bit her on the same side Rusty had hit. Immediately, Lauren stopped struggling and began to hum in pleasure.

After feeding for a few seconds, he stopped, and the punctures closed. Lauren was in a transport of ecstasy, unaware of her surroundings.

"Your venom's not very potent yet. When it's stronger, they'll give in right away," Gregor told Rusty. "She's sedated; try again now."

Although Rusty's lust had been broken by Lauren's response, the hunger was stronger than ever, and she didn't hesitate to plant her fangs again. The coppery blood held the slight sweetness Rusty recognized as the taste of her lover's venom; she gulped the hot blood that spurted into her mouth like water after a desert trek. When she'd had enough, Gregor took over and drained the prostitute's body of its remaining blood.

The exultation of the venom and the satiation of feeding filled Rusty with a warm glow until she looked at the empty vessel that was once named Lauren. She saw the dark hair stark against the bloodless skin, the nipples she'd been pinching no longer erect, and knew her life was over. Rusty was overcome with guilt, and she ran to the bathroom, where she vomited all the blood into the toilet bowl. Gregor wiped her face gently with a warm washcloth.

"You had no choice, my dear," he said. "Once I told you my secret, you were dead, one way or the other. We must feed to exist, like every other animal—to refuse is to die. If you are not a hunter, you are the hunted. The instinct to survive is the strongest urge we have—you adapt or you die."

They'd gone on to the Grateful Dead concert that night, but by the time they got out, Rusty was weak.

"I can't go through that again now, Gregor. Maybe we can try again tomorrow."

"Risha, if you don't eat before dawn, you'll be too weak

to get up tomorrow. You have none of your old blood left, and you threw up what you drank earlier. Get in the back seat. I'll bring you something to eat.''

He was gone for fifteen minutes, returning to the car with a hippie girl in tie-dyed clothes, a backpack with sleeping bag strapped to her back. He took her backpack and opened the back door of the car for her, and she climbed in next to Rusty.

''Hi!'' she said brightly. ''I'm Sunbeam. Wasn't that a groovy concert?'' Gregor leaned in behind the girl and bit her neck, injecting her with venom; she dropped into Rusty's lap, smiled, and closed her eyes.

''Go ahead,'' Gregor urged. ''She won't feel it.''

Rusty hesitated for only a moment before draining Sunbeam. ''She kept smiling right until she died,'' she marvelled to Gregor.

''Once your venom is up to strength, that'll happen most of the time. It's a very pleasurable way to go, Risha—you might even say it's humane,'' he laughed.

He started up the car and drove through the Presidio to the rocky point under the Golden Gate Bridge, where he threw Sunbeam's body and backpack into the chilly black water.

On the way back to Berkeley, Gregor regaled Rusty with a funny story about a feeder, hooked on the high, who kept coming back for more venom, unaware he was losing blood each time, until he was finally shot with a gun to prevent him from inadvertently crossing into vampirism.

''Maybe we ought to see if we can find you a live-in junkie, since your venom won't be strong enough to stimulate metamorphosis for several years.''

''Right,'' she laughed, ''we could keep him in the pantry

and have Elliott bring him in each night on a silver tray with the Bathory crest.''

Elliott was late leaving to pick up the mail Thursday because he had slept, uncharacteristically, until almost noon. He had been unable to sleep all night, never completely at ease unless he knew Risha was safe inside.

Although it was not unheard-of for her to be out all night, she usually was in before four, working in the darkroom, reading, or watching videotapes. When Elliott's bedside clock showed four-forty and Rusty still had not come in, he got up to check; perhaps he'd missed hearing her return.

A fruitless tour of the house increased his anxiety level exponentially. He knew she'd had another date with the guy in the Fairfax District that night, and he was afraid of a catastrophe—had she told him what she was and been staked or beheaded? Had she been arrested? Maybe the BMW had broken down and she couldn't get home—did she have her auto club card with her? They were so slow to arrive . . .

Maybe he should go out and look for her. Dawn would come too soon to wait much longer. Elliott started to throw on clothes. He knew the route she would probably take home . . . Maybe he should call. He dug through his sock drawer until he found the guy's name and number.

The phone rang four times before a sleepy male voice answered, ''What?''

Elliott panicked—what would he say? ''I'm sorry to wake you . . .''

''Who is this?''

''This is Elliott, Mr. Wilkins. I'm Risha Cadigan's assistant. Is she there, please?''

Elliott crossed all his fingers in childish superstition. There was a long pause before Marshall answered.

"You mean Rusty? She's left."

"How long ago did she leave?" Elliott tried to keep the panic out of his voice.

"I don't know—I was asleep. Is something wrong?"

Just then, Elliott heard the BMW pull into the driveway.

"It's okay—she just arrived. I'm sorry to have disturbed you." Elliott hung up, undressed, and went back to bed.

The mail service counterman exchanged a large package for the slip Elliott found in the mailbox the next afternoon. It was from Spiegel, addressed to R. Cadigan; she must have bought some new clothes. The rest of the mail included two envelopes from *City of Angels*—a check for $2,500 with an advance copy of the new issue, and an invitation to their Halloween party. Risha would be pleased when she woke.

Jace spent most of Thursday at the courthouse, testifying in a case from August—a man had bludgeoned his wife to death and claimed a burglar had done it—and it was after three when he got back to his desk. Liz was cross-referencing data in the computer, and looked up as Jace came in.

"I see by your outfit you've been in court." Jace was wearing a jacket and tie—not his usual attire.

"All fucking day—the Curtis case. The defense attorney was a real hotdog and he wouldn't take anything I said at face value."

"You've got such a nice face, too," Liz smiled.

"What's going on here?" Jace looked at the stacks of paperwork on his desk. Nothing new on the top layer.

"I've finished cross-checking Cabot's and Kaufman's

phone directories—no matches. I was just starting to enter the names and numbers from Avallone's black book."

"Probably won't give us anything either." Jace removed his tie, rolled it up, and put it in his pocket. "I think I'll go see what Vice might have to help us. If it's not too late, can you call that agent at the FBI—Brenner?—and let him know about this new twist with the blood?"

"Somebody will be there; the FBI doesn't close any earlier than we do." She picked up the phone as Jace left.

Liz was still at the computer when Jace returned at 4:30, her Charles Jourdan pumps under the desk next to her stockinged feet.

"So what did Vice have on violent drag queens?" she asked.

"Not much," Jace admitted as he dropped into his chair. "I talked with LoBrutto, but he thinks we may be barking up the wrong tree. T's—that's what transvestites and transsexuals call themselves—apparently are a remarkably nonviolent bunch; LoBrutto thinks it has to do with all the female hormones they take."

"The antidote to testosterone poisoning," Liz observed.

"Male basher. Anyway, knives are the T's' second choice of weapon when they do get violent."

"What's their first choice? Guns?"

"Fingernails. Usually they only fight among themselves, unless they're fighting off an attack. He couldn't think of any stone killers, but he said he'd check with Best at the West Hollywood Sheriff's and see if he knows of anyone. LoBrutto's got a snitch who's tapped into the subculture and he'll see if she's heard anything."

"Did he have any guesses on the AIDS-infected blood?"

"Just the same gruesome scenarios we've been afraid of—it constitutes a lethal weapon with hideous possibilities . . . and it's probably sitting in the killer's refrigerator right now. Death on ice."

"Sounds like a hockey game," Liz said. "You got dinner plans tonight?"

"Yeah. I was planning to nuke a TV dinner. You got a better offer?"

"Sandy's still up north, and I really don't want to spend the evening alone worrying about my marriage. I'll buy dinner if you buy drinks." She tapped a few computer keys and turned off the machine. "But I've got to warn you: I plan to drink a lot. I'll try not to embarrass you."

"In that case, you can take me to Cutter's and I'll drive. Pick you up at seven?"

"Wear the tie."

Jace and Liz were still hashing over the case when his Cajun chicken fettucine and her mesquite-grilled salmon filet arrived. In spite of her warning, Liz was only on her third glass of white wine and still appeared sober. She was wearing an apricot silk dress low enough to show the sprinkling of freckles on top of her pale breasts and clingy enough to show she wore no bra. Jace was having a hard time keeping his mind on murder. He ordered a second Harp Lager from the waiter.

"Has Sandy called since he left?" He picked the parsley off his pasta. Jace didn't eat green food.

"Last night. He's calmed down some, but it wasn't the warmest conversation we've ever had." Liz swallowed half her wine. "If he can get the depositions wrapped up tomorrow, he'll be home tomorrow night. I'm beginning to see why you avoid commitments, Levy.''

The waiter returned with Jace's beer. Liz ordered another glass of Chardonnay.

''All relationships are hard, Liz, but that's not why I don't want one. It's . . .'' his voice dropped a notch in volume, ''. . . the Huntington's. I can't put anyone through that—having to care for someone who deteriorates for years and then dies? And I can't father children. Maybe if I make it to fifty without developing it . . .'' Jace's voice trailed off and he turned his attention to his dinner.

Elliott had put the envelopes from *City of Angels* on the top of the mail stack next to the tub. At first, Rusty thought they'd made a mistake on the check—it was $625 more than she was expecting—but then she saw the note paper-clipped to the advance copy of the new issue: ''Great response to Part One, so we decided to run four photos for the second series. Good work!'' It was signed with an illegible scribble, but the heading indicated it came from David A. South, editor-in-chief of the magazine.

Toweling dry, Rusty was elated—her career was taking off. She wanted to celebrate somehow, and regretted again that she couldn't share her success with Gregor. She walked over to the dresser, topped by a framed print of the only photograph she had of him. Taking a picture of a vampire had been a challenge—almost all cameras involve mirrors and vampires don't reflect. She had snuck Gregor into the school photo studio one night before she crossed over and took the picture with the big view camera with the black hood that was used for portraits. The finished photo called to mind a description of Sir Richard Burton: ''Gypsy eyes like a wild beast . . . fierce, proud, and melancholy''; though Burton was dark and Gregor fair, it fit him as well. He'd been flattered when she added the print to her first show.

''You always told me my photography would bring me fame,'' she told the portrait, ''and you were right!'' She sighed. It wasn't the same as talking to him in person.

She put on an oversized Grateful Dead T-shirt; wearing nothing else, she went downstairs to call. She'd never had need of a bedroom phone.

''Laboratory.''

''Marshall Wilkins, please.''

''Rusty?'' Marsh sounded pleased to hear from her.

''Hi, Marsh. How are you?''

''Not bad, considering you and your assistant kept me up all night,'' he laughed.

''Elliott? What are you talking about?''

''He called around five this morning looking for you. You photographers sure keep weird hours.''

Rusty realized that Elliott must have been concerned when she was late getting home, but she wished he hadn't done that. ''God, I'm sorry he woke you. The water heater burst, and he must have panicked,'' she improvised.

''Any damage?''

''Nothing serious, but I did have to get a new one.'' She paused to shift subjects. ''I just got a note from *City of Angels*. My first trio of photos was so well-received that they're running four in the new issue.''

''That's great! I can't wait to see them. I'm off tomorrow night—why don't we celebrate?''

''That's just what I hoped you'd say.'' She made a mental note to change the ''date'' with a feeder from Friday to tonight if she could. "Can I interest you in a movie? I haven't seen *Thelma & Louise* or *Terminator 2* yet."

"Let's make it *Thelma & Louise*—I've already seen the Schwarzenegger. I'll pick you up and we can see it on the Westside—what's your address?"

Rusty hesitated a second—no one knew where she lived— but if she and Marsh were going to get anywhere, she was going to have to trust him. "Do you know the Beverlywood area?"

John Howard rushed around his living room, trying to pick up the mess before Rusty arrived with the pizza at eight to watch TV. He threw everything on the bed and closed the bedroom door, but then had second thoughts: If she was eager enough to move their date up a night, she might put out. After all, that's why women placed those ads, wasn't it? And it sure as hell was why he answered them. He grabbed everything off the bed and threw it in the closet, shutting the door quickly to keep the pile from tumbling out. He made the bed for the first time since he'd changed the sheets two weeks previously. He took a fast shower, shaved, and put on a yellow polo shirt with his brown double-knit slacks and fastened the self-belt. He looked at the clock: 7:50.

He sat on the couch and looked at the front door. Any time now. How should he handle the money for the pizza? Pizza and TV had been her idea, and he didn't think he should have to pay for the whole thing since she was going to eat half. Half the money should be okay. What if he didn't have the right change? He checked his wallet: a twenty, a ten, and a single. His half shouldn't be more than six or seven dollars— would she give him change if he gave her the ten? Maybe he

should write her a check. When should he offer the money—
as soon as she came in? ("Hi, how much is my share?")
After dinner? ("Here, let me pay my half.") Just before she
left? (No, that'd be too much like she was a hooker, particularly if they fucked first.) Maybe it'd be easier to say nothing—she could ask for the money if she wanted it; otherwise,
he'd let her treat and he could buy the pizza for their second
date, if they had one. He looked at his watch again: 7:56.

He got up to look out the front window. His Culver City
street was deserted. He sat on the couch again. What if she
insisted he wear a rubber—a lot of chicks did. He rushed into
the bedroom and rummaged through the bedside table, finally
producing a packet of three condoms with only one missing.
He put the packet on the top of the table next to the bed, then
went to the bedroom door to check the effect. Too obvious.
He was putting the rubbers back in the drawer when the
doorbell rang.

John Howard patted his hair, sucked in his gut, and went
to meet his fate.

CHAPTER
Ten

Jace's concentration was broken by a demand from Cosentino for a briefing on progress and tactics on finding the killer, whom Liz had dubbed "The Westside Vampire." A half an hour and four sticks of gum later, Jace returned to find Liz working at the computer.

"'Bout time you got in," he said, dropping into his chair. "You just missed briefing Cosentino."

"Be still my heart," she grinned. "I was hung-over."

"From five glasses of wine? You're a real lightweight, aren't you?" He summed up the meeting for her, adding, "He got a chuckle out of 'The Westside Vampire,' but said to tell you if he ever sees that term in the press, he'll have your shield."

"He can have it. I'll become a housewife like Sandy wants." She continued to tap computer keys. "So, what's next on the agenda?"

"Well, I want to go see Ronnie Schaffer and take over the

crime-scene photos in case she can tell from the pictures if blood was missing from any of the others. I also thought I might go talk to Erica Michelle again. Maybe she can shed some light on our drag-queen theory . . . or turn me on to someone who can.''

"Good idea. I'll call King and see if he's got the HIV results from the other vics. It'd be nice to know if this blood thing is really part of the Vampire's pattern.''

She picked up her phone while Jace called the lab on his to confirm that Ronnie was available. He hung up and stood to leave, but Liz, still talking to King, held up her hand to him to wait.

"Cannon, Kaufman, and Cabot were HIV-negative; Flores was positive; Garcia is still unknown—King said the samples from him have been 'misplaced,' which probably means 'lost forever.' "

"I guess we should be grateful they've only misplaced one.'' Jace sat on the edge of the desk. "If AIDS-infected blood is the link, how is the Vampire getting the info? It can't be very accurate if she—or he—missed on at least three out of six. See if you can get a list of AIDS-testing facilities in L.A.—both where blood samples are taken and the labs that do the actual testing. We might get lucky and turn up a link; maybe the Vampire works at a lab—it would explain having the know-how to draw blood.''

Liz nodded thoughtfully as she made notes. "We won't be able to get a list of their patients and test results with anything less than a Supreme Court decision, but they might be willing to give us any matches if they see our list. It might be easier to get employee rosters, but I wouldn't count on it.''

"You know how most serial killers are caught?'' Jace

asked, standing again. He dug the file of crime-scene photos off his desk.

"The three S's—shoe leather, scotch, and snitches?"

Jace shook his head. "Chance, Liz. It's usually by accident. See you later." He left for the lab.

Ronnie studied the photos carefully, both by eye and with a magnifying glass. "This one," she said, pointing to the photos of the Cannon crime scene Jace had gotten from the Santa Monica Police Department, "is impossible to tell, because the body was on sand. Similar problem with this one," she indicated Garcia, the crack-head, "the one on a lawn."

Jace had the least hope for those two anyway. "What about the others?"

"This one's on bedding on a waterbed. The bloodstain on the bedding might be small, but there's no way to see how much blood collected under the bedding or may have spilled between the water mattress and the frame. We've got the same situation with this one in the bunkhouse, too, because the blood flowed down his arm and through the floorboards. I'm not sure it would have been evident that there was blood missing even if you'd been looking for it at the time."

"This one"—Jace indicated the crime-scene photos from the Flores murder—"was on the paved walkway at Venice Beach, but after the murder, the body was tossed into a trash bin."

"I remember this scene—I took the call," Ronnie said. "There was virtually no blood in the trash bin with the body. Where are the pictures of the walkway?" Jace handed them to her, and she studied them closely. "It's nothing you could use in court," she warned.

"What? What do you see?"

"I don't think there's enough blood here. I can't even tell you how much is missing. It's like the one in Griffith Park last week—this just doesn't look like five-six quarts to me. This is weird, Levy. A victim's blood is in the body, near the body, and/or where the body was when the murder occurred. I can't think of a time when we found an appreciable amount of blood missing from all three places."

"Robinson's started calling the killer The Westside Vampire."

"She's been reading too much Stephen King. Why do you think the killer is taking blood?"

"I don't know, Ronnie, but I'm worried. This is the only other vic that tested HIV-positive."

Marsh Wilkins woke up Saturday morning with an erection and a full bladder. He was lying on his back; Rusty was curled up next to him, her head on his chest, her left leg bent across his. The digital clock on her bedside table read 6:32—past dawn, yet the room was as dark as it had been two hours earlier. Marshall thought if his curtains were as efficient as hers, he'd need an alarm clock to ensure that he made work by 3:30 in the afternoon.

He began to stroke Rusty, running his palm slowly down from her shoulder across her chest to stop briefly to cup and caress her breast, rubbing his thumb across the nipple. She slept on, her body unresponsive, and he continued to trace his hand along the side of her belly, down her hip, and up the inside of her thigh to her cool inner lips. She didn't move, not in pleasure, not even to shift away from his questing fingers.

"Rusty," he crooned softly in her ear, and again, "Ruuusty." Nothing. Marshall was starting to get concerned. "Rusty!" He spoke her name aloud, the urgency in his voice enough to embarrass him if she responded "What?" But she didn't. He put his hand on her shoulder and shook her none-too-gently. "Rusty, wake up!"

Nothing! And he couldn't see anything in the blackened room. He reached across her inert body for the bedside lamp. He got his fingers on the switch, but as he turned it, he lost his balance, and pulled the lamp off the table; it fell to the floor, its ginger-jar base crashing loudly upon impact. Under him, Rusty's body didn't even twitch at the sound.

Marsh grabbed her wrist and felt for a pulse—her room-temperature skin was still. He moved his hand to her neck—no pulse there either.

He tried not to panic as he turned her over and began to perform CPR, counting as he worked to convince her lungs to take a breath on their own. "Breathe," he yelled between counts, "breathe, damn it!" He'd seen people brought back from death many times at the V.A. Hospital where he worked; he knew it could be done. "Breathe!"

Suddenly, the bedroom door flew open and the room burst into full illumination. Elliott was standing in the doorway, dressed in pale-blue striped pajamas, maroon bathrobe, and leather slippers, one hand holding a forgotten coffee mug, the other on the light switch.

"Call 911!" Marsh yelled at the gaping assistant, "she's stopped breathing!"

Elliott didn't move, dumbfounded at the man administering CPR to a vampire. Had he never noticed her lack of breath before?

"You idiot! Don't just stand there, man—go call an ambulance! Do you want her to die?"

Elliott stood his ground. Marshall assumed Rusty's assistant to be paralyzed by shock and he looked frantically about the room in vain for a telephone, all the while trying to push air into Rusty's lungs.

"Where's the phone? There must be a phone!"

Marshall jumped up and grabbed Elliott's shoulders so roughly that the smaller man's coffee sloshed over both of them. "The telephone," he shouted into his face, "where is the telephone?"

With his free hand, Elliott pointed vaguely downstairs. Marsh pushed Elliott out of his way with one hand and charged down the stairs, tripping over the living-room cocktail table before finding the light switch; the heavy drapes were still shut. There was no phone in the living room, and Marsh barrelled into the study, slamming the wall on both sides of the doorway before finding the light. There, across the room on the desk, was a phone.

"I'm sorry, I can't let you call an ambulance." Elliott appeared at the door from the kitchen.

"You're crazy," Marsh yelled. "If I don't call, she'll die." He lunged for the desk and grabbed for the phone, but Elliott yanked on the cord and the phone dropped off the desk and out of Marshall's immediate reach.

"Leave her alone," Elliott insisted, "and she'll be fine."

"She won't be fine, fucker," Marsh said, diving for the phone, "she'll be dead!"

He frantically jiggled the switch trying to get a dial tone, and never saw Elliott pick up the bronze reproduction of Michelangelo's David that sat on a bookcase. Marshall felt an explosion at the base of his skull, the last thing he knew.

Elliott straightened Risha's body and carefully covered her nakedness with the blanket. Next, he cleaned up the broken lamp while he thought about how to handle the body in the study. Obviously, he was going to have to attend to disposal before dark when she would wake. Although it was not the first murder Elliott had ever committed, he worried how Risha would take it; she'd been awfully fond of Wilkins.

He picked up Marshall's clothes and found the man's keys in his pants pocket. One of them was a Ford key. Downstairs, he looked out the living-room window: There was a blue Taurus parked out front. He generated his plan while he dressed.

He moved the Honda from the driveway to the street; the BMW was in the garage behind the house. He scooted up the seat of Wilkins's Ford to reach the pedals and carefully backed it up the driveway and around the house until the trunk was right outside the kitchen door. He opened the trunk and looked around. No one would be able to see him; that would make it easier. He wouldn't have to dress the corpse or wrap it up.

Dumping Marshall's clothes in the car, Elliott found his wallet and searched the contents for references to Risha; there were none. He left the money and I.D. intact and tossed the wallet on top of the clothes and went back for the body.

It was a good thing it was in the study instead of upstairs, Elliott thought as he hefted Wilkins's dead weight; the man must weigh two hundred pounds. He grabbed the outstretched arms and dragged the body to the back door. After a short breather, he'd deposited it on top of the clothes and slammed the trunk shut. He looked around again; no witnesses.

The Ford was low on gas, but had enough left to get where it was going. Elliott got on the southbound San Diego Freeway.

Lot C was the long-term parking lot for Los Angeles International Airport; cars parked there for weeks at a time, sometimes for months. No one would pay any attention to the Taurus for quite some time. Elliott took the automated ticket at the entrance and parked in a far corner of the enormous lot.

He lowered the sun visor and a slip of paper fell into his lap. He looked at it: it had Risha's address and directions on it. Elliott's heart began to pound as he realized how close he'd been to leaving a major clue; he was going to have to think more clearly. Even though his fingerprints weren't on file in California, he rubbed the steering wheel, visor, door handle, and the outside of the trunk with his handkerchief. He locked the Ford and walked two sections away before catching the tram to the front entrance, where he boarded the free shuttle to the airport.

He got out at the United-Delta Terminal and went inside to deposit Wilkins's keys and parking stub in far-separate trash cans.

He returned to the curb and caught a SuperShuttle for home. He had the driver drop him at the Westside Pavilion Mall and walked the two miles back to the house. It was still before noon.

Jace was looking forward to a weekend of drinking beer and reading; he hadn't had time to read all week. He had found a special on Harp Lager and picked up a case; he was eager to finish the Andrew Vachss novel on the living room chair.

By the time he actually got out of bed, the mail had arrived; all window envelopes. He made himself a peanut butter and banana sandwich and settled into the chaise on the patio, three beers in a cooler at his feet.

He was on the third beer and the last chapter when he realized the doorbell was ringing insistently. Had it been ringing long? Jace peered out the curtain next to the front door.

"It's me, Jace; let me in." Liz was wearing a navy jumpsuit with red belt, earrings, and sandals. Jace thought the trim picked up the red in her eyes very smartly.

"Liz, what—"

"I must have been ringing for five minutes," she said as she entered.

"I was outside. You want a beer?"

"Yeah, what the hell." She sat down heavily on the couch while he went into the kitchen to retrieve two bottles.

"You want a glass?" he yelled.

"Only if you have a clean one."

Jace washed out a glass, thinking again that he really should get someone in to clean. By the time he returned to the living room, Liz had kicked off her sandals and had her feet tucked up on the couch.

"Sorry to bust in on your weekend like this," Liz began, "but I needed to see . . . talk to you, and I didn't want to wait 'til Monday."

"That's what friends are for, remember?" Jace handed her the glass and sat in the chair facing the couch. He took a swig of his beer and waited for her to continue. She stared into her glass, not drinking, silent.

"What's up?" he finally prodded.

She dug into her pocket and pulled out a folded piece of paper which she handed to him. It was a receipt from a hotel in San Francisco summarizing room charges for Mr. and Mrs. Sanford Baker Glass.

"I found it on the bedroom floor this morning," Liz explained. " 'Mr. and Mrs.,' it says."

"Yeah, I see." Jace drank. "Maybe the typist made a mistake."

"Right. Just like there was a mistake with a room-service breakfast yesterday for thirty-two dollars. Sandy doesn't usually eat breakfast. Thirty-two dollars worth of breakfast would have to include champagne, don't you think?''

"Did you ask him about it?"

"I did. He said he had breakfast in the room with 'some other lawyers,' but his story fell apart when I pressed for details." She took a long draught of beer. "He finally admitted he spent the night with a stewardess he met on the plane."

"Oh, shit," Jace said.

"Deep shit. I don't know if that's the truth, either; for all I know, he has a girlfriend up there. I don't even know that this is the first time he's done this. He says he used a condom, but he could have lied about that, too."

Liz polished off her beer and held the empty glass out to Jace. He took it into the kitchen for a refill. He didn't know what to say to Liz, what advice (if any) he should offer. He brought the glass back and sat down opposite her again.

Liz stared at him. "You know," she mused, not quite casually, "a little extramarital sex sounds like a good idea to me right now."

Jace felt a little surge of adrenalin, then pushed it down. "Don't you think you're overreacting? You're hurt and looking for revenge," he pointed out. "Infidelity is a major trauma, I hear."

"It doesn't seem to bother you and Ellen Fisher."

The reminder that he felt comfortable being a back-door man didn't help him distance himself from this situation. Was he imagining things—or was she actually suggesting they go for it after all these years?

"That was different; Ellen and Dennis have—had—an open relationship. She wasn't lying to him about me."

"Would it have made any difference to you if she had been?"

Jace knew the answer was no; Liz read it in his face before he could lie. It wasn't the first time he was uncomfortably aware of the flexibility of his morals.

"Why are we discussing this, Liz? If you want revenge sex, why tell me?"

Liz took a deep breath before she spoke. "Let's do it, Jace. No strings. Just a couple of friends making love."

It took him a few seconds to push out a response. "Jeez, Liz, I don't know; I mean, we work together . . ." Maybe she'd agree—that had been his best attempt at resistance.

She put down her beer and stood. "Strictly a one-after-noon-stand, okay? Never to happen again. I need . . . to feel loved right now."

He couldn't turn her down.

In the bedroom, Liz was voracious, all mouth and hands, radiating heat, already wet when he placed his hand on her vagina. Their lovemaking was hungry, frantic, and incredibly intense. But as soon as she'd climaxed, she burst into tears.

Jace held her while she sobbed, stroking her back, trying to will away his erection.

"Kind of bittersweet, huh?" he said as she wound down.

She wiped her eyes. "I'm sorry. I didn't know that was coming. It's not you; I guess I'm more upset about Sandy than I thought."

Jace nodded. He pulled off his condom, a little ashamed that he hadn't said no . . . but it'd been her idea, and he wasn't a saint. Hell, it wasn't *his* marriage. So why did he feel guilty? ·

"Forget it, Liz—it probably wasn't right anyway." He got out of bed and extended a hand to pull her up. "It didn't happen, okay?" He smiled. "Get dressed; I'll have a beer waiting for you in the living room."

CHAPTER
Eleven

When Rusty woke, she was surprised to find the bedside lamp missing. She got up and went into the bathroom. The bathtub was empty; no stack of mail awaited her. Something was wrong. She grabbed the robe off the back of the bathroom door, putting it on and tying it closed on her way downstairs.

"Elliott?"

He wasn't in the living room, nor in the study. Rusty peered into the kitchen and darkroom, then went to his room. She knocked on the door. A second passed, then he opened the door.

"Are you all right?" she asked.

"Yes. I'm sorry. I lost track of the time." He came out, closing the door behind him. They walked to the study. "Would you like me to run the bath? The mail's on the desk—I'll get it."

"That's okay. I'll go through it down here while the tub's filling." Elliott turned to go upstairs, but before he reached the door, Rusty said, "What happened to my bedroom lamp?"

Elliott stopped. Rusty saw his shoulders drop an inch before he turned back to her.

"The . . . guest . . . you had over last night broke . . ." he began.

"Marshall? Did he wake you when he left?"

Elliott suppressed an inappropriate urge to laugh. "It's a little more serious than a broken lamp. I'm afraid I had to kill him."

Rusty sat at the desk and tried out a smile; tentatively, because Elliott must be kidding, even though his sense of humor was virtually nonexistent. "Breaking a lamp isn't a capital crime—"

"He discovered you weren't breathing and he tried to call an ambulance. I had to stop him. I didn't mean to kill him. I'm sorry." Elliott avoided her eyes, staring instead at a spot of blood he'd missed on the carpet. He'd have to take care of that while she was bathing. "I'll take care of that bath now," he said, but he didn't move.

Marshall's death overwhelmed Rusty, exacerbated by unresolved anger over the loss of Gregor, and she exploded at Elliott.

"You didn't have to kill him!" she yelled. "You did it because you were jealous, didn't you? For two years, you've had me to yourself, and you couldn't stand me getting close to another man. You could have stopped him without killing him, couldn't you? Well, I'm not going to let you stand in the way of my happiness again—you can count on that!"

Elliott winced at Risha's tirade, more painful to him than any physical attack could ever be. He shrunk into himself, looking down at his feet, unable to meet her wild, pale eyes, and remained silent.

"Get out of my sight, Elliott—before you find out what death feels like!"

"I'm sorry," he mumbled as he left for his room, "I had no choice. I had to protect you, Risha."

She heard his door click closed as she headed up the stairs. The anger stopped as fast as it had come, and Rusty was left with guilt. It wasn't Elliott's fault. He was trying to protect her, and whether from jealousy or not, she couldn't blame him for that. If Marshall's death were anyone's fault, it was hers. She hadn't thought through the consequences of allowing him, however inadvertently, to stay with her past dawn, unaware of what she was. It had been so comforting to be held again . . .

She decided to apologize to Elliott before she left for the night.

Besides Elliott, there was only one person who had survived the knowledge that she was a vampire.

King Voodoo Palace on the Caribbean island of St. Thomas was not a tourist club, in spite of the fact that it was a scant ten-minute walk from where the cruise ships docked in Charlotte Amalie. Residents of the island tried to avoid town on Thursdays and Saturdays when the ships vomited their cargo onto the streets: tourists searching for duty-free bargains in china, watches, liquor, and tobacco, who never saw the tropical beauty around them. The club didn't even open until eleven P.M., long after the big ships had taken their spenders to another island.

Tucked in the back of a never-completed shopping center, King Voodoo Palace was a deep, dark storefront, undecorated except for the miscellany of tables and folding chairs. It had a gallery on the second floor which held a couple of wooden picnic tables with beer stains and attached benches. The stage and the dance floor were the same bare floor area; merely a neighborhood bar with entertainment.

The fifty-or-so patrons were island residents and hotel staffers, the crowd mostly young, mostly black, but all were welcome. It was a friendly place to party out the night, usually closing sometime between four A.M. and dawn. Between shows (there were two each night: midnight and two A.M.), the crowd drank and danced to canned reggae and ska.

Gregor and Rusty had arrived minutes before the first show; there was no host. Rusty confirmed with the bartender that she could take photographs; Gregor got them a ringside table. The show, like the bar itself, was a family operation: King Voodoo and his two lovely daughters, twenty and twelve, were the sole entertainment. After the girls had shown off their agility by limbo-ing under a bar which was scant inches above the floor, it was time for the main attraction.

King Voodoo was attired in soft, red cotton pants, rolled at the hem, multicolored ruffled sleeves but no shirt, and nothing else—not even shoes. He brought a box filled with empty liquor bottles to their table, so that Gregor could confirm for the rest of the audience that they were real glass; he had Rusty inspect the bottoms of his feet, which were moderately calloused but otherwise unprotected. While his older daughter smashed the bottles into dangerous shards, King Voodoo danced and flame-swallowed. When the broken glass had been spread on a cloth on the floor, King Voodoo began to step gingerly on it, moving slowly to the Caribbean music. As the tempo increased, so did his movements, until— to the wild applause of the audience—he was cavorting, pounding out his dance atop the perilous spikes. He brushed off the bottoms of his feet before leaving the perimeter of the cloth and coming once again to their table—this time so that Rusty could see that the soles of his feet were uncut.

"Think he's one of us?" she whispered to Gregor.

King Voodoo poured lighter fluid over the glass and asked Rusty to ignite it with a small torch his youngest daughter handed her. Although she hesitated, Gregor urged her on. King Voodoo didn't even wait for the flames to die off; to her amazement, he leapt onto the pyre to dance again. He played to Rusty's camera, finishing his act with a somersault towards her across the burning jagged glass fragments. The applause was thunderous. Rusty got an entire roll of good shots—two of which eventually ended up in her third gallery showing.

"How'd he do that?" she asked as they walked outside. "There wasn't a mark on him."

Before Gregor could answer, King Voodoo's youngest daughter came outside, looked around until she saw them, and came over.

"Sir, King Voodoo ask you an' de lady come back, talk wit' King Voodoo. Please, sir." Her island lilt was enchanting.

Rusty raised her eyebrows at Gregor and shrugged with a smile; Gregor nodded, and they followed the girl back inside, through the bar, and to a small room in the back, furnished with a couch, two armchairs, and a table. An ornate cross hung under a black velvet painting of Jesus. She asked them to sit and disappeared through a curtain at the rear.

Moments later, King Voodoo came in through the same curtain, a small tray with three brandy snifters in his hand. He wore the same outfit he'd performed in.

"You are new to Charlotte Amalie," he pronounced it *Amal-ya*. "You enjoy de show?"

"Very much," Rusty enthused. "I can't figure out how you did that."

"Fait', madam; my fait' keep me safe. In India, dere be mens who sleep on nails—it be da same t'ing: fait'—it just not be da same fait'," he chuckled. He offered them the snifters. "Dis be some very special rum, mon; she be age twenny-fi' year, you like dis."

Gregor inhaled the aroma, then tasted. "Very smooth, sir, very fine. Thank you." King Voodoo nodded. Rusty tasted hers—it burned all the way down and left her eyes stinging. King Voodoo laughed.

"You take more—she grow on you."

They sipped their rum in comfortable silence for a few moments, then King Voodoo put his glass on the table. He leaned forward, his hands on his knees, elbows akimbo, to look directly into Gregor's eyes.

"I know who you be, mon."

"You're mistaken—I've never been to the Virgin Islands before," Gregor said, taking another sip. Rusty was confused—they'd only been on St. Thomas for two days.

"I know *what* you be, an' your lady too, mebbe. Dead mon hunting by de moon, I know who you be—an' you be bad, mon." The man shook his head. "You be trouble for dis islan', mebbe for my fambly." King Voodoo put his hands together. "I beg you, mon, leave dis place; take your great hunger away. We have no home but dis home; you have many. What you want to go away, mon?"

Gregor put down his glass. "If I were what you think I am, you'd be in great danger talking to me like that."

"I know, mon; I know you kill me like dat," he snapped

his fingers. "If dat be your price to go an' leave my people in peace," he sat erect, "you take me, but den you leave an' you not come back. My fait' protec' my soul." King Voodoo waited to die.

Gregor stood, and towered over the man.

"I have no price and I make no bargains. . . . If you tell anyone, ever, I'll come back for you . . . and for your daughters. Do you understand?" The man nodded solemnly. Gregor looked at him closely; satisfied, he continued. "We have no particular need to stay here. We'll leave this island without a hunt, I give you my word." Gregor extended his hand to Rusty, who put down her glass and stood. He turned to the man again. "I do have a question before we leave: Have you met my kind before?"

"When my mama born, de Obeah woman tell my ol' gran'mama a walking dead mon come one day to Charlotte Amalie, an' she mus' stop him or people die. You late. Gran'mama dead t'irty year. She tell me watch for you."

"What made you think I was that man?"

"My fait', mon. I feel a grief when I see you wit' your lady, a grief so deep, dere not be enough in de worl' to fill it—dat be how I know, mon. You empty inside."

Rusty could tell that Gregor was stung by King Voodoo's observation. After they'd left, she asked him why he had agreed to leave the island . . . and why he had let the man live.

"He knew what we were, Risha—I don't know how, but he knew. This is a superstitious culture, and it's easy for them to believe. 'The strength of the vampire is that people will not believe in him.' Van Helsing said that in *Dracula*, remember? It seemed prudent to move on. Besides," he mused, "it isn't often one sees that kind of bravery. I just didn't have it in me to kill him.''

The depression hit Rusty hard on the way home. She might have had trouble seeing the road if she'd been able to shed tears. She pulled the car into the driveway at 3:30 and turned off the motor, but didn't get out. The house, which had always seemed to be her haven before, threatened her with emptiness. Her bed upstairs, shared the night before for the first time since Gregor died, now seemed too big, too symbolic of her loneliness.

She hadn't really realized how lonely she was until tonight. She knew the unconscionable lapse of permitting Marshall to stay past dawn was due to her need to share her life again, but it had been a fatal mistake. She was plagued by recriminations: if only she hadn't . . . if only Elliott hadn't . . . if only Gregor hadn't . . . He was beyond her reach now, and she feared she would never find another compatible man. Must she spend Forever alone?

A flood of despair washed over her and she sobbed tearlessly, her arms wrapped tightly across her chest as she rocked back and forth; needing comfort, having none. The emotions she'd refused to confront when Gregor died added fuel to this comparatively minor loss and she was overwhelmed with grief, self-pity, and anger. Anger at Gregor for dying, yes; and anger with herself for not being able to save him, for not being Enough, for not being perfect. He'd been the best . . . and she'd lost him.

Her sobs quieted, her head felt heavy; she knew it was getting close to dawn, time to go in. She took a deep breath—physically unneeded, but a habit established in life and unbroken by her death—and opened the car door.

She turned off the back-door light on the way in and tiptoed up the stairs so she wouldn't wake Elliott. He'd moved one of the lamps from the study to her bedside table, and her room beckoned with a warm golden light, gentler than the threatening image she'd wrestled with in the car. Her bed had been turned down.

Next to the lamp was a cut-crystal vase with half a dozen long-stemmed yellow roses, their perfume delicate in the room like the touch of soft mist, a reminder of dawns long unseen.

Liz went home a little after dark, and Jace finished the Vachss novel before he showered. He thought of beginning another book—there was a Robert Parker on the bedside table he hadn't read yet—but the puzzle of their case kept nagging at him. He got out his notes and the summaries that Liz had prepared and sat down at the dining room table to work.

"King? Levy. You're working Saturday night?"

"That Ol' Man Death, he just keeps rolling along. What can I do for you, Detective?"

"I've been going over my notes and I've got a gap you can fill. You remember that orange smear on Avallone's neck? You thought it might be lipstick and you said you'd check."

"Shit, didn't I call you back on that?" the medical examiner said. "Yeah, it was lipstick; not a cheap brand, either—no paraffin."

"Custom-made?" Jace asked hopefully.

"What—you want it handed to you on a platter? It wasn't anything that couldn't be bought over-the-counter in any department store in town."

Jace thanked him and hung up. Lipstick. Consistent with

a woman or a drag queen. Suddenly, he remembered something the hype in Venice had said about the Flores murder, and he flipped back to Spiker's interrogation.

"She was kissing his neck." Spiker had said it at least twice, Jace remembered now. She was kissing Flores's neck before she stabbed him. Before?

"Very strenge," Jace said aloud in his Inspector Clouseau accent, "very strenge."

Was it possible the killer drank the missing blood? Were they dealing with someone who wanted to contract AIDS, for some sick reason? But why choose this method, when there were easier ways to get it?

Or just as crazy, was the killer under the delusion that s/he was a vampire?

Jace thought a little research was in order. He was sure he had a copy of *Dracula*; although he couldn't locate the book, he did have the 1931 Lugosi movie in his video collection. He called Jacopo's and ordered a pizza, then took his notebook and a beer into the living room and started the tape.

The deputy at the desk handed Jace and Liz visitor badges and directed them to Sergeant Best's cubicle.

Jace's pager had beeped a little after two A.M., but it didn't wake him; he was back at the dining room table, engrossed in his notes, his cup of coffee forgotten in the kitchen an hour earlier. He had called the displayed number—it turned out to be the West Hollywood Sheriff's Station—and had been told they were interviewing witnesses to a knifing by a drag queen, and that Best had thought he'd want to know. Jace said he'd be there in under half an hour.

A very sleepy male voice picked up after the first ring.

"Sandy, it's Jace. Sorry to wake you, but I need to talk to

Liz." He felt awkward and tried to forget he'd slept with the man's wife that afternoon.

Silence. Why wasn't he saying anything? Did he know? "Sandy?"

"Yeah. Just a minute."

It took long enough for Liz to answer that Jace realized the couple wasn't sleeping in the same room. Had she told Sandy? He never asked her.

Best was waiting for them with a smile. "We just sent both witnesses home."

"Shit," Jace swore, "I wish you'd waited. You knew I was on my way."

Best put up a restraining hand. "Cool off, Detective. After the lineup, there was no reason to keep 'em."

Liz figured out what he meant first. "You picked up the knifer already? You have a positive I.D.?"

Best hooked his thumbs in his waistband and leaned back, a smirk on his face. "Two positive I.D.'s. You've been outcollared by the sheriff once more. You want me to tell you how we did it before you meet the African Queen?"

Jace was so put off by the man's smarmy attitude, he didn't notice the epithet. "Brag on, Macduff."

Best really drew the story out, but eventually explained to them how a homeless man had been stabbed by a transvestite; the man was hospitalized, but was expected to live. The attack had been witnessed by a waiter and his tennis-pro lover as they left a West Hollywood nightclub, subtly called Balls. As near as the witnesses could tell from across the street, the derelict had said something to the drag queen as s/he passed, and the queen had pulled out a knife and stabbed the man before running away. Deputies picked up the assailant a couple of hours later, following an anonymous tip about someone washing blood off himself in a gas station restroom.

"Where was the wound?" Liz asked.

"Puncture wound above the left collarbone at the base of the neck, long slash up the left arm."

Liz looked at Jace, who shrugged.

"Get a statement from the queen?" he asked.

"Full confession after the lineup. Said the man pissed her off," he laughed, "but wouldn't tell us what he said. You want to give it a try? Maybe use some secret LAPD line of questioning?"

Jace had had just about enough of Best. The worst of Best, he thought with a smile. "Sure. Where is he?"

Best took them to the interrogation room, and pointed through the one-way glass. "There she is, Miss America."

Jace looked. He saw a tall, skinny man in fluorescent-yellow hot pants with matching blood-spattered halter-top and knee-high vinyl boots. He wore a dark-red wig and plastic earrings the size of his fist. The earrings were blowfish.

"Cute, huh?" Best said.

Jace turned to leave. "Not ours. Thanks anyway."

Best's face fell, ruining his smirk. "Whaddya mean, not yours? I thought you were looking for a knifer in drag on the Westside."

"Yeah," Jace tossed over his shoulder as they walked out, "but ours isn't black."

When Jace finally woke up, it was almost noon. He threw on his bathrobe and started a fresh pot of coffee. Pain in the ass, spending half the night on a wild goose chase.

He thought about Liz. She hadn't broached any personal

subjects the whole time last night. Jace had followed her lead, but he was curious as hell about what she wasn't saying. He wondered when she and Sandy had stopped sleeping together.

He got the Sunday *Times* off the front step and read the funnies while he waited for the coffee to percolate. He wanted to be alert for the crossword puzzle; he was determined to ace it today. It was something he had control over—and he needed to feel in control of something, anything.

He turned on the TV, more for background noise than for content, and was stunned at the conflagration before him. Berkeley and Oakland were in flames, massive walls of flame that consumed drought-dried brush, beautiful homes, and people with the same mindless abandon.

As he watched and listened to the reports of the catastrophic losses, injuries, and deaths, the homicide detective cried.

CHAPTER
Twelve

"Look, all I'm asking is if you recognize the names of specific murder victims—they're already dead, ferchrissakes!"

"Have other AIDS clinics cooperated with you?" The doctor knew the answer before he asked. Jace shook his head. "I expect you knew they wouldn't, going into this—why are you wasting time trying to get information no one will give you?"

Apparently, the question was meant to be rhetorical, because the doctor finished it over his shoulder on his way out of the room.

Jace jammed his notebook back in his pocket and left the clinic. He looked at his watch: 3:30. That was the last clinic on his list—in the last two days, he'd gone to seventeen AIDS-testing facilities while Liz covered a similar number on her own. No one had been willing to even look at the names he'd brought, much less consider checking them against their files. He took small consolation in the realization that if The Westside Vampire didn't have legitimate access to testing records, s/he'd run into the same wall Jace found.

He didn't know if it was just fatigue, but he was beginning to think AIDS was coincidental, and not integral to the killer's motive. "The blood is the life, Renfield," he quoted to himself as he got into the car.

But, what *was* the killer's motive anyway? And, most confusing of all, why didn't any of the victims have defense wounds? If they all knew their assailant, Liz would probably have found some link on the computer by now. This was the most challenging case he'd ever had . . . and it was frustrating the hell out of him.

As he drove out of the parking lot, Jace had every intention of returning to the station, but he was much closer to home. He decided to call it a day.

The new issue of *City of Angels* was in the mailbox when he got in. He tossed it on the recliner and went to check his phone machine.

Liz's voice: "I struck out, Jace. If you got anything, page me—I'm going to Bed Bath and Beyond to pick up some pillows and then home. I'll see you in the morning."

New pillows. Jace suspected things were getting worse in the Glass-Robinson household. He kicked off his shoes and got a Harp out of the refrigerator.

Cadigan's "After Midnight in the City of Angels" was right after an interview with Jonathan Kellerman. Apparently, the theme this time was play: The first photo was of four college students playing cards at a card table . . . set up on the traffic island at Wilshire and Federal, the illumination provided by the overhead light pole. Jace laughed—he remembered his sophomore year in college. He'd gone to pick up Marcia at her dorm, and when the elevator opened, he found three students playing hearts on a card table in the elevator, their chairs taking up the remaining space. They told him he had a choice between sitting in for a hand or taking the stairs; he'd trotted up eight floors to avoid being late for his date.

The next picture was of two punks embracing in front of the Roxy on Sunset—it was impossible to tell their genders. Both were clad in an odd combination of black leather and torn cloth. One had spikes sticking out of one side of an otherwise-shaved head, while the other wore a trio of mohawks. They both wore multiple earrings. On second glance, Jace decided the one with the spikes was female; her jack-booted foot was raised daintily behind her as she was being kissed.

The third photo was taken at some shitkicker bar—a pretty blonde with a neckerchief was framed by two men in cowboy duds holding mugs of beer. One of the men had his cowboy-booted foot on the bar rail, his head thrown back in laughter.

Jace didn't get to the last picture in the series. The man laughing in the bar was Teece Cabot.

"Mr. South can see you now." The secretary indicated the closed door with the highly polished brass letters reading "David A. South, Editor-in-Chief."

South stood as Jace opened the door, his hand extended across the expanse of his rosewood burl desk long before Jace had time to cross the large office to shake it. South was the type of man women would kill for: impeccably groomed with graying hair worn long, an Armani suit that he wore like it was one of dozens, a Rolex watch, and a tan that could come only from owning a boat.

"Detective . . . Levy, was it?" he said. Jace nodded. South indicated a comfortable-looking chair in front of his desk. "Please sit down. Can I get you a drink or some coffee?"

"I'd appreciate some black coffee, thank you," Jace said as he was enveloped by the chair.

South sat down and pushed a button, "Two coffees, Amanda." Then to Jace: "Jamaican Blue Mountain acceptable?"

Jace nodded. He'd heard of the coffee, but had never tasted it—too expensive. He looked around South's office. The thick rose-and-sand-colored carpeting probably cost more than Jace's house. Two of the sculpted walls bore framed blowups of *City of Angels*' covers, but the wall behind South displayed the obligatory photos of South with various dignitaries; Jace recognized Mayor Bradley, Robert DeNiro, Magic Johnson, and Mother Theresa. The exquisite desk was clear in the middle, but manuscripts were neatly stacked a foot high to South's left and right. South followed Jace's gaze.

"I usually don't have this mess here, but our deadline's this Friday. I've got a lot of reading to do." He gestured to the stacks.

"I won't keep you, then," Jace said. "I need some information for a case I'm working on." His eyes fell on the title page of the Xeroxed manuscript closest to him. *White Jazz* by James Ellroy. It looked like at least five hundred pages. "Is that the sequel to *L.A. Confidential*?"

"It certainly is. You a fan?"

Amanda came in with the coffee on a silver platter. She poured for both of them, and left the service on the sideboard on her way out. Jace was too impressed with the manuscript to notice the taste of the coffee.

"I've read everything he's written," Jace admitted.

"Then, by all means, you must have this one," South said, handing it to him. "Otherwise, you'll have to wait until next fall when it's published."

"You sure? I'll return it as soon as I'm done." Jace was thrilled to have the Ellroy, but that wasn't what he had come for. "Look, Mr. South—"

"David. Please."

"David. I need to find this photographer, Cadigan." Jace indicated the magazine he'd opened to the photo essay. "They told me downstairs that you were the only one who knew how to contact him."

"I'd like to know what this is about before I start handing out phone numbers. You understand." He smiled the kind of smile that said no one ever successfully messed with him.

"This man," Jace pointed to Cabot's photo, "was murdered last month. It's possible that Cadigan may have been one of the last people to see him alive."

South leaned forward, fascinated. "No kidding?" All of a sudden, his manner was no longer that of a suave executive; now, he seemed like an impressed boy. "You're a homicide detective? No shit?"

Jace laughed. Imagine this guy being impressed with *his* job! "Yessir, got a gold shield and everything." He flipped open his I.D.

"You ever write, Levy? I'd love to have an article by an LAPD homicide detective!"

"I don't have time to write—maybe when I retire. But right now, I've got this case . . ."

"Oh, right. Just a second." South flipped his Rolodex and wrote on a slip of paper while smiling and shaking his head.

"It's kind of weird, but I've never met Cadigan. An assistant handles all the business and brings the pictures in. The checks are made out to R. Cadigan and go to a mail drop. Here's the box number and the telephone. The assistant is Elliott." South handed Jace the paper. "I don't even know if that's his first or last name."

Jace looked at the slip. The phone number was a West L.A. prefix. "Thank you, you've been a big help." Jace stood and shook David's hand. "And thanks for the Ellroy. I'll get it back as soon as I can."

"Keep it. Enjoy. And if you decide to do any writing, give me a call, okay?"

"Don't hold your breath," Jace said on his way to the door, "but I'm grateful to be asked."

"Oh, Levy?" South called after him. He grabbed a card from his desk and strode to the door. Handing it to Jace, he said, "We're having a Halloween party Saturday night. Bring a date if you like. Ellroy will be there."

"Is this R. Cadigan, the photojournalist?" Jace asked the male voice who picked up the phone.

"Risha Cadigan is not available. This is Elliott. May I ask who's calling?"

Risha? Cadigan is a woman? Jace was surprised, considering the *milieux* she shot in. "Detective Jacob Levy, LAPD. Can you tell me where I can reach Ms. Cadigan?"

"I'm sorry, Detective. I'll be happy to give her a message, however. May I tell her what this is about?"

"I want to talk with her about someone she photographed."

Jace gave him his home number after Elliott said she would get the message by early evening.

Jace was sixty pages into the Ellroy manuscript when Risha Cadigan phoned. He explained to her that he needed to see her about someone she had photographed and she gave him a Beverlywood address, not far from the home where Jace's mother had died. "Now would be fine," she'd said. Jace left the Ellroy on the recliner with regret, put on a clean shirt, and left.

Elliott showed Jace to a seat in the living room and said that Risha would be down in a moment. Jace wandered the room, admiring the few photographs on the walls. One was signed by Brassaï, another by Stieglitz. A print of a fat man in a dirty shirt, slumbering on a chair next to a baby carriage, was signed Model, but Jace didn't recognize the name.

"Isn't that one wonderful? Lisette Model took that on Delancey Street in the early forties."

Jace turned. Risha Cadigan was a very attractive woman, her auburn hair settling like clouds over her shoulders. She was wearing jeans and an oversized, burgundy silk sweater which revealed her nipples better than it hid her rounded hips. Jace pulled his eyes away from her chest, only to encounter a pair of stunningly pale eyes, smiling the way women do when they've caught men staring at them.

"Detective Levy, I presume?"

"Jace." He knew that was unprofessional, but he said it anyway.

"Good. I'm Risha. Now, what's this about someone I shot?"

Jace was momentarily confused by her syntax, until he realized she was talking about shooting with camera, not gun.

"This photo of yours," he said, showing her the magazine. "Do you remember when you took it?"

"It was about a month ago at the Topanga Corral. Do you need the exact date?"

"Please, if you have it."

Risha left the room. He could hear voices, but couldn't make out what they were saying. She returned a moment later.

"Jace, it was September twenty-eighth. I think that was a Saturday."

Jace knew it was. It was taken the night Cabot was killed.

"This man"—he pointed to Teece—"was murdered that night after he left the Corral."

"Oh, how awful! But you don't think I had anything to do with that, do you?"

"No," Jace smiled, "but you might have seen his killer. Do you remember that night?"

"I was there for a couple of hours. That guy and his friends were having beers at the bar. I didn't talk with them, though." She shrugged. Jace watched her nipples move. "What do you want to know?"

"Did you see him leave?"

"No. But he wasn't there when I left—the place had mostly emptied out by then." She thought for a moment. "But I saw these two leave," she said, pointing to the woman and the other man in the picture. "I got a photo of them going out the door. He had his hand on her ass," she smiled.

"So you took other pictures that night besides this one? Can I see them?" Jace was jazzed—this might be the break he'd been waiting for; maybe she'd photographed the killer.

"They're just on contact sheets," Risha warned him. "I'll

bring you a magnifying glass, but they'll be small.'' She left the room again.

When she returned, Elliott was behind her, hovering protectively as he glared, none-too-subtly, at Jace.

"Would you like something to drink, Jace?" she asked.

"Just a soft drink, if you have one."

She looked at Elliott, who turned and left. She handed Jace two sheets with about two dozen photos on each, and a magnifying glass.

"Sit here. The light's better." She indicated the place next to her on the couch. "Not all of these were taken at the Corral. Just the last two strips on this page, and the first one on the next."

As he examined the photos, Jace could smell Risha's perfume, a dusty rose scent that was somewhat familiar. He looked carefully at each one, and didn't notice when Elliott re-entered with his Coke. Finally, Elliott cleared his throat, and Jace looked up. He was sure Risha's assistant was angry at finding them sitting so close.

"Thank you." He took his drink. He guessed Risha wasn't having anything.

Elliott still didn't leave.

"If you want prints of those, it wouldn't take long—maybe an hour," she offered.

"Could you? That would be very helpful, Risha."

"Elliott, will you please print these for Detective Levy?" She pointed out the Corral shots to him.

Elliott mumbled something unintelligible, took the contact sheets, and left, glaring at Jace on the way out.

"Charming fellow," Jace observed.

Risha laughed, "Don't let him get to you. He just doesn't

like strangers. Is there anything else you want while you're waiting?''

You, naked on a bed, Jace thought. "Actually, if you wouldn't mind, I'd like to see some more of your photos. I really liked the ones in *City of Angels*.''

"Thank you. I'd be delighted to show you some of my work. Why don't you come into the study?''

The room appeared to have been converted from the house's original dining room. Two love seats flanked a cocktail table, one of them lit by a reading lamp which craned over the back. A desk on the other side of the room faced a wall of books. Risha indicated the illuminated love seat and pulled over a heavy wooden bin on wheels so it faced him. She sat next to him.

"These aren't in any particular order—they just happen to be the ones I have matted just now.''

After Jace looked at each print, he carefully placed its face against the front of the bin. The work was remarkable—he could tell she'd been inspired by the photographers represented in the living room gallery. Every so often, she would tell him where she got a particular shot: Amsterdam, Paris, Stockholm, St. Thomas, Budapest. She seemed young to have traveled so much. All of the pictures had been taken at night.

"I gather night shots are your specialty, Risha?''

"Yeah, I'm a real vampire,'' she smiled. "I never work in the daytime.''

"Okay, Ms. Comerro, why don't you start at the beginning?'' Liz said.

"When John missed work Friday, I figured he was just taking a long weekend, but he didn't show up Monday or yesterday, and that wasn't like him at all; I mean, he knew we had a deadline to meet. I must've called ten times, but I always got his machine, so I called the cops . . . uh, police . . . and I met them here. They saw him through the kitchen window. Do you know how he died?''

Liz ignored the question. "Where is work?''

"El Segundo. Whitlow Data Systems. I'm a systems analyst. John is . . . was . . . a programmer.''

While Liz questioned Sandra Comerro, Jace was in the Howard kitchen with the forensic team. John Howard was still sitting at the kitchen table, his head thrown back over the chair, an untouched pizza in front of him, two clean plates next to the box. He was completely dressed, his yellow shirt spattered with the blood that had sprayed from the knife hole in his neck.

"Well?'' Jace asked Ronnie Schaffer. "Is all his blood here?''

The serologist eyed the blood under the chair and on the table. "Uh-uh, 'bout half's missing again, maybe more. It'll take a while to get measures on this.''

Jace made sure Howard's body would be tested for HIV. Again, there didn't appear to be any defense marks. He looked closely at the wound. Was that another lipstick smear?

"Did you see this?'' Ronnie asked Jace.

She was lifting the lid of the pizza box. There was a slip of paper taped to the top. She slid it into a clear evidence bag and handed it to him. It was a receipt from an electronic cash register: Cosa Nostra Pizza #15, 101791, 19:24, lg. pep/mush/x-chees $12.48, Tom.

"The seventeenth was last Thursday,'' Jace said.

"He didn't show up for work on Friday,'' Liz added as she came into the kitchen.

"Looks like he was going to have pizza with the killer. See if you can find his calendar and phone book, Liz." He opened the yellow pages and found that Cosa Nostra #15 was on Sepulveda about a mile from the crime scene. He copied the address into his notebook—he'd go over there when they were finished here.

"Jace! In the bedroom," Liz called.

She was sitting at a computer terminal, John Howard's calendar on the screen in front of her.

"There's nothing on the calendar for Thursday the seventeenth, but look at Friday the eighteenth."

Jace looked. The only entry read "Pizza/TV w/Rusty 8:00."

"Looks like we've got confirmation on the name we found at Kaufman's. See if you can find his phone book."

She nodded. "The name fits, but I doubt anyone would pick up a pizza a night in advance, Jace. If Rusty killed him Friday night, why is the pizza dated Thursday?" She switched the screen to Menu.

Jace rubbed his face wearily. "Hell, I don't know, Liz. Maybe the date was moved up at the last minute. I'll requisition his phone records." He made a note.

The kid behind the counter at Cosa Nostra was wearing the staff uniform: a T-shirt printed to look like a black, pin-striped wide-lapel suit jacket over a black shirt and white tie, a silk-screened red carnation at the buttonhole. Cosa Nostra was spelled in white machine-gun fire across the back. His paper cap was designed to look like a fedora. The gangster theme was offset by a face full of adolescent pimples and a high stuttering voice.

There were no customers in the takeout pizza place; a

similarly attired teenager lounged in the kitchen area, his feet on a stool, a comic book in his hand. They call them "graphic novels" now, Jace reminded himself.

He showed his I.D. to the counterman, and said, "I want some information about this order." He slid the bagged receipt across the counter. "Read it through the bag," he instructed the kid. "Let's start with this name here: Tom. Is that the name of the person who ordered the pizza or the person selling it?"

"It's m-m-mine. I'm T-T-Tom," he stuttered.

"Good, Tom. Now, this is the date and the time here, right?" Tom nodded. "That was last Thursday night at seven-thirty. You remember this order?"

Tom shrugged. "I t-t-take a l-l-l-l—oh, hell!"

"That's all right, son, take your time. I'm in no hurry." The kid looked grateful for Jace's patience. "It was a large pizza with pepperoni, mushrooms, and extra cheese. Do any of these codes tell you whether it was phoned in or ordered in person?"

"S-she c-c-came in to order. You can t-t-tell because I p-p-put a name and number on when they c-c-c-call."

"She? You remember the woman who bought this?"

Tom nodded. "S-s-she was p-p-pretty. She wa-waited over there. Read a b-b-b-book." He pointed to three chairs by the door. The phone rang and Tom yelled to the other kid, "I'm busy!"

"Can you describe her, Tom? What color hair did she have?"

"D-d-dark red."

"Was she white?" The kid nodded. "What about her eyes? Did you notice what color they were?"

Tom thought for a minute, then shook his head.

"Okay, how old was she, would you say?"

"Old. At l-least th-th-th-twenty-nine." Jace repressed a smile.

"Good. How about her height and build?"

"N-n-not t-tall, medium." He looked down with a shy smile. "She had g-g-great t-tits," he added.

"All woman, huh?" Jace asked with a male-bonding snicker. The kid nodded enthusiastically. Jace was certain he'd looked closely enough to make out a drag queen. "What was she wearing?"

"Black j-j-jumpsuit. T-t-tight. Unzipped." He pointed to a spot midway down his chest. "S-she was way hot for an old l-lady."

"Would you recognize her again?"

Tom responded with a vigorous nod.

CHAPTER
Thirteen

Elliott dropped off the new photos at *City of Angels* and was about to leave when the receptionist called to him. "Mr. South for you, Elliott." She held out a receiver to him.

"This is Elliott."

"There was a police detective here yesterday, looking for Cadigan," the voice came over the line. "I gave him your phone number. Did he reach you?"

"Yes, sir." There was a pause, like South was waiting for more information. If so, he was disappointed. "I hope everything's all right," he prompted.

"Yes, sir."

"Fine." Pause. "That's all I wanted to say, Elliott."

"Goodbye, sir."

On the way home, Elliott began to worry. With the police investigating one of Risha's feeders, it might be time to think about moving. At least, he should start shipping some of the valuables to the London home.

Risha hadn't traveled since Bathory died. Elliott couldn't remember ever staying in one place for so long before then. The old vampire had traveled constantly. Elliott figured if they stayed in L.A. much longer, eventually, someone was going to link her feeders or catch her in the act.

It was his duty to warn her, but he wasn't in the best of positions just now—it had only been four days since he disposed of Wilkins. If he angered Risha again, she might get rid of him, and he couldn't stand that. Finally, Elliott decided to take a wait-and-see attitude about bringing up the subject with her, but he could ship a lot out without disturbing her.

At least they'd be prepared if they had to leave in a hurry.

"So Rusty is definitely a woman. That makes sense with the lack of defense wounds," Liz said.

"Men do let women closer to them than men," Jace agreed. "But the neck wounds weren't made with any force. Some of them were only an inch deep. Why did the guys hold still while she was killing them?"

Liz leered, "Maybe they were too hot to notice. The cock hardens and the mind disengages." She looked up suddenly. "Jace! That explains Cabot, Kaufman, and Avallone's state of dress—they thought they were going to get laid right until they died."

Jace nodded thoughtfully. "Did you find anything in Howard's room about sex partners?"

"Just a stack of one-hand mags and sex papers in the closet. The magazines were heterosexual. I'll check out his computer disks."

* * *

When Liz came back from the computer room, Jace was studying the photographs he'd gotten from Risha Cadigan on Tuesday night.

"What're those?" she asked.

"Photographs taken at the Topanga Corral the night Teece Cabot was killed. I'd hoped they might show him with someone besides Charlie Haldeman and Rachel Lynn . . . like with a woman who can lift two hundred pounds."

"But?" Liz put her purse in her desk drawer.

"He's only in one photo—with the two of them. None of the women in any of these looks capable of lifting more than a bag of groceries."

"That's a chauvinistic crack, Levy," Liz sneered at him.

"Write it off to testosterone poisoning."

Any retort Liz might have made was cut short by the summons from Cosentino.

There was someone already in the homicide coordinator's office when they entered. Frank had a mouthful of gum—before he could shift it to his cheek to speak, the other man stuck out his hand to Liz.

"Detective Robinson? I'm Agent Brenner, FBI."

Brenner was in his early thirties, with curly light-brown hair and a thin build. He had a New Jersey accent he was at some pain to conceal.

Liz shook the man's hand. "We weren't expecting you, Brenner. This is my partner, Jace—Jacob Levy."

He shook Jace's hand. "I had to be in L.A. on another matter, so I thought I'd find out what's been happening here and tell you what we've been coming up with on the profile for you."

Cosentino added, "I told Agent Brenner about the d.b. yesterday, but I don't have any details. Why don't you fill us in?" He gestured to chairs, and everyone sat.

Jace explained about John Howard, the pizza, and the description of Rusty.

"Any prints?"

"Nothing fresh, except the vic's," Liz answered.

"Was there anything . . . unusual about any of the crime scenes?"

"There's been remarkably little evidence of any sort," Jace said. "What kind of unusual were you thinking of?"

"Any indications of devil worship, black magic—anything ritualistic?"

Cosentino's head turned from one to the other like at a tennis match.

"No, nothing like that. Why?" Jace asked.

Brenner shook his head. "Something is out-of-kilter here. This just doesn't add up."

"This is my top team, Agent. If something was at the scene, Levy and Robinson would have found it," Cosentino said. "They're not in the habit of overlooking major clues . . . or even minor ones, *capisce*?"

Brenner raised a palm in protest. "I'm not impugning the abilities of your detective and forensic teams, Lieutenant. It's just that this killer is completely outside the psychological profile parameters. Just about the only thing that would have made the pieces fit would be some kind of ritual."

"Could you explain what you're talking about?" Liz said in exasperation. "Have you got a profile for Rusty or not?"

The agent ran his fingers through his curls. Jace noticed that it didn't change the appearance of his hair one bit.

"Look—serial killers fall into types. By being female,

your killer is already out of type. By choosing victims of different races—you've had whites, blacks, Latinos, Jews—she falls out again. Serials almost always hit only one race, usually their own. By the care she's shown in avoiding capture—or even clues—we know that she is intelligent and organized. She operates well socially. Her reality testing is at a high level. This is not the work of a psychotic mind.''

"Don't you have to be psycho to do this kind of stuff?'' Liz asked.

Brenner shook his head. "Most serials get a sexual high from killing. The cooling-off period between murders lasts until the pressure to relieve the sexual urge becomes too strong to resist."

"Yeah, okay," Jace said impatiently, "so what's the problem with the profile? She's intelligent and organized. What doesn't fit?"

"A few things. What links the victims?" Jace and Liz shook their heads. "These killers choose their victims because they fit some criteria in the killer's mind. So far, you haven't found any hint of criteria—except for gender and availability. That's one.

"Two: what does the missing blood represent? If it's just a souvenir—they like to take mementoes—why blood? Given today's risks—both of being captured and of AIDS—this just doesn't fit an organized, intelligent, social type, *unless* some ritual is involved."

"Like with the Manson homicides?" Cosentino asked.

"Exactly."

"There's a theory that she may be drinking the blood," Jace pointed out.

"If she'd shown signs of being a disorganized asocial—or into some kind of ritual—that would fit, but it just doesn't play with the other indicators," Brenner insisted. "It's confusing the hell out of the team at Quantico, I can tell you that.

"Finally," he added, "there's number three: generally, by the process of killing repeatedly, the killer becomes comfortable with murder. It gets to the point where he no longer gets his satisfaction merely by killing, and the murders become more grotesque. So far, with the exception of Kaufman's mutilation, you've had no escalation here."

" 'We're up to our necks in dead bodies; what are you waiting for—the last act of Hamlet?' " Jace quoted from a Pink Panther movie. "So what can you give us that will help?" He was becoming somewhat belligerent.

"Not a damned thing, Detective, not one goddamned thing. I can tell you that we'd really like to interview this woman when she's finally caught, though."

Rusty hadn't been aware that it was October twenty-fourth until the date appeared under Peter Jennings's face on the evening news. Gregor would have been 309 today.

It's not a date he would have marked if he'd been alive— he told her that he'd celebrated his birth annually until he crossed over, then by quarter-centuries until he reached two hundred. The observation of his three hundredth birthday in 1982 had been the only one since.

"Birthdays cease to be special when you've had so many of them," he'd said. "There's something depressing about marking the passage of time, even when you're immortal. Looking back to see what you've accomplished gives no pleasure when you've had all the time in the world to do it. It ceases to have any meaning when you can fulfill all your dreams and still have more time ahead of you. The problem," he'd laughed ruefully, "is in coming up with new dreams. It's hard to find something new with this type of life, Risha."

Nevertheless, Rusty had insisted they do something special on his three hundredth birthday, preferably something Gregor had never done before. That was a bigger challenge than she'd ever imagined.

"Isn't there anyplace you've never been that you'd like to see?" she began.

"No. I've been everywhere. But I'll go wherever you'd like—in a way, I can see them in a different light through your eyes."

Not so easily deterred, she ran through lists of obscure places, wild adventures, sexual perversions—Gregor had long since tried them all.

"What about a visit to your birthplace?" she suggested.

"God no! You can't imagine how bleak the Carpathians are this time of year—how bleak they *always* are. They're inhabited by superstitious peasants who lock themselves in their houses at sundown and are working again at dawn. It's deathly boring there, Risha, and about as attractive as a canker sore."

That was when she came up with the idea of going to the Caribbean. Gregor had never been there—it had never occurred to him to visit a place that worshipped the sun. Rusty had heard there was an active nightlife on the islands, but the clincher came in a travel brochure she'd sent for.

"Have you ever gone scuba diving or snorkeling?" she asked.

"May I remind you that you're speaking of daylight sports, my dear?"

"Look at this, Gregor—there are night dives. They take underwater lights with them—look at the colors! A lot of fish sleep at night, just hanging in the water. We can hold a sleeping fish, Gregor!''

He'd laughed in delight then. "Risha, you're amazing. You've come up with something new for me. By all means, let's go hold a sleeping fish for my birthday!''

When Rusty called Elliott to do her make-up that night, he was surprised to find her wearing a very short lavender dress, low-cut with long, loose sleeves, fastened at her wrists. With her hair down, she looked like one of the hippie chicks that had populated Berkeley the year they had lived there. Without make-up, she looked even younger than usual.

"Another date this evening?" he asked.

"No, I'm just going out to eat, maybe take some pictures. Why?''

"You look very pretty, if you don't mind me saying so.''

She laughed. "I never mind a compliment. Thank you, Elliott. A little heavier than usual on the eye shadow, please. I want to turn heads tonight.''

Rusty parked her car at the airport and took the free shuttle to the hotel. She walked through the lobby to the bar and took a seat in a dimly lit booth.

The waitress delivered a drink to a man at the next table, dodging the hand he sent groping under her short skirt with a deft maneuver before coming to see what Rusty wanted.

"Do you have any port?"

"I don't think so. You want a glass of sherry?"

Rusty told her that would be fine, and the waitress left to get her drink. Rusty got up and went to the ladies' room, sashaying her hips as she passed the leering customer.

When she returned, the waitress was putting her sherry on

the table. "It's already paid for," she said. "The guy in the sweater." She tilted her head toward the groper.

Rusty smiled her thanks at the man, an invitation evident in her eyes. He immediately picked up his drink and headed over.

He looked like a yuppie in his cotton sweater, but the careful styling of his hair didn't conceal the sparseness of it.

"May I join you?"

When he sat down, Rusty noticed the white line on his left ring finger. She suspected his wedding ring was in his pocket. Five minutes of small talk produced the information that "Al" was in L.A. "about some real estate ventures I have here" and that he was staying in the motel around the corner, which had no bar of its own.

Twenty minutes later, Rusty was having dinner in his room.

The motel maid found Alvin Zamel's body the next day at one. She'd finally ignored the "do not disturb" sign, determined that a late sleeper wasn't going to delay her shift-end any longer. When the Inglewood detectives saw the body, they knew immediately that it was the work of Levy and Robinson's killer.

Liz had just come back from the computer center when the call came in. She told Jace what she'd found as they drove toward the airport.

"We've got six Rustys in the records—four of them male; one female is black, the other one would be close to sixty by now. Neither of the women was picked up for violent crimes—the black one was a prostitute, the white one a shoplifter."

"What about women fitting Rusty's description, regardless of name?"

"We don't have much to go on," she reminded him, "just that she's Caucasian with dark red hair, about thirty. And hair color isn't a constant—she might dye it or wear a wig."

Zamel had been in town from Sacramento for a one-day trip and had decided to stay overnight at the last minute, according to his wife, Terri, who had flown down to L.A. as soon as she heard. Al had come down to "inspect the premises and get the key" to a commercial building she'd inherited in Venice. There had been some problems with the last tenant, a science-fiction bookstore at the end of a ten-year lease. The rent had been considerably below market price, and, although she couldn't afford a sizeable increase, the bookseller had pleaded to be allowed to renew the lease, saying they'd have to go out of business if they lost the space.

"Al didn't want to give them a lease at all—although he told her she could stay on a month-to-month basis at a 200 percent increase until we found a new tenant. We found one a few weeks ago and gave the bookstore notice. They closed last weekend, after several phone calls begging for a reprieve. You go see her," she'd insisted tearfully. "She killed my husband, I know it!"

Liz had given Jace the car to go see the bookseller while she got a lift back with Ronnie Schaffer so she could be at the Howard autopsy.

Maureen Carr's apartment was in a forty-unit building in Santa Monica, near St. John's Hospital. Although there was a security door at the building's front, it was propped open with a brick. Inside, the building was a warren of inner walkways; many of the apartments had balconies jutting into the center space. The atrium was filled with center apartment units piled one atop another for three stories. The plastic flower-filled planters were faded and dirty, the whole effect depressing. Jace could smell dinners of several different nationalities cooking.

"Who's there?" the woman's voice came from behind number 223.

"Police, Ms. Carr." Jace held his I.D. to the peephole.

"Just a minute." Locks disengaged and the door opened to reveal a short, middle-aged woman in a robe and slippers. She was thick-waisted and chunky, her short dark hair streaked with gray and uncombed. Her eyes were red, as if she'd been crying . . . or drinking.

"May I come in?"

"Yeah, sure." She stepped back to let him through the tiny entryway into a book-filled living room. A bearded red-haired man in cutoffs sat cross-legged on the couch, an open paperback in his hand.

"Are you Maureen Carr?" She nodded. "You owned Strange Land Books on Venice?"

"*A* Strange Land," she corrected automatically. "Look, if this is about the money I still owe Random House . . ."

"No, Ms. Carr. I'm not here to collect on your debts. Is there somewhere we can talk in private?" Jace looked pointedly at the man on the couch.

"I'll go in the bedroom. Call me if you need me," the man said to Maureen as he got up. He took his book with him.

When the door closed, she turned back to Jace. "This is as private as it gets, Officer."

"Detective," he corrected. She responded with raised eyebrows. "When was the last time you saw Alvin Zamel?"

"Yesterday, when he refused to give back my security

deposit.'' She picked up a half-empty drink from the cocktail table and took a good swig. ''I don't suppose he's sent you around with it?''

Jace shook his head. ''What time yesterday?''

''I don't know. Early afternoon. Why?''

''Where were you last night, Ms. Carr?''

''Right here, doing this,'' she indicated her glass. ''I'm . . . in mourning. This would've been my store's fifteenth anniversary, if it hadn't been for that money-hungry . . .'' She started crying. She gave in to sobs for a minute, then wiped her eyes with her sleeve. ''I'm sorry. I really loved that store—the customers, the staff, the whole business. And it's the middle of a recession—how am I going to find work? I feel like my life's over.'' She polished off her drink. ''The future used to be my forte—now I'm afraid of it.''

Jace felt her grief, palpable in the room, but the questions had to be asked. ''Were you alone last night?''

She barked a short mirthless laugh. ''My friends won't let me be alone. I think they're afraid of what I'll do. Judith and Jordi took me to dinner at the Bicycle Shop Cafe. Ted stayed the night. I haven't been alone since I closed the store.''

''Is that Ted?'' Jace pointed to the bedroom door. Maureen nodded.

''You gonna tell me why you're asking?'' she said as she refilled her glass with scotch.

''Was anyone else there when you saw Zamel yesterday?''

''I told you I haven't been alone all week. Ted was with me. I'll get him if you want to ask him.''

''In a minute. Alvin Zamel was murdered last night at a motel near the airport.''

Maureen's face showed a quick play of emotions, from shock to a faint smile. ''I can't say I'm sorry to hear that,'' she said, "it'd be a lie. I hope they took their time. I hope he suffered a lot. I'm sorry for Terri, though—she seemed to be a nice person, even if she couldn't convince Al to let us stay."

Questioning Ted confirmed Maureen's story. Jace's gut told him this was a dead end—the bookseller had nothing to do with Zamel's death, nor did her taciturn boyfriend. He knew this was Rusty's work . . . and Carr wasn't even close to Rusty's description.

"I'm sorry to have bothered you, Ms. Carr," he said as he headed for the door.

"No bother. You probably won't understand this, but your news actually made me feel better."

CHAPTER
Fourteen

Rusty couldn't understand why she was still hurting. Gregor's loss was as painful to her two years later as it had been when it happened. She'd once believed the adage about time healing wounds, but now she doubted it—he was gone and never coming back; why couldn't she get on with her life?

Whenever she wasn't actively involved in something, he came to mind—his voice, his face, the time they'd spent together. Sometimes it was just his name whispering in her mind, a ghost of the man, almost as evocative as a complete memory: Gregor.

In spite of the joy she'd felt with him, his intrusion now brought no happiness; it merely served to reinforce the reality that he existed only in her memories. Memories that, perhaps, weren't even accurate; she no longer knew. Perhaps everything between them had not been as wonderful as she remembered, but the only person capable of a reality check was Gregor . . . and he was gone, his silence deafening.

It wasn't that they'd never had a disagreement; there had been plenty, although their arguments seldom had any personal components. Rusty and Gregor enjoyed debating their views on movies, plays, politics—and even vampirism—but they rarely discussed their relationship. Rusty felt secure that they would spend eternity together, and so never needed the reassurance of a formal commitment. However, she realized that there were things Gregor kept to himself.

He never talked about his life before he crossed over. Once, when she'd pressed him, he'd snapped, "I don't want to remember it—don't ask me again."

He never told her who had made him a vampire, nor anything about his previous mates; she didn't even know for sure that there had been any, much less what might have happened to them.

He was reluctant to discuss his feelings and emotions, responding to her queries with thoughts and logic, or by changing the subject entirely. She felt he was uncomfortable with even her emotions—if he didn't have a neat solution to give her, he seemed to feel helpless. She didn't know if it was just her own paranoia, but she felt he almost blamed her for having conflicts or doubts that he couldn't fix. It was as if he were feeling responsible for her well-being, and if she were temporarily unhappy, it reflected badly upon his ability, his masculinity. He never seemed to believe her when she said that all she needed was to be held and comforted when she was blue, as if that couldn't be the right thing to do—after all, what did it solve? Even now, that's all she wanted: for Gregor to hold her, to be there for her. She didn't need him to tell her everything, not about his past, nor his emotions; she didn't need solutions, she didn't want another man. She needed him to not be dead.

Gregor.

* * *

"Here's your costume," Liz said, handing Jace a garment bag. "Make sure you get the tux cleaned and pressed before I put it back in Sandy's closet. The cape is mine, so it might be too short—"

"Doesn't matter." Jace stood back to let Liz in. She stayed on the stoop. "Aren't you coming in?"

"I can't. I promised Sandy I'd come right back. He wants to talk," she shrugged. "I am sorry to miss the sight of you in a tuxedo, though—see if you can get someone to take a picture."

"You're coming to the party with me, remember?"

Liz shook her head. "I can't, Jace. This is the first time all week that Sandy's shown any desire to work things out. I can't leave."

"Chrissakes, Liz, it's not a date. I don't want to go to this thing alone. Bring Sandy, if you want."

Liz laughed. "Not a good idea, Levy. Besides, then he'd know I loaned you his tux without asking. I'm afraid you're on your own tonight. But have a good time, hobnobbing with the hoi polloi of film and literature."

She turned to go, but before she got to the sidewalk, she called to him, "Oh, Jace, I forgot to give you something."

"What?"

Liz rummaged in her purse and brought out a small bag from Sav-On Drugs. "The crowning touch for your costume—I picked it up on the way over. Leave it under a light for an hour before you go."

She got into her Miata and drove off with a wave.

Jace took the costume inside and hung it on the closet door. He looked into the bag Liz had given him.

It held a set of glow-in-the-dark plastic fangs.

* * *

Jace gave the car key to the parking valet and entered the hotel lobby. A sign announced that the *City of Angels* party was being held in the rooftop ballroom. He shared the elevator with Mikhail and Raisa Gorbachev; the man's port-wine stain was shaped sort of like South America. Jace slipped in his fangs and smiled at them.

The elevator opened onto a foyer. A black velvet-draped table was next to the entrance to the ballroom, manned by a clown. Jace waited while the clown dealt with the Gorbachevs.

"Name?" the clown asked. It was a woman's voice, the only indication of the clown's gender.

"Jafof Lefy." He took out his fangs and tried again. "Jacob Levy." He waited while she scanned her list.

"I'm sorry, I don't find your name. Do you have your invitation with you?"

He pulled it out of his pocket and handed it to her. "Maybe as Jace, instead of Jacob? David South invited me last Tuesday."

"He probably just forgot to put your name on the list." She handed him an orange plastic token with 152 stamped on it in black. "This is for the door prize drawings—don't lose it, there's some really neat stuff gonna be given away."

The ballroom was impressive, and not just because of the elaborate "costumes required." A combo was playing soft rock on the small stage while a few couples danced; a magician was doing card tricks on a folding table for a dozen interested party-goers; at another table sat a woman dressed like a Gypsy who appeared to be telling fortunes; a photographer was taking portraits in front of a black backdrop, a white one ready next to it. One entire wall was taken up with a buffet and bar.

Jace wandered over to get a drink and check out the food. Finding his fangs in his hand, he put them in his pocket.

"Yessir, what'll it be?" The bartender was wearing a pirate costume. He looked familiar; Jace realized he'd seen him on TV.

"Beer—imported, if you have it. Are you an actor?" Every waiter in L.A. was an actor.

The man grinned at being recognized, "Did you see me last month on *L.A. Law*? I played the husband of the rape victim? Anyway, we have Coors, Dos Equis, Kirin, Anchor Steam. What can I get you?"

"Anchor Steam."

Jace took his beer over to the buffet table. There were cold shrimp in dill sauce, steak tartare, a whole poached salmon with cucumber scales, spicy chicken wings with sesame seeds, pasta salads, snow peas and water chestnuts in vinagrette, imported cheese platters—and that was just on the end of the table closest to him. At the far end, he could make out a sinful assortment of desserts. If nothing else, he'd eat well.

"You're not supposed to get in without a costume."

Jace turned and found David South next to him, a glass of white wine in his hand. South was dressed as Sherlock Holmes, right down to the calabash pipe and deerstalker hat.

"I am in costume—you think I wear a tux and cape every day? Whoops! Forgot my fangs." Jace fished them out of his pocket and put them in. "I don't talk fery well wiff fese," he explained.

South laughed, "Dracula with a speech impediment—I love it! Enjoying yourself, Detective?"

Jace took the fangs out to answer. "I just got here, but this is some bash. The food looks great."

South nodded. "Catered by Moller's," he said, as if Jace should recognize the name. "Let me introduce you to someone. Who do you want to meet? Arnold Schwarzenegger? Jessica Tandy?"

"Actually, I'd really like to meet James Ellroy."

South looked around and shook his head. "If Ellroy's here yet, I haven't recognized him in his costume. Ray Bradbury's over there—how about him?"

Jace had read a lot of Bradbury books when he was younger. "That'd be great."

South led him across the room where a deeply tanned white-haired man in a white suit was talking to Humpty Dumpty and Ali Baba.

"What about his costume?" Jace asked.

"That's his Wonderful Ice Cream Suit," South explained. When they arrived, Bradbury was finishing telling a story.

". . . so I'm sitting in the back of the classroom, listening while they discuss the symbolism of this and the meaning of that, finding all this dark Freudian stuff where there just wasn't any. I interrupted, trying to explain that sometimes a cigar is just a cigar, but they weren't having any of that, said I just wasn't conscious of the symbolism when I wrote it. Finally, I stood up and said, 'If you don't want to listen to the author on his own work, fuck you!' and I walked out."

Everyone laughed. Bradbury said something about getting some food, and broke away. South tapped him on the arm.

"Ray, I'd like you to meet someone. This is Jace Levy. He's a detective. Jace, Ray Bradbury."

Bradbury stuck out his hand and Jace shook it. "Mr. Bradbury, it's a pleasure. I'm a big fan of yours."

"Thank you. Call me Ray." South left them alone. "You're a detective? LAPD or private?" He looked longingly toward the food. Jace caught the look and nodded, and the two men headed for the buffet as they talked.

"LAPD—Robbery-Homicide," Jace answered.

"Fascinating," Bradbury said, picking up a plate. Jace followed suit. "I wrote a mystery—maybe you read it?"

They chatted about books while they loaded their plates. Then an overweight woman dressed as a cat threw her arms around Bradbury and screeched, "Ray! You naughty boy! How long have you been back from Paris?" and Jace faded off, leaving Bradbury to the cat-woman in the lumpy leotards.

He took his plate and beer over to watch the magician. For the life of him, he just couldn't get the hang of eating and holding a drink at the same time—it seemed to require a minimum of three hands. The magician was a rabbit. As the capper to his routine, he reached into an apparently empty top hat and produced a stuffed man.

Jace went into the bathroom to wash his hands. While he was standing at the sink, next to Bob's Big Boy, David South came out of one of the stalls with a man dressed as Nancy Reagan. Nancy giggled when he saw there were witnesses, sniffed ostentatiously, and left. South didn't seem to see Jace, but Jace noticed a smear of white on South's left nostril. Doing coke in the john with Just-Say-No Reagan?

Jace thought it would be terribly rude to bust the man at his own party, but he was pissed that he would have to overlook it. He stopped South on his way out the door.

"You'll want to wipe your nose before you go out, South."

The editor didn't even have the courtesy to be embarrassed;

he nodded, passed the back of his hand against his nose, and went back to the party.

Jace had just about decided to go home, but remembered Liz's request to get a picture. He went over to the photographer, a young woman with spiked green hair, dressed in a black leather jumpsuit with SATIVA SLUTS picked out on the back in metal studs.

She was shooting a couple in sixties hippie garb: tie-dye, bell-bottoms, headbands, and love beads. Jace thought they might have been under ten years of age when the look had last been popular. They mugged for the camera—beatific smiles, fingers in a V for peace. Jace put in his fangs.

When she finished with the throwbacks, the photographer turned to him. "Ah, the first vampire of the evening. In front of the light drop, Count."

Jace stood where she indicated. She took a light reading, then altered the angle of the white umbrella she used to bounce the light.

"Spread your arms and look menacing," she suggested.

When she was done, Jace said, "Can I arrange to get a frint of fat?" He took out his fangs. "I mean, a print of that?" he laughed.

"Well, I'm not supposed to . . . But I'll tell you what— there's a chick in a Peter Pan outfit someplace here. I think Peter Pan and Dracula sort of go together, you know? I mean, neither of them is ever going to get old, right? Anyway, if you get her over here for a picture of the two of you, I'll make you prints. Okay?"

Jace went in search of Peter Pan. He finally saw her profile between the Queen of Hearts and a talking strawberry. She was the bustiest Peter Pan he'd ever seen. When she turned, he saw it was Risha Cadigan, the photographer.

"Hello, Risha."

She smiled, surprised. "Jace! How do you come to be here?"

He told her about meeting David South earlier in the week, and his eagerness to meet the elusive Ellroy. "I did get to meet Ray Bradbury, though. Listen, can I buy you a drink?"

"It's a hosted bar," she pointed out.

"Allow me my fantasies."

As they walked over to the bar, Jace told Risha about the photographer's request.

"I don't think so, Jace. I don't photograph well."

"Strange thing for someone in your line of work to say. C'mon, otherwise no one will ever know what I look like in a tux and fangs."

Risha peered at his mouth. "I don't see any fangs."

He pulled them out of his pocket and popped them in. "Fey glow in fa dark." She laughed. "One ficture, flease."

"How can I resist someone who says 'flease'? But I warn you, it won't come out."

They went over to the photographer's area. She was delighted to see Dracula coming back with Peter Pan, and set them in front of the backdrop.

"I think it'd be best to have Dracula behind Peter Pan, bending over to sink your fangs into her neck," she told them. She took the reading and adjusted the lights.

Jace caught a whiff of dusty rose as he put his lips next to Risha's neck. He restrained the urge to nibble her earlobe.

"What kind of camera are you using?" she asked the photographer.

"I've got a Nikon and a Sinar view. You know cameras?"

"Some," Risha said modestly. "If you don't mind, I'd rather you use the view camera than the SLR."

"No prob." She switched cameras.

When they were done, Jace gave the photographer twenty bucks and his address for mailing the print.

The band was playing a fair rendition of "Nights in White Satin" and Jace raised his eyebrows and nodded to the dance floor; Risha smiled and followed him. It had been a long time since Jace had last danced—not since Liz's wedding. The pleasure of holding Risha close to him was offset by his initial anxiety about stepping on her toes. While they danced, they made small talk about the party, the band, and the costumes. Finally, Jace felt enough at ease to stop worrying about his feet, but the music stopped, and David South tapped on the mike.

"We're going to have a drawing for several door prizes, so find the little piece of plastic you were given when you came in," he announced.

There was a brief flurry of small activity while everyone searched for tokens stashed in costumes. Marie Antoinette stood next to South, holding a bowl full of tokens.

"The first prize is a cellular telephone. And the winner is . . ." South took the token from Marie Antoinette, ". . . number one twenty-six!"

"Mine! It's mine!" Jace turned to the shrill voice and saw the bulky cat-woman who'd ambushed Bradbury; she was rushing up to the stage, waving her token over her head, her ample body bouncing.

"Kind of wish I'd brought my camera," Risha said.

"It wouldn't be quite as good without the sound, anyway," Jace smiled.

Risha sighed, "You're probably right."

South gave away a weekend in Palm Springs, tickets to see the Lakers, tickets to the stage production *Two Trains Running*.

"Okay, only two prizes left, and then the band will play again. First is a pair of tickets to a screening at the Motion Picture Academy for *Rambling Rose*, a new film by Martha Coolidge with Robert Duvall and Laura Dern. Number one fifty-two!"

Risha looked at Jace's tile. "That's your number!"

Jace looked down. "So it is."

He went up to the stage to pick up the envelope with his tickets. By the time he returned to Risha, South was giving away the last door prize.

"Last, but not least, we have four tickets to an advance screening of Oliver Stone's *JFK*, starring Kevin Costner as Jim Garrison. Number ninety-six!"

"Shit—I really wanted to see *JFK*," Jace said as a bag lady claimed the tickets.

"I'm looking forward to it, too," Risha said, "but at least you won something. Anything with Duvall is bound to be good."

"Would you care to go with me?" He looked at the envelope. "The screening's on the thirtieth—Wednesday night."

She paused just long enough for Jace to think she was going to say no. "I'd love to."

Rusty thought it probably wasn't too smart of her to be going out with a cop, particularly one who was investigating the death of one of her feeders. But if Jace suspected her of being the killer, he wouldn't be asking her out on a date, would he? She thought he was kind of cute, and he was intelligent and articulate—a far cry from most of the men she'd dated lately. Besides, she thought, what better way to keep an eye on the investigation? If she got Jace to confide in her about his work, she'd know if she were in any danger of discovery in plenty of time to leave town. So, why not?

She realized Jace was talking. "I'm sorry. What?"

He smiled. "I suggested we go check out the sweets."

"I don't eat desserts," she said, "but I'll watch you."

They walked over to the table and Jace piled a small plate with cheesecake, chocolate truffles, and an almond square. "Can't I even tempt you with a taste?" he asked.

Sure, she thought, give me your neck. But she shook her head. "No thanks. I was fat once, and don't intend to be again. Enjoy them for me." While he relished his desserts, she asked casually, "Have you found the murderer yet?"

He looked startled at the question, and she thought she'd blown it, but then he said, "I forgot I met you in connection with a case. No, not yet, but I will. This is a tough one— it'll take a while."

"Can you tell me about it?"

He groaned. "Not tonight, Risha, please. I forgot all about it the last couple of hours—let me enjoy my weekend. How about getting our fortunes told?"

"I'll have to pass. I have some work to do tonight." Actually, she was hungry. She wanted to go home and change and go out for a meal. "But I'll see you Wednesday night."

"The screening is at eight. How about I pick you up at six and we'll get a quick bite to eat first?"

"I can't go out to dinner because of my diet. Would seven o'clock be okay?"

CHAPTER
Fifteen

"The HIV results came in on Howard and Zamel—both were negative," Liz told Jace. "It looks like you were right; the AIDS link is a dead end."

"Just as well, considering the problems we faced getting anyone to talk to us. Did King find lipstick on either of their necks?"

"Both of them. He said it's the same formula as the lipstick on Avallone, but only Howard's neck had the same shade of dark orange; the lipstick on Zamel was a paler color, sort of apricot."

Jace looked at Liz's lipstick, a clear red. "Do women choose lipstick to go with their complexions or with their clothes?"

"Both. I've got maybe four or five shades I use regularly, depending on what I'm wearing." She was wearing navy today. "But all of them go with my skin, hair, and eyes. The oranges Rusty apparently uses are consistent with dark auburn hair, if that's what you're asking, but they don't tell us much about her complexion or what she might have been wearing."

Jace sighed. Nothing about this case was coming easily. He couldn't remember ever having murders with so few leads. "Okay, so let's assume, for a moment, that she actually is drinking the blood—"

"That's a pretty wild assumption, Jace."

"Don't you think I know that? But that's what fits the evidence, Liz. Can you think of any other explanation that does?" Reluctantly, she shook her head. "Back to my assumption: If she's sucking their necks, shouldn't there be saliva traces?"

Liz looked up with a big smile. "Levy, have I ever told you you're brilliant?"

"Not often enough. I'll call King."

It was nearly two hours before King called back. In the meantime, Jace filled Frank Cosentino in while Liz poked around in Howard's computer files.

The medical examiner began with, "On the saliva, I've got bad news and weird news—which do you want first?"

"The bad, I guess," Jace said with trepidation.

"Your 'vampire' isn't a secretor; her saliva doesn't carry any genetic information. With one tiny exception, there is no way to differentiate her saliva from that of any other non-secretor."

"One tiny exception?" Jace probed hopefully.

"That's the weird news. There are traces of something odd in the neck wounds."

"Odd, how? You just said you can't tell anything about her from her saliva. You mean it's something she ate?"

"Well, I suppose that's a possibility. Some foods are secreted in the saliva, like garlic, but this doesn't look like anything I've seen before. The smear is probably too small to tell anything, but I've sent it on for tox anyway.''

"I know: six to eight weeks, if we're lucky. How about an educated guess?" King was silent. "Okay, I'll settle for a hunch." Still nothing. "C'mon, King, anything!"

"Look, there's nothing I'd put in a report, Levy, so this is completely off the record."

"I won't tell a soul. Now, what did you find?"

"There was no lipstick on the chest wounds, only the neck wounds. The amount of lipstick wasn't equal on the top and bottom of the neck wounds, like you'd expect if she was sucking the blood out of the knife hole. I thought she might have already worn off the color on her bottom lip when she mouthed Howard, but I noticed the same thing on Zamel. So it occurred to me that the knife wound might have been camouflage to cover teeth marks, and it was the knife that wiped off part of the lipstick.''

"Jesus—you mean we've got someone who's crazy enough to sink their teeth into someone's neck, but smart enough to cover the marks?"

Liz looked up from her computer at what Jace was saying, her eyebrows peaked, her curiosity piqued. "Is he trying to tell us we have a real vampire?" she laughed.

"I told you this is off the record, Detective. You didn't get it from me," King insisted. "Anyway, I've closely examined the wounds, and I found one strange anomaly on Zamel."

"Give!"

"On the anterior lower edge, a small scar, round. Could have been made by an ice pick, except it's far too shallow."

"Could it have been made by a tooth?"

"Aren't you getting a little carried away with this 'vampire' nickname, Detective? It wasn't made by a human tooth—it went too deep for that and had no adjacent tooth marks. Besides, it had healed over before he was stabbed. At a guess, it was maybe a month before the murder, but I'll be damned if I can figure out what caused it."

Jace thanked King and hung up. He turned to Liz. "Is Terri Zamel still in town?"

"She's staying at her uncle's house until the body is released. You want the number?"

Alvin Zamel's widow was waiting for Jace at Ships when he arrived. She was drinking coffee, and Jace ordered a cup for himself.

"Thank you for meeting me, Mrs. Zamel."

"I'm sorry I couldn't have you up to the house, but my uncle's not well, and I didn't want to upset him further. Are you ready to release Al's body?"

Jace shook his head. "I'm sorry, not yet. But, it shouldn't be more than another day, two at the most. Did your husband have any kind of injury recently, perhaps a month or so ago?"

"Injury? You mean like a car accident?" She looked confused. Jace didn't blame her; he felt confused himself.

"Anything that broke the skin, caused bleeding?"

"Not that I know of. He doesn't work with tools, if that's what you mean."

"What kind of razor did he use?" The mark King had described didn't sound like a shaving cut, but it didn't sound like anything else either.

"I don't know the brand. Is that important? It's the kind that recharges . . ."

Electric. Not a shaving cut. "Can you think of any way

he might have accidentally poked his neck with anything sharp?''

"His neck? What are you talking about, Detective? Are you trying to tell me you think that Al stabbed himself in the neck and died from it a month later? What kind of half-assed investigations do you people run in L.A.?''

"I know this sounds strange, Mrs. Zamel, but we found a recent scar on his neck . . .''

She stood up. "It isn't bad enough my husband is killed, but now you're worried about what kind of shaver he used? Is that the best you can come up with? Are you people totally incompetent? If you have anything else to say to me, you can do it through my lawyer. I'm going back to Sacramento. He'll call you to arrange shipping for Al's . . . body. If you ever call me again, it had better be to tell me you've caught the murderer.''

She turned on her heel and walked out.

Liz handed Jace a sheet of paper when he walked in.

"What's this?''

"A letter I found in John Howard's computer files. Read it,'' she ordered.

Jace sat at his desk and read the letter.

> *Dear #_____,*
>
> *I have never answered a personals ad before but your ad was very intriguing and I think we would get along fine. I hope you agree. My name is John Howard. I'm a senior programmer. I'm 26, 5'10", with light brown hair and brown eyes, and I live in Culver City. I*

*like movies but I usually watch them on video
because $7.50 is too much for most movies
nowadays. I enjoy nice drives out in the country
and sleeping in late on my days off, particularly
with someone special. I'm a non-smoker, but am
not bothered by people who do smoke, as long
as they brush their teeth (ha ha).*

*I'm looking for someone to share the good times
with, who will still be around if things are not so
good, and someone who likes sex as much as I do.
(I have no diseases, and hope you don't either!)*

*I would have sent you a photo but believe it or
not, I don't have any (other than a shot
including my ex-girlfriend, which would be real
tacky to send you). Mel Gibson I'm not, but if
you were seen in my presence, I don't think
they'd have to call out the dog catcher. If you
think we should get together for a date, you can
call me at 555-8152. The ball's in your court so
to speak, so have a real nice day.*

Sincerely,

"There's something smarmy about someone who begins a form letter with 'I have never answered a personals ad before,' " Liz observed.

"The box number here is blank, there's no date, and no address. Is any of that stuff in the computer?"

Liz shook her head. "Not that I've found so far. The file for the letter was titled *SEX.LET*, which seems to indicate what he was looking for. The original date for the file was 01-09-91, but that doesn't tell us what dates he printed them out. He could have been using the same letter to answer several ads, just plugging in the box number before printing out.''

''Do I remember correctly that you found some sex papers in Howard's bedroom? The closet, I think you said?''

''That's right, there were, but I didn't tag them. They're probably still there, unless his landlord cleared everything out.''

''There should still be a seal on the scene. I'm going to see what I can find. Maybe he kept the papers because he marked the ads he responded to.''

''From your mouth to God's ear,'' Liz called as he left.

Rusty pushed the play button on the CD player and adjusted the volume as Jerry Garcia started singing ''Touch of Grey.'' It had been nearly three years since she'd last seen a Grateful Dead concert; she'd have to make sure to get tickets the next time they were in town—assuming she had someone to go with.

When she turned to go into the study, she was stopped by the sight of the living room wall opposite the couch. The spaces previously occupied by the Model, Brassaï, and Stieglitz prints were now filled with three of her own prints. Her portrait of Gregor was neatly centered between an action shot of King Voodoo performing and a picture of a toddler straddling his father's shoulders to see fireworks over Edinburgh Castle, his finger pointed at the display.

She assumed Elliott had changed the pictures to tell her he disapproved of her dating this soon after Gregor's death. Elliott's messages generally tended to be heavy-handed; his placement of Gregor's photo was just that, but reminding her of Edinburgh was crass.

* * *

The last trip Rusty took with Gregor was to Scotland in the summer of 1989. A rented house near Edinburgh served as their base for the three weeks of the Edinburgh Festival, the extravaganza of concerts, plays, and circuses that brought in thousands of tourists annually. An additional Fringe Festival increased the number of events into the hundreds. Each night, they saw at least one event, usually two, chosen from the mind-boggling selection of talent from all over the world.

The constant ebb and flow of people throughout the city, people who often partied in the streets all night, provided plenty of low-risk feeders for the vampire pair. None of the bodies they abandoned in the surrounding countryside or dumped in the Firth of Forth had been found during their stay, and the variety of entertainment led Rusty to fantasize about settling in the area for a longer period.

The last Thursday of the Festival period was the big fireworks concert. On Princes Street, an orchestra played the 1812 Overture to a hundred thousand people below Edinburgh Castle while an hour-long fireworks spectacle blossomed over the castle. With cannons booming and skyrockets exploding, the castle looked to be under siege—indeed, at one point, some of the brush on the hill below the castle even caught fire, adding to the illusion.

"I wish we could see inside the castle," Rusty said wistfully.

"I know you do, but it's not open at night," Gregor said. "Anyway, if you've seen one castle, you've seen them all."

"I haven't, though. Have you ever seen inside a castle, Gregor?"

He laughed. "I used to live in one. Terrible place. Depressing, cold, and drafty, with uneven steep steps . . . and a mob howling outside. Not an experience I really care to repeat.''

A particularly intricate and bright skyrocket lit the air and the crowd cheered and applauded.

"Still," Rusty said, "it's a shame the Scottish castles aren't open at night."

"Pardon me, but did ye say ye'd be wanting to see inside a castle at night?" They turned to the voice and found a young man with long hair smoking a thick joint. "I might help ye oot with that," he added, "for a price."

"How?" Rusty asked him. "You don't look like a prince to me."

"Aye," he laughed, "I'm no prince. But I am a watchman at Stirling Castle. It's as old as this 'un, and it's vacant until it's been restored. Mary had her coronation in the Chapel, and her son, James VI, was baptized there. Aye, it's full of history, and for a price, ye can have it all alone for a night. Fuck in Prince Henry's quarters, if ye like," he added with a friendly leer, "though there'll be no bed."

They met Duncan Jellen at Stirling at midnight Sunday. He unlocked the gate in the outer defense and let them in, locking it again behind them. Gregor handed Duncan the fifty pounds he'd named as his price.

"I'll show ye aboot a wee bit, if you like, and then I'll leave ye alone to do as ye please. But, ye must split by dawn—the work crews come in early." He had an electric lamp and a flashlight with him. He handed the flashlight to Gregor. "I'll gie ye the lamp when I go—I ken my way aboot fine with the torch and I'll have no need of it to sleep—but I'll be wanting it back when ye go.

"Mind yer step—these stones can be treacherous in the dark. I dinna ken a lot aboot the history and all, but I can tell ye some things," Duncan explained as he led them through the lower square.

"What's that building?" Gregor asked, pointing to a towering wall festooned with fantastic statues and sculptures.

"Aye, are they no strange? Devils and gods. That's the palace itself. That way lies a courtyard known as The Lions' Den—the rooms aboot it were the apartments for the king and queen. Ye'll find some impressive fireplaces in there, but I'm afeared ye canna light a fire in them."

After a quick orientation tour, Duncan traded Gregor the lamp for the flashlight, and pointed out The Nether Bailey, the lower enclosure where he had his room. "If ye ha' na come by dawn, I'll have to coom looking for ye . . ." he warned.

"We'll be long gone by then, I assure you," Gregor said. "I expect we'll only be two or three hours."

"Ye ken where to find me then," Duncan said as he left.

It was actually even less time than that. Even with the lamp and their impressive night vision, Rusty and Gregor found it difficult to see the architecture. They looked into as many rooms as they could find, but they were bare, the tunnels and arched doorways hidden in darkness. Eventually, they settled for a tour of the Wall Walk which ran around most of the Castle.

They found the Grand Battery, with its seven huge guns pointing toward Abbey Craig and the medieval bridge. Rusty climbed onto one of the old guns, straddling it with her legs.

"Oh, Gregor! Wouldn't this have been a wonderful place to play as a child? Let's go up to the tower—I'll be the kidnapped princess and you can rescue me—'' She stopped when she realized he wasn't listening to her.

Gregor was facing out over the wall, staring into the valley with a pensive look. She peered down to see what he saw: a cemetery, its oddly shaped Celtic headstones gleaming in the moonlight.

'' 'To be really dead—that must be glorious!' '' Gregor said.

"What?''

"Nothing''—he turned to Rusty—''just a quote from *Dracula*. Are you ready to leave, my dear?''

She wasn't ready, and didn't want to leave, but she sensed Gregor's discomfort, so she agreed.

They found Duncan and he walked them to the gate. Rusty walked through, but Gregor stayed next to Duncan. He held out the car keys to her.

"Wait in the car, Risha, I'll be there in a minute.''

Was he going to kill Duncan? she wondered. It would be unlike Gregor to not share a meal. But she felt this wasn't the time to challenge him—the moody man she was with was a stranger to her. In a way, it frightened her.

It was nearly twenty minutes before Gregor got back to the car. He said nothing about what he'd been doing. In fact, he was silent all the way back to Edinburgh.

It was after three when they got back to the house. Gregor didn't get out of the car.

"You go in, Risha. I have something to take care of on my own.''

He kissed her and put the car in reverse. As he backed down the drive, he gave her a wistful smile.

Although she heard from him later, it was the last time she saw him.

* * *

John Howard had been a busy correspondent, judging from the personals ads he'd kept. Most of the papers were freebies: *The LA Reader, The LA Weekly, What's Up/LA*, but there were also a smattering of copies of *The Singles Register* and *Swingers World.*

Jace took the stack into the living room and sat on the couch with them. The papers dated back to August of 1990, the month Howard had moved into the apartment. He was obviously a pack rat, and Jace found the stack was already in reverse chronological order, the newest on top. There were weeks when he'd picked up several different papers, weeks when he'd only picked up one or another, weeks for which there were none.

Jace started with the most recent, an issue of the *Reader*, dated the week before Howard was killed. The personals ads in the back were divided into sections: Men Seeking Women, Women Seeking Men, Men Seeking Men, Women Seeking Women. The pages of Women Seeking Men had five ads circled, three of which were starred in the same pen that had circled them.

Were the circles the ones Howard was interested in and the stars the ones he actually answered? Or were the stars on women who'd called back about his response?

Three hours later, Jace had over seventy circled ads, about two-thirds of them starred, from four different papers, and that was covering just the last three months. No wonder Howard had his response letter on a computer.

He reminded Jace of a guy he knew in school. No one could figure out how Corish always had someone new to date, because he was unattractive, loud, and obnoxious. One day, Jace had asked him.

"The secret is in not minding rejection, chum. You come on to every woman you want to fuck, sure you're going to get turned down a lot—even laughed at—but some of 'em are gonna say yes. I ask a lotta women, so I get laid a lot."

Jace wondered if John Howard's letter got him laid a lot before it got him killed.

CHAPTER
Sixteen

It was too late in the day to reach anyone in Classifieds at the newspapers, so Jace took the stack back to his house. He sat at the dining room table, drinking Harp and reading personals ads.

It was difficult trying to come up with a common factor for the ads John Howard had chosen. Most of the women stated ages of thirty or under (or none at all), but one of the circled ads gave an age of "forty-ish" (placed by a "sexy, successful woman seeking a hot HIV-neg young man"). Few of the ads were as openly sexually oriented; Howard had circled many ads from women who wanted committed relationships as well.

The ads that had been starred seemed to have something a little out of the ordinary about them. One might begin with "For a limited time only, this very special offer . . .", or claim to be a "mythical creature" who could give the right man "something no other woman can," or state that the advertiser "loves to cook for my man." However, they had nothing else in common with each other. Jace decided that he would concentrate on the circled-and-starred ads; whether they were the women who responded to Howard's letter, or only the ads he had actually sent letters to, they were the ones he had contacted.

Jace got up for another beer, but as he took it out of the refrigerator, it slipped out of his hand and crashed on the floor. "Shit!" He got the broom and dustpan and swept up the broken bottle. As he soaked up the spilled beer with paper towels, it occurred to him it would be more ecologically sound to use the sponge, but he grabbed another handful of paper towels to finish the job.

Had he dropped the beer just because the bottle was cold and wet . . . or because Huntington's was affecting the grip in his hand? Jace clenched and unclenched his fist several times. Was that a tremble? He held his hand out, parallel to the floor, compared it to his other one. He couldn't tell. Finally, he decided he was making himself crazy over nothing, and he carefully got another Harp out of the fridge.

He tried reading some of the unmarked ads in each paper to see why Howard hadn't circled them. As far as he could tell, the unmarked ads were lacking nothing from the marked, save that some required replies from black or Jewish men only, for instance.

Jace was astounded at the specificity of some of the advertisers' requirements—he began to think of them as "must be's" "must be: 6'-6'3", 29–32, blond, slender, entertainment business . . ." Jace noticed that the "must be's" were always in multiples and usually physical; no one ever said, "must be over 130 I.Q." or "good at crossword puzzles."

So many lonely people.

* * *

He slept badly that night, tossing and turning. Just before dawn, he had the dream again.

He was trapped, his hands manacled to the floor by iron cuffs, unable to turn his head to see the monster he knew was looming behind him, its maw dripping in a voracious hunger only Jace's death could appease. Jace screamed for someone to save him, screamed until his throat was raw. The beast laughed—his mother's insane chuckle—and began to gnaw on Jace's hands. The sharp pain turned to numbness as his hands were devoured, and he continued to scream for mercy.

Suddenly, he was free! He slid out of the manacles and leapt up, turning to reach for his gun. He could see the gun next to him, but he couldn't grab it—he had no hands!—and the monster laughed again and lunged for him. Somehow, the beast had become Dracula, and his fangs were dripping blood. Jace ran for the door—he must get out!—but he couldn't turn the knob. He could feel the beast's warm breath on his neck and when he turned, it was on top of him, exuding the foul smell of stale beer.

He woke, then, covered in sweat. He couldn't feel his left hand! As he sat up, he realized it had been pinned under his body, and was relieved to find the familiar pins-and-needles sensation of feeling returning to his hand.

He took a quick shower to rid himself of fear-sweat. It was too early to get up, and too frightening to go back to sleep. He wished he'd confiscated more than one joint from the kid down the street; he could really use a few tokes right about now. If he didn't get some sleep, he wouldn't be very good company for Risha Cadigan tonight.

He got the Ellroy novel from the living room and took it

back to bed with him. He would read until he fell asleep, or until it was time to get up.

If only there were some way to stop the fucking nightmare.

Rusty had left two rolls of exposed film on the desk in the study, along with a note to Elliott asking him to develop them and print contact sheets. She'd ended it by saying she had a date at seven that evening, and to please plan to do her make-up as soon as she'd finished her bath.

Elliott wondered who the date was with. Wilkins was dead and she hadn't gotten any more letters from *What's Up/LA*. He hoped she wasn't getting involved with anyone else—it would only make it harder to convince her that it was time to leave L.A.

He finished packing up the valuable photographs from Gregor's collection; he'd ship them to the London house that afternoon. He'd already sent Risha's older negatives and most of the prints that she wouldn't need now. He looked around to see what else he could ship off, what couldn't be easily replaced if abandoned. The Bathory silver. She never used it anyway, so it really belonged in London.

He began to wrap the silver.

Maybe she met someone last night while she was out shooting. He'd have to see if the photographs told him anything. He put down the silver and took the film into the darkroom.

The sales manager at the *LA Weekly* looked at Jace's casual attire and the dark circles under his eyes, doubt obvious on his pudgy face. "You got some I.D. that proves you're a cop?"

Jace showed him his badge and identification card. The

man took a long time to examine the I.D. Jace wondered if he had a learning disability—there wasn't that much to read.

"If that's not enough, you can call Lieutenant Cosentino downtown, and he'll vouch for me."

"I guess I can check with the publisher. What do you need the names for, anyway?" He unwrapped a Milky Way bar and bit off half of it.

"I'm investigating the murder of someone who answered personals ads. Some of these women might have met him— one of them might even have been his killer."

The manager nodded as if that kind of thing happened every day. "How many different box numbers you got?"

"Seventeen."

"That's a lot of work," he complained. "I only keep the information for a month after the ad runs, you know. If they ran before that, I can't tell you anything . . . unless they're regulars, you know. These are transient ads—if I kept their addresses any longer, I'd need a warehouse to store them, and for what? It's not legally required, you know."

It was nearly an hour more before Jace left with the information he needed: the names of six women whose ads John Howard had starred in the last month. He glanced quickly at the list before he started the car. No Rusty. So, who said this job was going to be easy? He'd have to talk to all of them.

The woman at the *LA Reader* was more cooperative, but also had records on only the most recent advertisers.

"There's nothing says they got to give their real name and address," she pointed out.

"Without the right address, how would they get their responses?"

"Oh, yeah. Well, the names could be phony, anyway."

She handed him the information on thirteen box holders. Again, no Rusty. Jace thanked her and left.

As he was getting into the car, something occurred to him, and he went back in.

"Look," he said when he found her again, "it's possible the woman I'm looking for may have been answering the victim's ad. Can you look up his name and let me know if he ran a personal?"

She shook her head. "We're not cross-referenced by advertiser in the Matches section. Do you want to go through the box lists and see if you can find his name?"

Jace didn't, but he didn't want to leave the stone unturned. He sighed. "Yeah, that'd be great. Before I start, is there someplace I can get a sandwich and coffee around here?"

By the time Jace finished poring over the lists, it was after four. John Howard apparently hadn't placed an ad of his own in the *Reader* in the last month.

Jace realized he wasn't going to have time to go to *Swingers World* and *What's Up/LA* today, or he'd be late for the screening with Risha.

He decided to swing by the station and check in—he hadn't been there all day—and to give Liz Sandy's tux, which he'd picked up from the dry cleaner's that morning.

Liz was getting into her car as he pulled in.

"Where have you been all day?" she asked.

"Chasing my tail. What's happening?" He got the garment bag from the back seat and handed it to her.

"I got Howard's address file into the database—no matches with any of the others. Cosentino wanted to know where we were." She laid the bag in the trunk and shut it.

"What'd you tell him?"

"Nothing he wanted to hear. Ghiz left a message for you to call him. He said it wasn't urgent; you can call tomorrow. I won't be in tomorrow; I'm taking a personal day," Liz added.

"Anything wrong?" He wondered if Liz and Sandy had split up.

"No. Yes. I don't know." She shifted, turned to glance around, looked down at the ground. When she spoke again, her voice was quieter. "We're going to see a marriage counselor."

Oh. "Probably a good idea," he ventured.

She nodded reluctantly. "Probably is. I just feel weird, like we're going to air our dirty laundry in front of a stranger."

"Are you going to talk about . . . you know," he finished lamely.

"The Afternoon That Didn't Happen?"

He nodded.

"I don't think so." She paused. "I don't know, Jace, maybe—if that's what it takes."

Jace smoothed his slacks, straightened his sweater, and pushed the bell. A moment later, Elliott answered the door, and Jace could swear his face dropped a little when he saw who rang.

"Can I help you, Detective?"

"I'm here to see Risha," Jace said with a smile.

Elliott remained planted firmly in the doorway. "Ms. Cadigan has an engagement this evening."

"Right. With me. Will you tell her I'm here?"

It was another three seconds before Elliott stepped back and allowed Jace to enter. "Wait here." He left him in the living room while he went upstairs.

Jace saw the photographs on the living room wall had been changed . . . a new show in the home gallery? He recognized the calypso dancer as a shot he'd seen last week when Risha was showing him some of her work, but he hadn't seen the other two before. There was something almost hypnotic about the man in the center portrait, and something about his face that was vaguely familiar.

"Hi."

He turned. Risha was wearing her hair in a French braid like it had been at the party, but a few intentionally errant strands of auburn hair curled about the nape of her neck. Her white shoulders were bare above a pale-green silk peasant blouse, which was belted over a full, forest-green corduroy skirt. Her pale eyes caught and held him.

"You look terrific!" he said.

"Terrific, as in causing terror?" she asked with a smile. "Thank you," she added as he struggled for a comeback.

He laughed. "Shall we go?"

As they headed for the door, Jace said, "Who's the man in that photograph? He looks familiar."

He opened the door for her and they stepped out onto the porch. Jace was glad he'd had time to get his car washed.

"You wouldn't know him. It's my ex."

Why would Risha display a picture of her ex-husband? He hoped she wasn't carrying a torch, one of divorce's walking dead. He opened the car door for her and went around to the driver's side.

"He died two years ago," she explained when he got in.

Shit. A torch for a corpse—hard to compete with a dead man. "I'm sorry," he said as he started the car. "He looks young to have died."

"He was older than he looked," Risha said. "But let's not

talk about that and risk putting a damper on our evening. How was your week?''

Jace was almost sorry when the movie began because they had to stop talking. They discovered a mutual love of crossword puzzles, and discussed how last Sunday's had been one of Bursztyn and Tunick's best. He found Risha Cadigan to be a delightful, sexy woman, intelligent and funny. She seemed to be fascinated by his work, and begged him to tell her all about his cases. He had just been about to relate the story of the last twenty-four hours with the personals ads when the lights went down.

The movie had been excellent; they both agreed it was Academy Award material.

"I'm sort of glad you won passes to *Rambling Rose* instead of *JFK*," Risha said, "because I might have missed this one entirely otherwise.''

"You're probably right. I know you won't eat, but can I interest you in getting a drink? It's only a little after ten, and Kate Mantilini's is near here.'' He wouldn't have suggested Mantilini's if he'd had to buy dinner—it was beyond his dining budget—but for the price of a few drinks, he could afford to impress her.

When they were settled in a booth, Jace with a beer, Risha with a glass of port, he said, "You want to go see *JFK* with me when it opens?'' When she agreed, he continued, "I remember what I was doing the day he was assassinated like it was yesterday. My English teacher had sent me to grade papers in the vice principal's office—I was teacher's pet,'' he laughed, "—and he had a radio playing. When the news broke in that Kennedy had been shot, I ran back to the classroom, totally unable to speak. Later, the teacher told me that

I was white as a ghost when I came in; she thought I'd found out someone in my family had died. In a way, she was right.''

"I was in the library, shelving books," Risha said. "Suddenly, the head librarian screamed that Kennedy had been killed and the world was going to come to an end. She was completely hysterical and it took a while before we realized she hadn't gone over the edge, that it had really happened.''

Jace nodded, the hysteria of that day very familiar to him, even though he was fourteen when it had happened. Risha was so much younger, it must have been . . .

"How could you have been shelving books in a library? You must have been all of—what, two?—when it happened.''

Risha laughed. "Not quite that young—I'm older than I look. It was my grammar school library," she added.

Rusty mentally kicked herself. Good thing she hadn't volunteered the information that her junior college advisor had gotten her the job in the Oakland Public Library. The grammar school lie was credible—she could be eight years older than she appeared, but not twenty. She was going to have to watch what she said around Jace more closely, avoid giving firm clues to her age. She'd never had that problem with Gregor and Elliott and it hadn't even occurred to her to be careful before.

"Since you're into crossword puzzles," she said, "do you happen to play Scrabble?''

"God, I don't think I've played Scrabble since college! I used to be pretty good at it, though—I still remember one game where I played 'sequin' on the triple-word and got eighty points.'' He paid the bill and they stood to leave. "Do you play?''

"Gregor . . . my ex and I used to play all the time, but I haven't played since he died. I still have the set if you're up for a game."

Jace glanced at his watch. Eleven-twenty. "It's pretty late. Much as I'd like to, it's a school night," he explained with a laugh, "Can't solve crimes when I'm asleep. I'd like a rain check, though. How about Friday night? I shouldn't have to go in to work on Saturday and we can play all night if you want."

"You're on. But be prepared to be slaughtered," Rusty said. "I once played 'quixotic' for ninety-six points."

Although Jace had reluctantly declined Rusty's invitation to come in, they spent another hour talking in his car, parked in front of her house. Once during that time, Rusty saw Elliott peering at them through a tiny part in the living room drapes. Jace hadn't appeared to notice, but Rusty glared at the intrusion, and the part closed immediately.

"Have you ever had to kill anyone?" she asked Jace.

He nodded. "Once, when I was still in uniform, we were sent out on a family dispute—neighbors had called because of the screams. The woman had been beaten nearly to death by her husband, who was in shock, almost catatonic. When I turned to call an ambulance, the man grabbed my partner's gun and shot him. He had the gun to his own head when I killed him."

"You killed him to keep him from killing himself?" Rusty had an amused smile.

"I killed him for shooting my partner," Jace said matter-of-factly.

"Don't you trust the courts?"

"One way or another, that one wouldn't get punished. He had enough money to get a high-powered lawyer, psychiatric observation, the works. He was about to take himself out of the game, anyway. I just made sure,'' he shrugged.

"What happened to your partner and the wife?"

"The wife died the next morning from her injuries. My partner survived, but after he recovered, he quit the force and went to Alaska to work on the pipeline. Two weeks later, he was accidentally crushed to death at work.''

"How did you feel?"

"I guess it was just his time to go . . . Or did you mean about the guy I shot?"

Rusty nodded.

Jace paused to phrase his response as gently as possible. "The world is better off without some people—the man I killed was one of them.'' He turned to face her, his lips compressed. "Look, Risha, I deal with death every day. If I got emotionally involved, I wouldn't be able to do my job. Becoming hardened to murder is a job requirement, and it's the only way I can survive. If you can't accept that, we shouldn't go any farther.''

Rusty kissed him, felt his tight lips become soft and warm, the heat radiating from his body as he put his arms around her. When she felt her fangs tingle, she pulled her mouth away, but maintained the embrace.

"I can not only accept it, I can understand it," she whispered. "I'll see you Friday."

She went into the house.

CHAPTER
Seventeen

The night after their trip to Stirling Castle, Rusty awoke to find that Gregor wasn't next to her. It was unusual for him to wake before her, but not unheard of; perhaps he'd even slept in one of the other rooms.

There was a knock on the bedroom door.

"Miss Risha," Elliott called.

Rusty tied her robe shut. "Come in, Elliott." When he entered, she said, "Have you seen Gregor tonight?"

"No, ma'am. But there's a young man downstairs who says he has a message for you."

"For me?" They knew no one in Edinburgh, no one had their address there.

"I told him he could give it to me, but he said Baron Bathory instructed him to hand-deliver it to you."

"Please ask him to wait. I'll be down as soon as I get dressed."

A message from Gregor? Had he been too far away to

get back by dawn that morning? Perhaps he'd taken shelter, sending word that he would start for home at dark. Rusty put on jeans with the cashmere sweater Gregor had bought for her earlier that week, quickly ran a brush through her hair, and took the stairs two at a time. Gregor had been acting so strangely last night . . .

The man was standing in the drawing room, his back to the door, but Rusty recognized his long hair. "Duncan?"

"Aye." The watchman from Stirling turned to face her, a large paper bag in his hand. "He told me to come after dark and give ye this." He handed her an envelope.

"Gregor? Where is he?"

"I dinna ken. He give me fifty quid and said to bring ye the letter I'd find in the morn inside the last cannon."

Rusty looked at the envelope; her name and address were written neatly in Gregor's elegant copperplate. She wanted, simultaneously, to read the letter immediately and to never have to know what it contained.

"Thank you, Duncan. Just a minute, my wallet is around here somewhere—"

He put up a hand, "Nae. Your husband took care of me. I'll be going now." He stepped toward the door, then stopped, remembering the bag in his hands. "Och, almost forgot."

He held the bag out to her.

"His clothes," he explained. "He didna tell me to bring them, but they were at the wall when I fetched the envelope. I shook oot all the sand," he added as he left.

Elliott had built a coal fire in the drawing room. Rusty poured a glass of the Cachucha white port Gregor was so fond of, and sat in an armchair at the fireplace, the Black Watch tartan blanket over her legs, the envelope still unopened in her lap.

She took a sip, feeling the mellow warmth of the port in her mouth, almost as sweet as Gregor's venom. As long as the letter was unread, she could pretend he was still alive. She took another sip, staring into the glowing coals.

The glass was empty. It was time.

She opened the envelope.

My dearest Risha,

By the time you receive this, I shall have ceased to exist. Try to forgive me for saying goodbye in a letter—I could not stand to watch as I caused you pain, but neither could I go on. You must not blame yourself—with you, I found the happiness that had eluded me for centuries. The timing was poor, though, my dear; I had already had enough of life when we met. Undoubtedly, it is scant consolation now, but I stayed "alive" another twenty years because of you. With you, the world was almost new . . . for a while.

Don't take as long as I did to find love—when you hold off, thinking to wait for perfection, you lose What Could Have Been. What good is immortality if you are alone? We had two wonderful decades together, but nothing lasts forever, my darling, even for Us. Find someone to share with, for as long as you can both make it work, be it a century or a single year.

To the east, my long night is broken by a thin

band of light. I must go. It is time for me to see the dawn.

> *Gregor*

Jace heard from Ronnie Schaffer that a few clothing fibers had been found at the scene of Al Zamel's murder. "They don't match anything he had with him, so they might have belonged to the killer."

"Black velour?" Jace asked hopefully, remembering the fibers found at the Flores scene.

"Nope. Lavender rayon. You'll have the full report in a couple days—we're a little backed up here."

Jace thanked the criminalist and went back to trying to figure out how to work the computer on Liz's desk. He wasn't totally computer illiterate—he knew how to play games, and had a sketchy knowledge of word processing—but he was having a hell of a time trying to access the data base on the Westside Vampire. He wanted to cross-check the information he'd gotten from the *LA Weekly* and the *LA Reader* against the victims' phone books.

An hour later, he was still tapping keys in vain, punctuating each appearance of an error message with an exclamation of "Fuckshit!" It was grossly inconvenient for Liz to be out— she could have had the machine humming and the answer to the cross-check in minutes.

Jace wondered how the marriage counseling session was going. He hoped that Liz wouldn't mention him—if Sandy knew they'd been to bed together, he would certainly insist that she transfer to another partner, if not another station. Jace didn't want to lose Liz—partners were like spouses, lovers came and went. He thought about Risha Cadigan as a lover—her demeanor hinted at an intriguing combination of passion and reservation, the same combination that attracted him to Liz. He made a mental note to bring condoms for their date the next night.

The computer beeped in response to his last command, and displayed an error message that concluded with the options "Abort, Retry, or Ignore?" Jace chose "Abort" and turned off the computer with a sigh. Liz could handle it tomorrow.

Even though traffic on the San Diego Freeway was light once he'd passed the airport, it still took Jace an hour to get to the Orange County offices of *Swingers World*. The receptionist was classic bimbo, with big platinum hair and far too much make-up; the collagen injections in her lips were uneven, giving her a comical look, like a parody of Monroe's famous pout. She wiggled her long red nails in a cutesy hello to Jace, then stopped mid-wave to examine a tiny chip on her middle fingernail.

"Where's the advertising department?" Jace asked as she got a bottle of polish out of her desk.

"It's all advertising, honey. You want to place an ad? Through that door on the right." She shook the polish and Jace could hear the rattle of the stirring beads in the bottle. With her other hand, she pushed a buzzer that unlocked the door.

"Thanks." He stepped hurriedly through the door before she uncapped the noxious smell of nail polish.

A balding black man in loud plaid slacks that fit so badly the white linings of his pockets showed had his feet up on his desk behind the counter, a copy of the *Racing Form* in his face. Without looking over the paper, he muttered, "Fill out the form on the counter."

"I'm not here to place an ad," Jace began.

"We're not hiring," the man told his *Racing Form*.

"I'm not looking for work, either. I'm a police detective. How about putting that down and helping me," Jace suggested.

The man made a melodramatic sigh, put down his paper, and came over to the counter. "Your I.D.?"

Jace showed him.

"LAPD. No jurisdiction here." The man turned to go back to his paper as if that settled things. Jace grabbed his arm. "Hey!" The man jerked his arm back. "I'm not Rodney King—keep your fuckin' LAPD hands offa me!"

Great start. Jace knew he was going to have a problem getting this guy to cooperate. "Sorry, sir." He put on his most disarming smile. "I just need a little information you can give me." He slid a twenty across the counter, but it was ignored, pointedly.

The man sat down and leaned back, putting his feet back on the desk. "I ain't giving you shit, man. What are you going to do about it?"

"Where can I find your supervisor?"

"You're looking at him. Fuck off." The man buried his face in the *Racing Form* again. Jace pocketed his twenty.

"I'll just come back with a subpoena," Jace warned.

"You do that," the man told his paper, "and see where it gets you. Freedom of the press, asshole—I don't have to tell you nothing. Get lost."

When Jace got back to the lobby, the receptionist's desk was empty, the bimbo nowhere to be seen. He walked around to look at the security system—a series of three unlabeled buzzers that, presumably, unlocked each of the three doors from the lobby.

"Hey, Gates-lover!" The balding man stood in his doorway. "Get away from there! You got no search warrant and you're on private property. Now get out before I call the cops."

Once again, Jace opted for "Abort" and left. Two blocks away, he pulled into a Unocal station, and parked next to the pay phones.

"Ellen Fisher's office."

"Ms. Fisher, please."

"Who's calling?"

"Jace . . . Jacob Levy." While he waited for Ellen to pick up, Jace read the graffiti on the glass wall of the booth. DARYL GATES EATS SHIT. Apparently the L.A. chief of police was nearly as popular in Orange County as he was at home.

"I'm sorry, Mr. Levy, but Ms. Fisher isn't in right now." Jace knew the setup at Ellen's office; it wouldn't have taken that long to determine she wasn't in.

"It's Detective Levy. Tell her it's business . . . and important."

When Ellen finally came on the line, Jace ran down the problem with getting box holders' names from *Swingers World*, and asked her to get him "a subpoena or something."

"I'll see what I can do about getting you a material witness warrant, Jace, but it won't be fast." Ellen's tone was businesslike; she was not pleased to be talking to him.

Jace shook his head. Nothing ever went fast in this job. "What good will a warrant do? He was yelling about freedom of the press."

"He might be less concerned about the First Amendment after a night or two in jail, particularly when he finds out he can get out as soon as he turns over the information you want."

"Okay, get me one."

"I'll see what I can do, but no promises. Call me Monday morning. At work," she emphasized unnecessarily.

Jace decided he'd never understand women. He filled the gas tank and headed north, back to L.A.

The advertising manager at *What's Up/LA* was more cooperative . . . and more strangely dressed than the staff at *Swingers World*. His get-up was straight out of *The Rocky Horror Picture Show*—black corset and stockings over hairy legs, lipstick and eyeliner—and Jace was beginning to wonder if weird attire was a requirement for working at a local newspaper when the UPS man walked in wearing a gorilla mask. While Dr. Frank N. Furter handed Jace the information he'd requested, the UPS gorilla wished the newspaper's staff a happy Halloween. Jace was relieved to find he hadn't entered the Twilight Zone, he'd only forgotten the date.

He looked over the list when he got back to the car: *What's Up/LA* didn't keep the names of advertisers, only initials and mailing addresses. There were two with the first initial "R"—Jace wondered if either of them were named Rusty.

". . . so after I saw the photo in the newspaper, I knew it was the same dude who was in the bar last Thursday night," the waitress from the airport hotel told Jace. "I remember him because he tried to cop a feel on me."

The waitress, Betty Pohl, had been at Jace's desk when he had returned to the station. She'd been waiting for over an hour with information about Alvin Zamel's murder, and was just about to leave when he'd arrived.

"Was he alone?"

"Yeah, at first, but he bought a drink for a chick who came in by herself half an hour later. They left together."

"Tell me what you remember about the woman." Jace opened his notebook and shoved aside the papers on his desk to find a place to put it.

"She wasn't no more'n thirty, kinda pretty with long dark hair. She was wearing this clingy lavender mini-dress, a low-cut dealie with long sleeves. It's funny," she laughed, "but I thought she looked like one of them, y'know, flower childs from the sixties, but she drank like an ol' lady."

Jace looked up. "What do you mean, Ms. Pohl?"

"Call me Betty. Ol' ladies drink sherry, port, elderberry wine—y'know that sweet kinda stuff? She asked for port, but we don't get much call for that at the hotel, so she, like, settled for sherry." Betty shook her head with a "no accounting for taste" expression. "Me, I wanna drink, I'm gonna have me some Jim Beam. Takes forever to get a buzz off that ol' lady stuff, y'know."

"What else do you remember?" Port was an unusual request in California bars—Jace had been surprised when Risha had ordered it in Kate Mantilini's the previous night—but he thought it was probably a common drink in Europe. "Did she have an accent?"

"Can't say as I noticed one. They just had the one drink together before they left. The dude didn't even leave me no tip, not 'less you count the seventeen cents change they didn't wait for."

"Betty, do you think she could have been a man dressed like a woman, a drag queen?"

The waitress laughed, a full-throated chortle. "No siree, not a chance, not with that dress she was wearin'—it didn't hide nothin', y'know?" She laughed again. "But it would have served the dude right if he got her back to his room and found cock-and-balls under her panties, wouldn't it?"

Another round of questions and answers determined that Betty hadn't seen Alvin Zamel, nor the woman, before, although she was sure she would recognize the woman again and agreed to meet with the police artist.

"Thank you very much for coming in, Betty." Jace stood to escort the waitress to the door. "We'll be in touch with you."

"Sure thing—you come into the bar, have a beer on me. You cops have a rough job, y'know? Not as rough as mine," she laughed, "but you-all get a bad rap on accounta some bad eggs."

Jace opened the door for her, and Betty looked pleasantly surprised at the courtesy. He'd turned his back to return to his desk when he heard a tapping at the door. Betty stuck her head back in.

"I just remembered somethin' might help you some," she said. "When I give the dude the tab, I heard him call the chick Rusty."

Elliott was worried about Risha dating the cop—given her circumstances, he thought it was risky at best, and possibly dangerous. It was conceivable that she was using Levy to keep an eye on the investigation, but Elliott couldn't see the sense of it. Why didn't she just move out of town? What if Levy were seeing her because she was a suspect? (Did cops do that?) Elliott didn't like the situation at all—it wouldn't be easy to protect Risha if she insisted on putting her head in the lion's mouth. He vowed to approach the matter before she went out to feed that evening.

The line at the shipper's moved very slowly. Elliott was not surprised at their inefficiency—look how the counter help was dressed. Elliott thought Halloween costumes were silly on adults, and terribly unprofessional. The patron at the head of the line concluded his business, and everyone moved up one space. Elliott shoved the crate of silver forward with his foot. At this rate, he wouldn't be home before Risha woke— it was getting dark by five o'clock these days.

It was after four when he pushed the crate up to the counter and hefted it onto the scale. The clerk—a pear-shaped woman with gray pigtails and painted-on freckles—looked at the address label.

"I'm sorry, sir, but this is over the limit for overseas packages." She didn't sound sorry at all; Elliott detected a note of relief in her voice that she wouldn't have to lift the crate. "Here are the guidelines," she added, dismissing him with a brochure. "Next!"

"Just a minute," Elliott interrupted, blocking the next patron's access to the counter. "I sent the same size box to the same address two days ago. There wasn't any problem then."

"It's not the dimensions that are the problem, sir," she said wearily, "it's the weight. We don't take single packages this heavy. You'll have to break it down so that no one package weighs more than fifteen pounds. Next!"

Elliott stood his ground. "Well, what do you do if someone wants to ship a television overseas? You can't break a TV down into lighter packages."

"Appliances are accepted only at our offices at LAX. The address is on the brochure . . . sir. Please move aside so I can help the next person," she added with finality.

Elliott restrained the urge to punch out the silly-looking woman, and hoisted up the crate. On the way to the airport office, he got caught in rush-hour traffic exacerbated by a three-car fender-bender in the middle lane of the freeway. It took him forty minutes to travel six miles. He hated L.A. The only thing it had going for it was a large selection of movie theaters.

He finally pulled into the parking lot, and managed with some difficulty to wrestle the crate out of the Honda's trunk and up to the front door of the shipper . . . just in time to see the sign being turned to "closed." He tried the glass door anyway, but it had already been locked. The young man on the other side pointed to the sign, and mouthed "Closed," perhaps on the assumption that Elliott was illiterate. Elliott pounded on the door, but to no avail. The young man just walked away. Elliott kicked the door, picked up his crate, and struggled it back into the car.

On his way back to the freeway, he passed the offices of Federal Express. They were still open. Elliott parked in the handicap space next to the door and hauled the crate out again. His arms and back were aching from carrying the damned Bathory silver around, and he was surly when he shoved it onto the counter, daring the clerk to give him a hassle. This time, there was no problem—although the shipping cost more than he'd expected, the box would be in London by Monday.

He got back to the Honda fifteen minutes later. There was a $125 ticket on the windshield for parking in a handicap space without a permit.

By the time he got home, Risha had left.

CHAPTER
Eighteen

One of the nice things about the end of Daylight Savings Time was that the stores were open for several hours after dark, so Rusty could go shopping. She drove over to the Westside Pavilion and found a parking space right behind Nordstrom. She shopped only in upscale stores with private dressing rooms; it wouldn't do to try on clothes in a common room—someone might notice that her skin cast no reflection in the mirrors. Three hours and seven hundred dollars netted her several colorful additions to her winter wardrobe, although it was still too warm for her to wear much of it yet. She was particularly fond of the ivory leather granny boots and the matching cashmere mid-calf dress. She was tired of wearing black all the time, and vowed that her black clothes would be worn only for hunting for a while.

She put the packages in the trunk of the BMW and slammed it shut. Although she generally waited until after midnight to feed, she was hungry, and didn't want to wait. She needed to find a part of town that was fairly deserted this early, and decided to head out to the West Valley. Most of the people there were yuppies with families and they tended to stay in evenings. All the trick-or-treaters were safely home by now, gorging themselves on candy.

She was cruising west on Ventura Boulevard when she passed a former 7-Eleven that had been boarded up. A large sign on the front directed customers to the new location two blocks away. Rusty parked her car in the lot, and walked north on Balboa Boulevard. She knew there was a park at Balboa and Burbank which was likely to be inhabited only by homeless at this hour.

She saw no other pedestrians on her twenty-minute walk, even though Balboa was a major Valley street with a fair amount of car traffic. People in the Valley walked even less than those who lived in town, and often drove even short distances.

Balboa Park was large, boasting a baseball diamond, tennis and basketball courts, and brick barbecues, but any gatherings there that evening had already ended, and the few lights that were still on illuminated little of the park. Rusty headed past the tennis courts, trolling an area obscured from the boulevards.

"Hey, *mamacita*, joo lookin' for a li'l treat for Hall'ween?"

Two Mexican men in their twenties were lounging on a park bench, passing a joint back and forth, a cooler full of beer next to them on the ground. The skinny one wore a black hairnet low over his forehead, his pomaded hair gleaming through the net even in the low light. The other one had spoken; his T-shirted belly hung over his dirty jeans, the sides of his head shaved so his hair looked like a bird had dropped a toupee on top of his head.

Rusty smiled and walked over to them. "Could be. What did you have in mind?"

Hairnet hooted and Toupee held out the joint to her. "Joo wanna *cerveza*?" Hairnet offered.

Rusty accepted the joint and the beer with a grin.

"*Gracias, amigos*. Mind if I sit here?" She backed up to the bench and wiggled her ass between them to make a space.

Toupee copped a feel of her ass as she settled in, his grin exposing a gold tooth in the front of his mouth. "Joo can sit ri' here, mama," he said, patting his crotch. Hairnet hooted again.

"Don't mind if I do," Rusty said, climbing onto Toupee's lap. She put her arms around his neck and planted her lips hard against his.

"Do it, honey!" Hairnet whooped. "I'm nex'!"

Toupee shoved his hand up under her sweater and squeezed one nipple roughly while he ground his groin against her ass, his tongue invading her mouth. She felt Hairnet's hand under her skirt and pulled out of the kiss.

"Uh-uh—one at a time." She turned to Toupee. "Let's go over there," she pointed to a dark area under the far trees. "When we're finished, I'll fuck you," she promised Hairnet as Toupee picked her up to carry her to seclusion.

"Doan take too long, homie," Hairnet called to them. "I'm a'ready hard!"

"Jus' hol' it, man—I gonna take as long this pussy wan'," Toupee yelled back.

He deposited Rusty in the grass under an oak and pushed up her skirt, moaning in pleasure when he discovered she wore no panties. He unzipped his jeans and pulled out his short thick penis. "Joo wanna suck this, mama?" He dropped his jeans to his ankles and stroked his cock in front of her face.

"Umm," purred Rusty, "I want to sit on that, honey. Get down here with your back against the tree."

When he was seated, Rusty straddled him. He grabbed her ass with one hand, while the other reached under her sweater for her breast. He found the bowie knife she had against her lower back, pulled it out, and tossed it on the grass near them.

"Joo doan need tha' here, *mamacita*," he explained as he tried to penetrate her. "I ain' gon' hurt joo . . . unle' joo wan' me to."

Rusty moaned theatrically and kissed Toupee while she squirmed away from his cock. As he attempted to reach his target again, she sunk her fangs into his neck. He roared in pleasure and Rusty felt him spurting simultaneously from cock and carotid.

When she was full, Toupee had lost consciousness and his cock had gone soft under her. She climbed off his limp body and straightened her black skirt and sweater.

When she turned to find her knife, she saw Hairnet standing a few feet away, rubbing his own erection, excited by what he'd been watching.

"Now me, baby—I fuck joo mo' better. I fuck joo all ni' 'til joo can' see," he promised. "Joo can watch me now, homie—see how a real man do pussy," he said to Toupee's unmoving form as he reached for Rusty.

Rusty was no longer interested in games, nor in further feeding. She hit Hairnet with a strong uppercut to the jaw, and heard the sound of bone breaking as he went down and lay still.

It took her a minute or two to find her knife in the grass.

She was heading over to Toupee's body, the knife in her hand shimmering in the moonlight, when she heard an inarticulate yell from Hairnet.

She turned to see him holding a gun, pointing it at her with a shaky hand. He fired once—the shot went wild. She turned and ran, but wasn't out of range before he got off another shot.

Rusty felt the bullet enter her back like she'd been hit with a sledgehammer. She stumbled and dropped the knife, the pain spreading like fire across her torso, but she regained her feet and took off in a panicked burst of speed.

Liz apparently didn't feel much like talking; since she'd dropped her purse in her desk drawer, she'd answered Jace in monosyllables, and had avoided eye contact. He didn't push, figuring she'd tell him when she was ready. She spent the hour cross-checking the advertiser names against the computer.

Jace had planned to spend the previous evening contacting women who'd placed personals ads, but had found that five of the first six addresses on his lists were private post boxes or work addresses that weren't open at night. The exception was a thin blonde named Gay Dozois—Jace guessed her to be anorexic; she was 5'7" and weighed about 110—who was painfully shy and embarrassed about having run a personals ad. She still had the eight responses to her ad, including the form letter from John Howard, but she had never gotten up the nerve to meet any of them. After the shock of being contacted by the police, she never would.

"No matches," Liz announced tersely.

Jace nodded wearily. They would have to interview all the women in person.

Liz read his mind. "I'll do it, Jace. They're more likely to talk to another woman." She scanned the three lists. "You want to get names and home addresses on the box renters?"

"Yeah, as soon as I see Ronnie Schaffer. She called this morning—they've got the tox reports on Cabot, Flores, and Kaufman. There are links, but she said it was too complicated to explain over the phone."

Liz looked interested for the first time that day. "A tox link? Like drugs?" Jace shrugged. "I'm coming with you." She slid her feet into her pumps and got her purse.

When he started the car, Jace said casually, "So, how'd it go with the marriage counselor yesterday?" He'd pulled out of the parking lot before she responded.

"Okay, I guess. The doc's pretty sharp and we both felt comfortable with him, but it's not going to be a quick fix. We'll be going every Tuesday night for a few months at least." She stared out the passenger window like the view wasn't something she had been seeing several times a day for years.

"Did you . . . ?" Jace left the question hanging.

Liz sighed, looked straight ahead. "No. I lied."

Jace parked the car in the lot behind the crime lab and they got out. Ronnie was in a meeting with the director, so they waited, Liz thumbing through a coffee-stained issue of *Forensic Journal*. Jace stared unseeing at the framed blood classification chart on the wall, relieved that at least Liz wasn't putting in for a transfer.

"I hope you're in the mood for puzzles," Ronnie said when she returned to her cubicle.

"We live for puzzles," Jace answered. "What have you got?"

"We found some alcohol in all three of them, small traces

of cocaine in Kaufman's body, and methedrine in Flores's. The amounts were too small to cause death . . . or even unconsciousness,'' she added, anticipating the question on Liz's lips. "But that's not the puzzle." She handed them copies of the three lab reports. "Look at the highlighted parts."

Jace read over Liz's shoulder. "Unidentified protein in carotid wound." Liz flipped over the Cabot report and Jace saw the same wording on the Flores tox, then again on Kaufman's. He looked up at Ronnie. "Give it to us in layman's terms, Ronnie. I don't understand what this means."

"Unfortunately, neither do we. There was a foreign substance in each of the neck wounds, but not in Cabot's or Flores's chest wounds or at Kaufman's penis amputation, so it wasn't something on the knife. It was a protein, but nothing that's been recorded. It had some chemical properties similar to hallucinogens like mescaline, but also to venom like you'd find in poisonous snakes or spiders. As near as we can tell, it's not plant protein; it's animal, and possibly human. Did you find any indications that the vics were involved in any kind of weird religious practices that maybe involved cannibalism?''

"Nothing," Liz said, shaking her head. "Could the knife wounds have been concealing bites?"

Ronnie shrugged. "Ask King—bodies are his bailiwick. But I can tell you the protein doesn't match any of our known venoms. You might check exotic species importers or with the zoo. Hell, maybe it's some new designer drug that's injected directly into the carotid." She scratched the back of her head, scrunching up her face. "There's something else. The protein slightly altered the cells it contacted, changing the size and shape of the nucleii."

"Carcinogenic?" Jace asked.

The serologist shrugged again. "Dunno. The samples were too small. But whatever it is, it's intensely concentrated and powerful—it changed any living cells it contacted, without disturbing the cell wall . . . either that, or it instantly heals the point of entry. Maybe your vampire works in a biomedical research lab or does secret testing on chemical warfare?"

"You got something that spells this out in scientific language we can take to the Army?" Jace looked at the reports again.

"All ready to go." Ronnie handed Jace a manila envelope. "There're two copies of everything, plus the numbers of some serologists I know who do government research. Tell 'em I sent you, maybe it'll cut through some of the red tape. But, I warn you, they're a closemouthed bunch. Try Bob Tiedge at UCLA first—he quit government research several years ago, and might be willing to talk off the record. Also, he's an entomologist, knows all about insects."

While Liz went to interview women who'd placed personals ads, Jace headed over to UCLA. The department secretary had made an appointment for him with Dr. Tiedge after his eleven o'clock seminar. He could start running down the box holders' home addresses after lunch.

Robert Tiedge looked like an aging hippie—mostly bald on the top, his wispy gray-brown hair tied into a thin ponytail that trailed eight inches down the back of his worn tweed jacket. He wore a small yin-yang earring in his left lobe. Jace tried to remember which ear meant the wearer was gay, but gave up. After all, it didn't matter.

Tiedge leaned back in his chair to read the toxicology reports, parking his feet on his desk. His brows knit, and periodically, he would flip back to check something on a previous page.

"Well?" Jace prodded. "Do you know what it is?"

"A real conundrum, Detective. Make yourself comfortable, this may take a while." The entomologist pulled a reference book off his shelf and paged through it rapidly while Jace moved a stack of papers off the other chair and began to lower himself into it.

"Freeze!" Jace stopped mid-squat. Tiedge reached under Jace to the seat, then said, "Okay, now you can sit. So that's where you've been," he said to something in his hand.

Jace stood to look. Tiedge held a palm-sized black spider which he dropped into a terrarium on the bookcase, latching the lid.

"I don't know how he got out, but he's been missing for two days. Sorry I yelled, but you could have killed him."

"You were worried about the spider?" Jace scanned the bottom, back, and under the chair before gingerly sitting down. "What about what he could have done to me?"

"He's not poisonous, and you're heavy."

Tiedge went back to the report, comparing it to the reference book. He flipped more pages, then slammed the book shut and got another one, finally closing it with a shake of his head.

"Any of the people involved spend time in unexplored areas of South America or Africa?" he asked Jace hopefully.

"Not the victims. Is the protein from there?"

"Fuck if I know. All I can tell you is that it's not from any classified insect or arachnid species. It's not my field, but it doesn't look like snake venom either. Can you get me a sample?"

"Let me use your phone." Jace called Ronnie at the lab,

but she was out to lunch. He left a message for her to call Tiedge.

"What can you tell me, Doctor?"

"Not much without studying a sample. But this isn't a man-made chemical, if that helps—it's animal venom—but I'll be fucked if I know what kind. Maybe after I study the sample . . ."

"How long will that take?" Jace stood, looking carefully where he put his feet.

Tiedge shrugged. "If we're lucky—and the sample is big enough for all the testing—couple months, maybe. It'd help to see the bite marks—can I get photos? Color would be best."

"If there were bites, they were obscured by a knife afterwards, but I'll get what we have to you."

Tiedge shook his head. "Leave me your number. If you haven't heard from me by the end of the year, give me a jingle."

Risha put the tiles on the board. "TOXIC. Sixteen, nineteen, twenty-two, twenty-four, twenty-seven," she announced, recording her score. "That puts me twenty-one points ahead."

"What's OE?" Jace asked, forcing himself to study the board. He'd been admiring her hair in the light from the fireplace and restraining the urge to reach over to stroke it.

"Is that a challenge? You'll lose your turn if it's a word," she reminded him. She had sensuous lips, Jace noticed.

"I'd settle for hearing you use 'ou-ee' in a sentence."

"No problem." She thought for a second, and a mischievous grin quirked her lips. "Ou-ee ou-ah-ah ting-tang walla-walla bing-bang," she sang.

Jace laughed aloud and sang along for the next line—

except for emphasis, identical to the first. "If that's the best you can do, I challenge you—I know lyrics from "Purple People-Eater" aren't in the dictionary."

Risha reached over the couch for the Scrabble players' bible, giving Jace a nice glimpse of her ass. He realized there was no panty line under her jade-green jumpsuit.

"Right year. Wrong song. It's from 'Witch Doctor.' " She grinned and handed the book to him. He flipped pages with a smug smile, which fell when he found OE after ODYSSEY.

" 'A whirlwind off the Faeroe Islands,' " he read aloud. "How the hell did you know that?"

She grinned. "I don't suppose you'd believe I've been there? You lose a turn, Detective." She drew five tiles.

Elliott came into the study in an obviously shammed preoccupation with finding something in the desk in the corner. After rustling aimlessly through drawers while surreptitiously casting sidelong glances at the pair on the couch, he finally chose a stapler to carry out of the room with him, muttering "excuse me" as he left, leaving the door open.

"I don't think your assistant likes me much," Jace said. "Is he jealous or does he just not like cops?" He got up and closed the door again.

"He thinks he's being protective. Think of him as my bodyguard and pretend he doesn't exist," she suggested.

"Kind of small and old for a bodyguard, isn't he? He reminds me more of a chaperone at a school dance. You know, the one who made sure you weren't dancing too close?"

Risha laughed, her lips parting momentarily to show glistening teeth. Jace shifted the Scrabble board and sat down so that their thighs touched. He could smell the dusty rose scent of her perfume. God, he wanted to kiss her! He was just about to do so when he realized she'd spoken.

"What did you ask? I'm sorry—I was thinking about kissing you."

"My question can wait," she smiled.

He kissed her, enveloping her in his arms, shifting his body against hers. He felt the same electricity as when they'd kissed in the car the other night, the passion she was keeping just below the surface, and it excited him. His hand moved partway down her back—no bra!—and around toward her breast as his tongue moved past her teeth. She continued to respond to the kiss, but softly stopped his hand's progression.

He moved his mouth to the side of her neck, and she made an almost-inaudible gasp, putting both arms around him. He could feel her nipples hard against his chest. He ran his left hand up the nape of her neck, deep into her loose auburn hair, and gently pulled her head back, moving his lips to the base of her throat, while his right hand cupped her breast. His thumb toyed with her nipple, which became more erect. She shifted, unconsciously thrusting slightly with her pelvis as his tongue trailed down her breastbone. He felt, more than heard, her moan, and his cock hardened. She pulled away, her eyes glittering, and licked her lips.

"We shouldn't do this," she protested weakly.

Jace unbuttoned the top button on her jumpsuit and slipped his hand inside to her breast. Her eyes closed slightly. "Why not?"

She put her hand over his to move it, but didn't. "Elliott might come back in." She squeezed his hand.

"Where's your bedroom?" He unbuttoned two more buttons and pulled her breast free, bending his head to suck the nipple. This time, her moan was audible.

* * *

Rusty idly twirled a finger in Jace's damp chest hair and then kissed him behind the ear, feeling her fangs tingle at the heat of his blood. Each of the several times she'd come, she'd had to pull herself back to keep from biting into his neck. Once she'd bitten the pillow instead, leaving two small punctures wet with venom. Well, they weren't the only wet spots on the bed.

The sex had been wonderful, more exciting and satisfying than it had been with . . . She couldn't remember his name. Marshall. She was sure she hadn't made love this intensely since the night she crossed over; if she didn't know better, she'd swear she could feel the throbbing of her pulse in her vagina as she basked in the afterglow.

"I've got an idea," Jace said, stroking her hair.

"Is it as good as the last one you had?—or should I say the last two?" she smiled.

"Let's sleep for a few hours, and then drive up to Santa Barbara for breakfast." He yawned and stretched. It was after two.

Rusty remembered that basking in the afterglow could lead to problems.

"I can't, Jace, I still have to work tonight. I'm afraid you can't stay over."

"I'll watch you work . . . or you can wake me up when you're done. I know you won't have any problem getting me up," he leered comically.

She pushed him firmly toward the edge of the bed. "It'd be too distracting with you here. Go home, stud."

He sat on the edge of the bed and looked at his clothes scattered across the floor. "I'll pick you up for breakfast when you're done, then," he said.

"I've got to sleep sometime," she protested.

He turned around to kiss her. "How soon can I see you again?"

"Tomorrow night, if you want." She kissed him. "Now, go before my watchful chaperone tells you to leave."

Jace sighed getting up, and pulled on his slacks. "If you insist. But it means I'll be spending tomorrow working instead of playing with you. Helluva way to spend a Saturday."

CHAPTER
Nineteen

It was eleven-thirty when Jace finally woke from a deep, dream-free sleep. He stretched in luxury, smiling as he replayed the evening with Risha Cadigan. The memory hardened his semi-erect cock; he touched it, then decided to "save it" for her that night, and got out of bed to piss.

He was fascinated with Risha. She made love with passion and abandon, yet he felt there was something she held back—he didn't know what it was, but he longed to break through her inhibition to experience it. He hadn't felt that just in bed, either. Even her conversation, apparently open and candid, hinted at the untold. A secret past? He realized she hadn't mentioned her history directly at all, merely as background to tales of visits to other places. He still didn't even know if she had been married to Gregor, nor how long they'd been together. He ought to do a little conversational prying.

He got into the shower and let the massage head pummel his back until he began to feel guilty about the amount of water he was wasting. He thought about going over to Risha's—if she were still in bed, he could surprise her by climbing in with her—but he knew he'd have a helluva time getting past Elliott. Besides, she'd seemed pretty firm about expecting him no earlier than six.

He turned off the water and heard a male voice in the living room. ". . . here for another hour if you get in." The answering machine clicked off as he got to the phone. He went to replay the message. It was from King. He had another victim of The Westside Vampire.

"The autopsy is scheduled for Monday, but I wanted you to see this," King said as he pulled open the refrigerated drawer that held the body. He pulled the sheet back.

Jace saw no wound. "What makes you think he's one of ours?"

"Look carefully at the right side of his neck." He handed Jace a penlight.

"I see two round scars. No knife hole."

"He was brought in to Sherman Oaks Community Thursday night, his blood pressure and pallor indicating he'd experienced significant blood loss. The cause of death yesterday morning appears to be massive myocardial infarction, following a stroke—caused by the blood loss. Those two scars are the most recent by a year, and seem to be the only possibility for the blood-loss site. They're teeth marks—fangs, to be exact. Notice there are no teeth marks between them, like you'd see with, say, a wolf or dog? If it weren't for their size and spacing, I'd guess snake because of their configuration."

"These scars are more than two days old," Jace protested.

"Remember the weird round scar on Alvin Zamel's neck last week? Plus, if tox finds that same protein in the punctures

. . . The reports indicated it may have instantaneously healed the cell walls it contacted; it could have done the same thing, larger scale, to the skin and carotid punctures. The substance could be a miracle healing drug if it isn't fatal—I wish we knew what it was.''

King covered the body and shoved the drawer shut. Jace scratched the stubble on his cheeks as he followed the M.E. to his desk.

"Blood loss, fang marks, magic venom, incredible strength. If I didn't know better, I'd swear you were all pulling some massive practical joke on me—you know, wouldn't it be funny to watch Levy trying to hunt down a real vampire?" He sat on the corner of King's desk—which he thought to be remarkably neat and clean.

"It's a helluva mystery to me, too, but I'll be damned if I'm going to be responsible for the uproar if you list this as a vampire attack.'' King scribbled on a piece of paper and handed it to Jace. "Here's the name of the investigating detective at West Valley. She's got a witness.''

Jackie Stanford was typing the report with one finger when Jace entered. "Shit!" She backspaced and retyped a letter. "My partner usually does the typing, but he's out of town 'til Monday.'' She stood up to shake hands. "Levy, right? Darrell King said you'd be over about the Jorge Martinez case.''

"He told me you had a witness." He sat in the chair she offered.

"Yeah, but questions-and-answers are a muther with him—his jaw is wired shut and he's mostly been unconscious since he was brought in. I was about to go back to the hospital to give it another try—if you want to come along, I'll fill you in on the way.''

* * *

"I got the call midnight Thursday after the uniforms had responded to shots fired at Balboa Park about eleven," Stanford said as she drove east toward Van Nuys Boulevard. "They found Martinez under a tree in a coma—smiling, for Crissakes!—his pants around his ankles. Juan Figuroa was lying fifteen feet west with a shattered jaw and a freshly fired Saturday night special in his hand, two shells spent. We recovered one of the bullets yesterday morning twenty feet south of where the men were, but the other's nowhere to be found. I'll be damned if I can figure out what happened."

"Figuroa wasn't shooting at Martinez?" Jace was getting a headache.

"Negative. We also found a knife not far from the shell. No one was stabbed, either, and there didn't appear to be blood on the bowie, but the lab's got it." She shook her head. "I've got two weapons, a vic with massive blood loss, and no point of entry. They didn't cover this at the academy."

Jace perked up. "A bowie knife? Make sure Ronnie Schaffer is on it, will you? It could be the weapon used in a pattern we've got."

"King told me about your serial—I'm sorry I missed the meeting last month. My partner's got the bulletin someplace, but I haven't had time to look for it since this happened."

Jace filled her in on the background, finishing as they reached the nurses' station.

Stanford quickly determined that Figuroa was conscious and they took a pad of paper and pencil into his room. It was impossible to tell what he looked like because his head was swathed in bandages, only his sunken eyes and a patch of dark hair visible through the white.

"Mr. Figuroa, I'm Detective Stanford, and this is Detective Levy. Do you speak English?'' The mummy nodded. "We'd like to ask you some questions if you feel up to it now.'' She placed the pad and pencil on the bed next to him. "Just write your answers here.''

Figuroa picked up the pencil and printed in block letters: JORGE DED—CUNT KILD.

"Martinez was killed by a woman?'' Jace asked, moving next to the bed. Figuroa nodded vigorously. "Did you see it happen?''

He nodded again and wrote furiously. Stanford moved to the other side of the bed so they both could see as he wrote. CUNT FUCK HIM—MI TURN NEX—CUNT HIT ME—STRONG— HAD NIFE—YO SHOOT. He began to hand the pad to Jace, but then pulled it back and added SELF DEFENS!

"She broke your jaw?''

He nodded.

"With what?''

Figuroa balled up his right fist and pointed to it with his left.

"A woman shattered your jaw with her fist?'' Stanford's doubt was blatant. "How many times did she hit you?''

Figuroa held up one finger, shrugged.

"Glass jaw,'' Stanford muttered.

Figuroa shook his head and pointed with the pencil to STRONG on the pad, then underlined it twice.

"Could the woman have been in drag? A man dressed like a woman?'' Jace asked.

The mummy shook his head, vehemently.

"Did you fuck her?'' Jace asked.

Figuroa held two fingers tightly together in front of Jace's face, then wrote, COPPED FEEL.

"You were gangbanging some chick in the park and she

cut Martinez and punched you out, is that right?'' Stanford's tone was hostile.

Figuroa was becoming agitated. He wrote fast: NO CUT—FUCK JORG—HIT ME—THEN NIFE—I SHOT 2 TIME HIT 1.

Jace looked until he understood. ''You hit her with one of the shots?''

Figuroa moaned, nodded, dropped back against the pillows.

''Are you sure it hit?''

He nodded again.

''Where did it hit her?''

He sat up again, groaning, and pointed over his shoulder at his back, then to a place midway down his chest, then over his back again. He dropped heavily back to the pillows, closed his eyes.

The nurse came in and told them the patient had to sleep now and that they would have to continue another time. She moved the pencil and pad to the side table, and lowered the upper half of the bed. Jace tore off the used pages and pocketed them before they left.

As he and Stanford walked back to her car, Jace asked if there'd been any gunshot victims reported since the Thursday night incident.

''I'll check into it, but I don't think much of his story. Anyone who was shot in the middle of the back isn't going to get very far before they die, and there weren't any other bodies in or near the park, and no blood. Besides, he didn't explain how Martinez lost all that blood.''

Jace said nothing. He didn't want to sound like a fool. Did vampires fall into the category of Impossible? Or merely Improbable?

* * *

". . . and now that that cop Levy is nosing around, it just seems risky to stay on here," Elliott finished as he took out the eyeshadow palette. He'd just started packing books when she called him.

Rusty didn't want to hear it. She liked the L.A. house, and the warm evenings, even in winter. Her series in *City of Angels* was just taking off, and she needed to be in L.A. to complete it. There had been little in the papers about her feeders, and no one had connected them, so what was the problem?

"Is the lavender dress back from the cleaners?"

"I picked it up last week," Elliott said, moving the applicator over to the purple eye shadow. He frowned. Purple wasn't her best color. He swabbed up copper instead. It would go with anything in her wardrobe, even that revealing mini-dress if she insisted on wearing it.

Rusty smiled. Besides, there was Jace. She'd run a personals ad and had met mostly losers, and then hit it off with the cop investigating one of her feeders. She wasn't ready to stop seeing him yet.

Of course it was risky, but she thought she could get Jace to talk about the case, so she'd know whether the investigation were turning in her direction even before he did. Hell, it could be years before he connected the kid in Topanga with any of her others—why deny herself the pleasure of him in the meantime?

"I'm not ready to move yet, Elliott, but I appreciate your concern. Don't worry," she said, noting his look, "I won't get caught—but even if they manage to convict me, they can't execute me."

She laughed when his look of distress turned to panic. She

patted his arm. "I'm kidding. It'll be fine, Elliott. Leave my hair down. Jace likes to play with it."

Elliott had stoically returned to boxing books when Jace arrived. Elliott left him in the living room—the nerve of the man, saying something about "popping upstairs" before Elliott had firmly headed him off!—while he went to announce his arrival to Risha.

Jace didn't hear her enter the study behind him, so engrossed was he in a book he'd picked up. She wrapped her arms around him from behind and made a tiny wiggle against his buttocks. "Hi there, sailor—new in town?"

He turned and embraced her, planting his lips on hers. It was a long kiss—lots of tongue—and Jace dropped the book, startling her out of the kiss.

"Whew," she laughed, "what a wonderful hello! Can I get you a drink or something?" She smoothed down what there was of her lavender dress.

" 'Or something' sounds good," he responded, reaching for her breast.

She dodged him playfully. "I meant a joint . . . oops. Forget I said that, Officer." She tried out a mock worried expression to go with the fishing expedition. He bit.

"I'm off-duty, Miss. Fire it up."

He looked delighted at her surprised expression, and sat on the couch, his arms along the back in wide-open invitation. Rusty got a joint out of the silver cigarette case in the desk—it had the Bathory crest on it and Elliott kept it filled for her—and leaned over Jace for a light.

He fumbled in his pockets for a match, his eyes glued all the while to the nude body revealed by the gaping neckline of her dress. As he lit the joint for her, he said, "I warn you—grass makes me horny."

"Being awake seems to make you horny," she grinned. She passed him the joint and he took a toke. They'd talked about going to hear some music tonight, but Rusty wasn't averse to a roll in the hay first. "What were you reading?"

He let out the hit and passed her the joint. "Vampire stories." He picked her book off the floor and handed it to her. "I've developed an interest in vampires."

"Ah, so that's why you were dressed like Dracula the other night. That's a good anthology—if you want, I'll lend it to you when I'm done." She took a hit, held it.

"That reminds me: I got the prints from the photographer today; they're in the car—I'll give you one when we go out. So, you know much about vampires?" he asked.

Still holding her hit, she nodded, and passed him the joint.

"Tell me everything you know," he said, taking a hit.

She remembered to exhale in a rush. "You just want me to rattle on so you can bogart the joint. What do you want to know?"

He spoke while holding his hit. "How come vampire stories don't deal with geometrical progression?" He exhaled. "I mean, let's say Dracula bites someone, turning them into a vampire. The next night, each of them bites someone, turning them into vampires. It wouldn't take long before the whole world was overrun by bloodsuckers."

"Robert McCammon wrote about that in *They Thirst*—did you read that?" Jace shook his head. "Well, anyway, it started out with one vampire, and within a week, I think, the entire city was vampiric. It took a major disaster to save the country. You ought to read it. It takes place here in L.A." She attached a roach clip to the joint and took a toke before handing it back to him.

She noticed his hand was shaking. "Nervous?" she teased.

He looked at his hand as if it belonged to someone else. Worry wrinkled his brow so briefly, Rusty wasn't sure she'd seen it.

"Nothing to worry about—it's just a fatal genetic disease," he said cavalierly. He transferred the joint to his other hand and took another toke.

"Now, there's something vampires don't have to deal with."

"If we don't get dressed now, we'll miss the ten o'clock show," Jace pointed out, making no move to get out of bed.

Risha ran a fingernail lightly up his thigh.

"Is that the last show tonight?"

Jace felt his cock twitch. He felt twenty years younger. He was sure he could get hard again in another ten or fifteen minutes . . . and maybe get it on again after they went out. He surreptitiously checked his right hand—the tremors had stopped. Maybe the cure for Huntington's was sex-and-drugs-and-rock'n'roll.

"Naw," he grinned, "there's another at eleven-thirty."

"Good." Risha hooked her left leg over his right and snuggled into him. "Tell me about your work. Did you ever catch the guy who killed the cowboy from the Topanga Corral?"

"Cabot? No, we hit a dead end. It was probably someone who went home with him, but no leads." He stopped toying with her lush hair and flexed his arm to show his bicep. "But never fear, ma'am, the LAPD is on the case, and we'll solve it eventually. We might get a lead from another case." Jace returned his hand to Risha's hair, drawing it across her throat like an auburn choker. She had a very long white neck. "Do you ever wear chokers?"

She pouted seductively. "Do you find them sexy? Bring me one and I'll wear it for you."

Jace knew just what kind of choker he'd bring—an inch-wide ribbon of black velvet. He imagined Risha wearing it, her hair loosely pinned up with errant strands all around, pouting like that. He kissed the pouting lips, which responded, soft and surprisingly cool. A black lace teddy, garter belt, and stockings with seams. His cock twitched again. High-heeled satin mules. It would cost a fortune.

She smiled at him, her eyes half-lidded.

It would be worth it.

CHAPTER
Twenty

Jace yawned. His schedule of late seemed to consist of days hunting the Vampire and nights with Risha Cadigan, leaving little time for sleep. There had been a time he could have run indefinitely on the adrenalin that both activities stimulated, but middle age (and Huntington's?) had slowed him down, and he realized he had to cut back or fail miserably on the case and the romance.

He couldn't cut back on the case—it was just starting to pop. The autopsy on Martinez Monday had confirmed that the victim was missing half the normal complement of blood and that the neck punctures had been the exsanguination site—toxicology for the mysterious substance would take weeks more. The artist's rendition of the woman Betty Pohl had seen with Al Zamel had come in, although it was too generic to be of much use—the woman looked like a dark-haired Rebecca DeMornay . . . or maybe a young Ingrid Bergman. Ronnie Schaffer had done only the preliminaries on the knife found at Balboa Park, but its dimensions matched the victims' wounds. The knife had two sets of prints—one set belonged to Jorge Martinez, the victim, but they were found only at the top end of the hilt, indicating that he'd touched it but hadn't used it; the other, indicating a right-hand grasp, failed to match any in the NCIC computer, but would prove invaluable should a suspect ever be arrested. Jace thought with a smile that he was going about it all wrong—he was spending his days tracking a creature that came out only at night.

On the other hand, he didn't want to cut back the time with Risha, either—in fact, he wanted more. He couldn't understand why she'd never let him sleep over; although he'd taken that for granted with Ellen, Risha had no mate expecting her. Maybe her bedroom had emotional associations with Gregor that she found difficult to overcome. Jace had straightened up his house in a few hours grabbed late Sunday afternoon—maybe tonight might be a good time to take Risha to his place; he reminded himself to change the sheets before he left to see her. He pictured her as she'd been last night when she came out of the bathroom in the lingerie he'd bought her, an image every bit as exciting as he'd forecast.

"I have what you want," her voice said.

Jace snapped to when he realized it wasn't Risha's voice. "I'm sorry?"

The small white-haired woman handed him a card. "The name you wanted—Box 2900. Can you just copy it down? I need the card."

Jace looked at the registration card. *What's Up/LA* had forwarded responses here to the ad placed by R.H. Robyn Hursh. An address in Torrance. Westside. Jace copied the information from the mail drop's record, thanked the woman, and left.

Back in the car, he added the information to the envelope for Liz to follow up on and checked off the ad from its list. So far this week, he had gotten forwarding addresses for all of the *LA Weekly* and *LA Reader* ads, and Liz was busy interviewing all the women they'd located; he still had two names left from the *What's Up* list—R.C. and E.B.—and twelve names from *Swingers World.* (The ad manager had decided the First Amendment wasn't worth a night in jail and had turned over the names yesterday . . . as soon as Jace had shown up with a warrant.)

R.C.'s mail drop was in West L.A., the logical next stop, but that would mean getting caught in rush-hour traffic out to the Valley to get E.B.'s name and address, so he decided to do that one first. He could swing by Sherman Oaks Community and ask Figuroa some more questions—like, had he or Martinez answered a personals ad lately?

His envelope thickened by the name of advertiser Edwina Bryant—and any connection between victims thinned by Figuroa's negative response—Jace identified himself to the teenaged girl behind the West L.A. mail drop counter and requested information on R.C., box holder number 1212.

"Ooh, I know who 1212 is—that old nerd. He never says hello or thank you or nothin'." The girl's jaw worked her gum as she shook her head, perhaps bemoaning the lack of courtesy pandemic in today's society, but more probably to show off her nose ring.

"It's not a woman?" Jace asked in surprise.

"No way. You still want the name?"

Jace nodded. He was having a hard enough time with this

case as it was without throwing in an old man who placed ads as a woman. He remembered Liz's comment about looking for an eighty-year-old transvestite vampire. On the other hand, who knows what the counter girl would consider to be old?

She opened a three-ring binder and flipped pages until she came to the one headed with the number 1212.

"Here it is," she said, turning the notebook to face him. "You need paper?"

Jace indicated his open notebook with a smile and turned to copy down the "old nerd's" name.

Risha Cadigan.

The young Mexican girl pushing a baby carriage took one look at the man sitting in the parking lot with his car door open and crossed to the other side to pass him. No sense taking chances.

Jace's left foot still touched the pavement—he'd forgotten to draw it into the car with him. He looked at his notebook again. The name was still the same. The address was the one he'd been visiting nearly every night. The "old nerd" was undoubtedly Elliott.

Coincidence. So she placed a personals ad, big deal. That didn't mean she was the killer, any more than the dozens of other women on his lists, any more than the hundreds who placed ads each week. He still had twelve names to check out from the *Swingers World* list—any one of them could be Rusty, any of the ones Liz was interviewing. It didn't have to be Risha.

Jace looked in the envelope for the ad Risha had run, knowing it wasn't there. It was still in his dining room, in the stack of newspapers taken from John Howard's house.

He put his notebook in his pocket without putting Risha's name in the envelope for Liz. He lived only a couple of miles away.

It took nearly half an hour to relocate the ad—he'd forgotten that he already knew it was in a recent issue of *What's Up/LA*.

WHAT WOULD YOU DO TO LIVE HAPPILY EVER AFTER? MYTHICAL CREATURE SEEKS MATE WHO CAN BELIEVE. I AM PRETTY SWF, INTELLIGENT AND SUCCESSFUL. YOU ARE SWM, BRIGHT, ARTICULATE, FUN, AND CAPABLE OF SERIOUS LONG-TERM COMMITMENT. I CAN OFFER THE RIGHT MAN SOMETHING NO OTHER WOMAN CAN—WOULDN'T YOU LIKE TO KNOW MORE? LETTER WITH P.M. PHONE.

An ad a killer would place? In spite of the intellectual "must-be's," it didn't sound much different than the hundreds of ads he'd read. "Mythical creature." Like a vampire? Jace got up to get a Harp out of the fridge, leaving the newspaper open on the counter next to him as he removed the cap. He took a deep swig and read the ad again. "Serious long-term commitment." Nothing unusual about that.

Even if Howard had responded to Risha's ad, that didn't mean she killed him, or even that they'd met. Coincidence. Jace looked at the clock—it was probably too late to check out any of the *Swingers World* mail drops and still make it to Risha's in time for their date.

He finished his beer, trying to ignore the unlikelihood that the same person would have coincidental contact with two victims of the same killer. He was unsuccessful. He left the empty bottle on the table and got the envelope with the photos from the *City Of Angels* party from the bedroom. He'd given

Risha one of two prints of the picture of them together. He took the other back into the kitchen and got an X-acto knife out of the utility drawer, carefully excising the image until only Risha remained.

He slipped the picture of Risha into his wallet and returned to the dining room files to find the witness statements. He had three witnesses who could identify Rusty—Tom, the kid in the pizza parlor from the Howard investigation; Betty, the hotel bar waitress who'd seen Rusty with Alvin Zamel; and Juan Figuroa, the mummy who'd copped a feel of Jorge Martinez's killer.

He started flipping through the file. His hand was trembling again. This time, there was no mistake. He stopped and held out his hands. They were both shaking uncontrollably; he realized his knees were weak, and he dropped into the chair, knocking the file off the table. It dumped its contents onto the rug, but Jace didn't notice. He was staring at his hands.

The shaking had never been this strong before. Jace was frightened, but he wasn't entirely sure that it was only Huntington's he feared. Was he sleeping with a suspect? Worse yet—a question he hadn't asked before—was he falling in love with Risha? He remembered something his mother said to him once: "If it occurs to you that you might be in love, you probably are."

He shook off the thought and tried to steady his hands. When the shaking began to subside, he turned to the file again, and found it scattered under the table. Jace got down on all fours and started to pick up the photocopies of forms, notebook pages, reports and faxes, shoving them into the file in no particular order.

He stopped, a police artist's sketch in his hands. He stared at the face of a suspect from a case thirty years ago in upstate

New York. He'd seen the same face recently, no older than this picture.

It was Gregor.

Elliott finished packing the last of the books from the study to ship to London and sat down for a breather. All the reaching and stooping had gotten to him—his lower back was killing him. Risha had been dismayed to find the library emptying, but she had just sighed, saying nothing, so he'd completed the job. He looked at his watch; a little past four. Not enough time to take the last boxes to the shipper. There was time to go to the mail drop, though, and still get back before Risha awoke. He'd just sit for a little while. Lord, he was tired!

Tiffany saw the old nerd at box 1212. She was about to tell him a cop was just in there asking about him—she'd love to see him spooked—but stopped to think about it again. The cop didn't tell her why he was asking for the box holder's name—maybe the old nerd was, like, some grotty pervo or something. She was alone at the mail drop, about to close for the night. What if he, like, raped her or something gross like that? She could spook him another time . . . like when one of the dudes who worked mornings and weekends was around in case he got heavy. In the end, she let him leave without speaking to him.

Tom looked at the photo and shook his head. "Sh-sh-shit, man, I d-d-don't know. Maybe I coulda tole you th-th-three weeks ago, b-b-but now . . . I only remember her t-t-t-tits."

"Look at the eyes," Jace suggested. "She's got really unusual eyes. Do you remember her eyes?"

"N-n-nope. She was wearing d-d-dark g-g-g-glasses."

Jace realized he wasn't getting anywhere, thanked the kid, and drove to the airport hotel.

"What can I get you?" The bartender put down a napkin. The hotel bar was beginning to fill with suits arriving for happy hour. Jace didn't see Betty Pohl.

"I'm looking for Betty," he said, pushing the napkin back across the bar in refusal.

"She's off." The bartender turned away.

Jace stopped him, showed him his I.D. "It's important that I talk to her. Where can I reach her?"

The bartender looked curious. "Something wrong, Detective?"

Jace ignored the question. "Do you have her home address or phone number?"

"The manager has it, but she's not home. Her son was in a car accident in Texas Monday and she flew out to be with him."

Two down, one to go. Back to the Valley.

"Mr. Figuroa already has two visitors," the nurse informed him. "You'll have to wait until one of them leaves before you can go in."

Jace paced the floor nervously, eyeing the door while the hospital bustled around him. An orderly got off the service elevator with a large cart holding patients' meals and checked in at the nurses' station before pushing his cart down the hall. The large clock on the wall read six o'clock. He was expected at Risha's in an hour.

Why would she kill these guys? What's the motive? Hell, what's the method? Why hadn't Gregor aged—and what did a dead man have to do with the case? Could he arrest her if she turned out to be Rusty? Did he love her? Jace's head was pounding.

"Have you got any aspirin?" It seemed like an inane question in a hospital.

The nurse frowned. "We're not supposed to dispense any drugs without a doctor's order."

Jace rolled his eyes and made a face, as if she were taking rules too far.

"Got a headache, huh?" She rummaged in a desk drawer. "I have some Advil in my purse." She came up with a small tin. "I'm not giving you this as a nurse," she announced clearly when she handed it to him.

"I'm not a nurse, I'm a cop," he said, swallowing two tablets dry.

The nurse looked confused, then shrugged slightly and pointed to the drinking fountain down the hall. Jace was returning when he saw a middle-aged Mexican couple leaving Figuroa's room.

"You can go in now," the nurse confirmed.

Figuroa's bed was surrounded by things that hadn't been there two hours earlier—a saturated-color picture of Jesus in a gaudy gold rococo frame, a yellow candle filling a sixteen-ounce glass painted with an image of the Virgin Mary, a rosary with a silver plastic cross, a mylar helium balloon with a puppy's face on one side which rotated to show GET WELL SOON on the reverse. The patient's face was still swathed in bandages, the eyes startled to see Jace again so soon.

The orderly with the food cart stopped outside the door, checking the room number against his clipboard. He moved on without entering. This patient's meals were served through a tube. Figuroa sighed heavily.

"I'm sorry to bother you again so soon, Mr. Figuroa, but I need a moment of your time."

The mummy nodded wearily. Jace switched on the reading

light over the bed, and took Risha's picture out of his pocket. This wasn't proper procedure, showing the witness only one photo, no lineup—Jace knew a decent defense lawyer could overturn the case if it hinged on the I.D.—but he had to know before he saw Risha again.

Without explanation, Jace showed the photo of Risha to the mummy. Figuroa's dark eyes widened—he nodded emphatically while poking the photograph hard with his finger.

"You're positive this is the woman you saw?" Jace asked unnecessarily.

The mummy repeated his movements, adding grunts this time for emphasis. There was no way Jace could mistake the response.

CHAPTER
Twenty-One

Rusty browsed the *Victoria's Secret* catalog while she soaked in her bath, the cloud of Ombre Rose scenting the room. Jace had been so thrilled with the lingerie last night, she thought it'd be a good idea to order more. She dog-eared a page with a sexy emerald green negligee, then stepped out of the tub.

She wondered if it would be appropriate to wear her new ivory dress and boots tonight. According to Elliott's note, Jace had called earlier to tell her to plan to go out tonight, but he hadn't said where. As she looked longingly at her new granny boots, Rusty hoped he didn't have a night hike or bowling in mind. Hell, she'd wear the new outfit—if he had something more rugged in mind, he could tell her when he arrived.

She looked for the ivory comb with the Bathory crest, but couldn't find it. She called down to Elliott to come fix her hair and make-up and continued to rummage in the dressing table drawer. Shit. She couldn't find the silver one, either. She hoped Elliott hadn't packed them. He'd been in a real frenzy the last week—she was afraid she'd have to go to London just to get her stuff back.

As soon as she opened the door, Rusty knew she'd have to change. Jace had obviously come straight from work—his shirt was wrinkled, as were his pants, and his beard stubble was at least twelve hours old, his hair finger-combed. He appeared startled to see her . . . or perhaps it was only her outfit that surprised him, but he wasn't smiling.

"Jace? Something wrong?" Rusty stood back to let him in. Smokey Robinson and the Miracles were crooning from the speakers about "a lifetime of devotion."

"What? No, nothing's wrong. It's just been a long day and I'm a bit wiped." He came in, looked around, and stood awkwardly in the middle of the living room. He hadn't kissed her hello. "How come Elliott didn't answer the door? I thought he screened all your visitors?"

Rusty shrugged. "I think he's in the darkroom. Do you want a drink or a joint before we go?"

Jace looked as if she'd been speaking Martian. "Go?"

"Sit down before you fall down. Elliott said you called earlier to say we were going somewhere," she explained as he dropped into a chair, his eyes fixed on the portrait of Gregor on the opposite wall.

He shook his head, apparently to bring himself back to the present. "Oh, shit, I'm sorry, Risha—I fucked up." He glanced down at his clothes, rubbed a hand over his stubbled face, and smiled at her sheepishly. "I planned to take you to the Improv tonight, but I got so busy today, I plain forgot. We can swing by my place and I'll do a quick shower-and-shave . . ."

"You don't look like you really have the energy for that. How about I change my clothes and we just go for a drive up the coast, maybe take a walk on the beach?"

He looked grateful, apologized again, adding, "You look gorgeous, Risha—you sure you don't mind saving it for another time?"

"Not at all. Unzip me and I'll be changed in a flash."

She turned her back to him and felt him draw the zipper down her back, then his fingers massaged a small circle between her shoulder blade and spine.

"Where did you get this scar?" he asked offhandedly.

She realized the wound left by Hairnet's bullet last week must not have disappeared yet. Could Jace recognize it as a bullet scar?

"That? I had a mole the doctor thought might be malignant—he did a real hatchet job to make sure none was left. I'm surprised you didn't notice it before."

She trotted upstairs, changed into jeans and a sweater, and was back to Jace in minutes.

"Shall I drive? We can open the beamer's moonroof and you can lie back and enjoy," she suggested.

Jace smiled. "Let's find a secluded beach and I'll 'lie back and enjoy' you there. Driving actually relaxes me, unless it's rush hour on the freeway. An open moonroof sounds good though—would you allow me to drive your BMW?"

She tossed him the keys. "Go for it."

Jace beeped off her car alarm with the key ring and let her in before climbing into the driver's seat. He reached under the seat to release the latch and slid back a foot. He fastened his seat belt, adjusted the side and rearview mirrors, and drove toward Pacific Coast Highway. "Malibu? Zuma? Farther?"

"Wherever you want—I'm just along for the ride."

Jace didn't say much on the drive. She figured he was trying to distance himself from a bad day and she kept quiet, enjoying the view. He readjusted the inside mirror two or three times during the ride, apparently never getting it quite right, but by the time they'd passed Topanga, he seemed content.

Jace watched Risha spread the plastic dropcloth from the car trunk on the sand in the secluded cove. The moon was only a sliver, yet her skin seemed to glow in the darkness. He wanted to make love to her, now, before they talked, without thinking. He wanted to plunge into her body and never have to ask questions again. He took her in his arms and kissed her hotly. She responded avidly, and they tore off each other's clothes, throwing them to the sand, laughing as they followed them down.

In spite of the urgency he felt, Jace took his time, not unaware it might be his last. He trailed wet kisses from her neck to her breasts; he teased the nipples with his tongue, nibbled them gently with his teeth. She moaned, arching toward his mouth, and his cock surged into full erection. His hand cupped her vagina, which was cool and very wet; he ran his tongue down across her flat stomach and replaced his fingers with his mouth, teasing her into a frenzy.

"Ohgod-yes-ohJace!-mmm-let me . . ." A symphony of pleasure escaped her as she shifted to envelop his cock with her lips, the coolness bringing him almost over the top. She seemed to somehow simultaneously trace her tongue over his glans and suck the shaft to the back of her throat, inhibiting his orgasm with fingers clamped at the base. She pulled her mouth away, and he felt the cool breeze against his hot erection.

"FuckmeJace-now-Ican'twait-now-now-now . . ."

He rotated his body to enter her. She was as tight as a virgin, clamping him inside her. "Ohgod-yes!-that's it . . . right there . . ."

They exploded together, her scream in harmony with his roar as the sea crashed behind them.

Afterwards, they lay entwined, the gritty sand in the sweat between their bodies ignored in the afterglow. Jace trailed the ends of her lovely auburn hair over her still-erect nipple. "Rusty," he whispered.

She shuddered in orgasmic aftershock, then laughed in delight. She opened her eyes and looked at him, smiling. "What?"

"Tell me about Gregor."

"Now?" she laughed. "What do you want to know?"

Jace sat up, and she laid the back of her head on his lap; he stroked her cheek softly. "How did you meet?" he said casually, although his heart was pounding so loudly he was sure she could hear it.

"He was a visiting professor, I was a naive college student. He swept me off my feet . . . the same way you are," she added with a grin. "He was charming and handsome and rich, and we traveled constantly. The last two years in L.A. are the longest I've spent in one place since I met him."

"How did he die? Do you mind me asking?" Jace half-expected to hear "with a stake through his heart." ("Older than he looked," she'd said once.)

She stared past his face to the stars and he thought he saw tears glisten in her pale eyes. "He killed himself in Scotland."

"Why?"

She shrugged. "He was tired of living."

"That must have been very hard on you." He drew her up next to him, smelling the blend of rose and sex and salt mist on her skin, touched.

"It's been difficult to get over him, but I have a long life ahead of me without him and it's time to go on. I miss having him to travel with." She stretched, her breasts glowing white even in the nearly moonless night. "Do you like traveling?"

Jace had never been out of the U.S., except for one excursion to Tijuana in high school. He and three buddies had driven down for a weekend to see the famous sex show with a woman and a donkey, but he didn't think that really counted as a trip out of the country.

"I'm sure I would if I ever got the chance. A cop's salary doesn't leave much room for vacations, but I've always wanted to see Italy and London . . . and Africa and the Orient," he added laughingly. "Give me a few minutes, I'll come up with more. It doesn't cost anything to fantasize."

Risha kissed him. "Gregor left me a house in London. If you can get some time off in the spring, I'd love to take you on a trip." She appeared to read something in his expression. "Would it make you uncomfortable if I paid?"

"It's fun to talk about, but it wouldn't be fair, Risha—I couldn't pay you back."

She shook her head. "Don't worry about it—I can easily afford it, and it would be delightful to have a traveling companion again. Elliott isn't the best company, you know."

Elliott. Jace wondered how he fit into all this. "Did he know Gregor?"

"He was Gregor's valet when I met him. I guess Gregor left me Elliott, too. Hey! You've got goosebumps—let's get dressed, go for a walk, okay?"

They brushed the sand off each other, shook out their

clothes, and got dressed. All the while, Jace tried to think how he was going to bring it up, knowing this would be a life-or-death situation as soon as he spoke.

As they walked barefoot down to the tide line, listening to the waves crashing on the beach, Jace thought back to the car ride. Try as he might, he hadn't been able to find Risha's reflection in the rearview mirror. He remembered something she said the night they'd met. He'd made some comment about all her photographs being night shots. She'd responded, "Yeah, I'm a real vampire." At the time, he'd thought she was joking.

He took her hand as they waded in the edges of the surf, then stopped to turn her toward him. He looked into her deep pale eyes.

"I think I'm falling in love with you, Risha Cadigan," he said.

Her smile grew; even in the dim light, her eyes danced. "Is that so bad?"

A question Jace had no answer for, in spite of having asked it of himself several times already.

"I know why you kill."

Her smile disappeared.

"Are you planning to arrest me?" she asked after he explained to her how he'd found her out.

Jace laughed bravely. "Near as I can tell, that's not possible, m'lady. You're much stronger than I am, and I'm alone and unarmed." He turned his empty hands palms up.

"I don't understand: I hold your life in my hands, but you seem calm. You don't expect to be able to blackmail me, do you? What did you expect to happen now?"

He read the confusion in her eyes. "Let's go sit down. We need to talk."

She looked startled at his affection, but followed him warily back to the blanket. When they sat, he took her hand, squeezing it reassuringly.

"Are you really immortal?" he wanted to know.

She found her voice. "For all intents and purposes, as they say."

"You're not affected by disease or injury?" She shook her head, just as he'd hoped. Finally, an escape from the Huntington's monster. "Are you very old?"

"Probably not much more than you. I was born in 1941. I crossed over in 1969, when I met Gregor."

Jace nodded. "Do you regret becoming a . . . crossing over?"

She smiled. "You can say 'vampire'—I'm not sensitive about the term. And no, I don't regret it. The advantages outweigh the drawbacks. Why are you asking me all this, Jace?"

"Humor me. We both know you can kill me any time you want, so it doesn't matter if you tell me, right?" She nodded. "Okay. So what are the drawbacks?"

"No daylight activities and a monotonous diet."

No more Killer Shrimp. "That's it?"

She shrugged. "If you expect me to feel guilty for feeding on people, you've got a long wait. Believe me, they go happily."

He was surprised. "Does that have something to do with your venom?"

It was her turn to be surprised. "How do you know about the venom?"

He explained, and she again seemed impressed with the thoroughness of his investigation. "Why haven't all your . . . feeders? . . . become vampires? Or have they?"

"It's not that easy. It takes repeated exposure to the venom during periodic small feedings. As far as I know, I'm the only vampire left since Gregor died."

Jace took a deep breath; holding her hand with both of his, he looked directly into her eyes. "Would you ever consider another mate?"

She smiled broadly then, for the first time since he'd told her he was falling in love with her. Was that a yes? He relaxed some then, and kissed her.

She pulled out of the kiss. "Hey, wait a minute. You're not the only one with questions here, you know."

Jace prayed that she wouldn't ask him why—or if she did, that she would accept love as his sole motivation. "What do you want to know?"

"What are you going to do about your investigation?"

"Obviously, I'll have to quit, take early retirement. I can say it's job stress or health; they're both common causes of burnout. I could be clear of the job in a couple of months without arousing suspicion."

"But doesn't your partner know about me?"

"No, and there's no way she'll find out. None of the stuff that led me to you is in the files; it's all up here." He tapped his temple. "The case will go on the back burner eventually, as long as there aren't any new victims."

"I can't promise that, Jace. I have to eat every few days or I could drop into a coma. After you cross over, we can share feeders, but it's still 2–3 bodies a week."

"Don't worry, I can help. I know how to dispose of bodies. I also know some feeders who wouldn't be missed. You wouldn't mind killing some career criminals, would you?"

Risha laughed, "No, the nastier the better. Oh, Jace, this could be fun!"

Epilogue

The taxi driver carried the luggage up the stairs and waited for Elliott to unlock the door before he deposited the load in the foyer. Elliott tipped him five pounds—although the trip from Victoria Station was not expensive, the baggage was heavy and he was grateful that he didn't have to carry it any farther. He waited until the taxi had disappeared through the front gate before he turned on the lights.

The grandfather clock at the base of the stairway chimed the hour ten times—the caretaker had obviously remembered to keep it wound. Elliott thought he might be able to get the house ready in time after all—if the caretaker had wound the clock, the rest of the house might also have been kept up. He entered the parlor on the left—all of the furniture, except for the chair next to the fireplace, was covered with sheets. As Elliott swept them off, revealing the lovely antiques that had been in the house the first time he had seen it, he was suddenly overcome with fatigue. He dropped into the love seat he'd just bared, and let his head drop to rest against the silk brocade back. It was good to be in London again.

His eyes fell on the Lisette Model photograph over the fireplace, its juxtaposition with the antiques a bit startling, but what really surprised him was that it was one of the items he'd shipped from Los Angeles during the previous winter. Had the caretaker shown enough initiative to unpack everything that had been sent? He got up from the love seat with a groan and crossed the foyer to the library door.

The light was on when he walked in, the books he'd sent partially unpacked.

"It's about time you showed up." Gregor stood from the high-backed chair across the room, a book in his hand. "When boxes started arriving in November, I thought you'd be here by the end of last year. Where's Risha?"

"She'll be arriving tomorrow night," Elliott said. "She won't be expecting you, sir," he added, knowing it was a gross understatement.

Gregor smiled. "Then it'll be a surprise, won't it?"

"She's not alone, Baron."

Elliott prayed that Gregor would leave before they arrived. He didn't want to think of how devastated Risha would be to find out that he had faked his suicide to leave her. Elliott had kept the secret to protect her feelings on Bathory's word that he wouldn't contact her again. He didn't doubt that Risha would be delighted to see Gregor again, but Elliott knew that she could—should—no longer trust the old vampire; he'd betrayed her once, and he could do it again.

Gregor looked surprised, then shrugged elegantly. "It's a large house, Elliott—we can accommodate guests. I take it her companion is male?" Elliott nodded warily. "Well, she won't need to spend every waking minute with me then, will she?"

Gregor put down his book, went over to Elliott and shook his hand. "It's good to see you again. Thank you for taking care of Risha while I was away. I was bored, Elliott, but now I realize that it was a mistake to leave. Things can be like they were before."

Elliott was amazed at Gregor's insensitivity. He had forgotten how people can change . . . and obviously expected them to forgive him without a second thought. Elliott, at least, was not able to forget the hurt Gregor had inflicted on both of them with his departure.

He realized Gregor was still talking. ". . . I'm going out shortly and I don't expect to be in much before dawn. I'm in the master bedroom. Make up the room across the hall for Risha's young man."

Tired as he was, Elliott was still awake when he heard Gregor close the front door and go up to bed. Risha had been happier with Jace Levy than he'd seen her since Gregor left, and Elliott had no doubt that Jace would be better for her than Gregor. It was very hard for Jace to sell out his profession for Risha, and that, more than anything, had proven to Elliott that Jace truly loved her. Levy had made sacrifices for Risha, and Gregor could not be allowed to ruin their happiness— not Risha's, not Jace's . . . and not Elliott's. Having finally decided what to do about the situation, Elliott slept.

It was early afternoon when he woke, and the clouds had parted to allow the sun to warm the western side of the house. The side with the master bedroom.

Elliott got the garden shears and went upstairs. Before he could properly clean the bedroom, he had to open the heavy drapes.

SHERRY GOTTLIEB is the author of HELL NO, WE WON'T GO! Resisting the Draft During the Vietnam War, a nominee for the PEN USA West Literary Award in Nonfiction.

A bookseller for nineteen years, she owned A Change of Hobbit, the oldest and largest speculative-fiction bookstore in the world.

LOVE BITE is her first novel. She lives in Santa Monica, California with her boa constrictor, Wrinklesnakeskin. She is working on another erotic vampire novel.